Ch

Book Two
Passions in the Park Series

BY
JL Redington

©JL Redington 2014

To my friend Jackie!
Happy reading!
JL Redington

No part of this publication may be reproduced, or
stored in a retrieval system, or transmitted in any form
or by any means, electronic, mechanical,
photocopying, recording or otherwise without written
permission of the author.

I would like to dedicate this book to my girls, Nicole, Melody and Steph, my own personal Wolf Pack. Their laughter and love has sustained me through many a dark day. I love that they grew up together and never forgot each other. I love that they include me every now and again in their den. I wish for all of you the kind of love and acceptance these three girls, now women and mothers, have given me in my life. What a blessing they are to me.

Table of Contents

Prologue
Chapter One
Chapter Two
Chapter Three
Chapter Four
Chapter Five
Chapter Six
Chapter Seven
Chapter Eight
Chapter Nine
Chapter Ten
Chapter Eleven
Chapter Twelve
Chapter Thirteen
Chapter Fourteen
Chapter Fifteen
Chapter Sixteen
Chapter Seventeen
Chapter Eighteen
Chapter Nineteen
Chapter Twenty
Chapter Twenty-One
Chapter Twenty-Two
Chapter Twenty-Three
Chapter Twenty-Four
Chapter Twenty-Five
Chapter Twenty-Six
Chapter Twenty-Seven
Chapter Twenty-Eight
Chapter Twenty-Nine

Chapter Thirty
Chapter Thirty-One
Chapter Thirty-Two
Chapter Thirty-Three
Chapter Thirty-Four
Epilogue

Prologue

The man stumbled into the city park, bleeding and in pain. He was hateful and angry, his fury burning inside him like molten lava. He wanted to kill whatever stepped into his line of sight, but he didn't have the strength. He needed help; he needed to get to a doctor, to get this bullet out of his shoulder. With no car, no money, no way to get anywhere and exhausted from the two days it took him to make his way north, he collapsed onto the grass, and leaned himself up against a tree.

He'd missed his chance to kill them. He'd *needed* to kill them. The whole plan was ruined, and now there was a big hole in the fabric of his life. How could he ever get himself back on track, back to the lovely sweet joy of watching a life slip away? He would figure it out. Somehow, it always worked out.

But that wasn't good enough. Having things 'work out' wasn't what he'd planned and he gritted his teeth in rage and frustration. He wanted to hurt someone; he wanted to do more than kill, but what else was there? His very soul was hatred and he wanted his revenge. He wanted them to feel as frustrated as he felt. He wanted them to pay for making his plan ineffective, and they *would* pay. The whole *world* would pay. They had no idea who they were dealing with.

Anger consumed him, fed him, kept him alive, and he wanted to lash out at something, at someone.

"Mister? Are you okay?"

She was filthy, but young and sweet. Her face was beautiful with delicate features, dark hair and eyes like large chunks of coal. He could tell she needed him, her eyes were hungry and he could feed her. She could fix him; she could make him feel important again. He could help her, as well. It would be a mutually beneficial relationship. This could work. He wondered if she'd ever been with a man before and inside his dead, dark heart, he could feel a grin begin to pull at the corners of his mouth. But he couldn't let it show on his face. He couldn't let her know she'd just fulfilled his own prophecy.

Like the closing and opening of a camera lens, his demeanor changed. He was suddenly sweating and breathing hard, frightened and alone.

"Somebody shot me!" he said, breathlessly, his face a mask of terrified innocence. "I was just passing through the park on my way home and he just stepped out and shot me. I'm visiting here. Is there a clinic that you know of where I could get some help? He stole my wallet and all my identification. I have no money, no proof of insurance. I don't know what to do…"

Chapter One

Gentry Beauchene brushed his light brown hair off his forehead with a sigh. His blue-green eyes focused on the phone sitting on his desk as he spoke into the receiver he held in his opposite hand.

On the other end of the line was his older brother, Greyson. Greyson was stabbed two months previous by a serial killer who escaped custody, the Evergreen Killer. He was concerned now that this maniac would come after his brother. Gentry never doubted for a minute a killer like that would use Glacier National Park. All the rangers were on high alert, hoping they wouldn't have to deal with that part of life, but steeling themselves for the task, should it come up.

"Well, if it isn't the old married man."

Gentry smiled remembering the evening of their wedding.

"You've been chained for, what…a whole month now? How are you feeling?"

"Don't knock it 'til you've tried it, bro," laughed Greyson, "Thanks to a very dedicated soul mate, I'm doing great."

"Now Greyson, you know I could never cheat on Baby that way. Shame on you."

"You have an unnatural affection for that horse, you know."

"Unnatural? You're a sick man, you know that, right?"

The two brothers shared a laugh and soon the conversation became serious.

"I want you to be careful, Gentry, very careful. We don't know where Bantus is, but I can tell you from experience he wants to even the score, probably due to his not-so-successful encounter with my wife and me. It just makes me worry about you. Don't stop looking over your shoulder until we know he's under lock and key, got it?"

"Wow, you got bossy when she put that ring on your finger."

Gentry chuckled, but he knew his brother was serious.

"I hear you, big brother, no worries. I'll take care."

They ended the conversation and Gentry hopped in his car and headed to his ranch about ten minutes from the station. He had a beautiful barn there that housed his beloved friend. He and Baby would go have a look around.

Located not far from the Hungry Horse Ranger Station, his small fifteen acre ranch was perfect for what Gentry needed. The house was a beautiful, well kept four bedroom log cabin with a sweeping view of the valley surrounding the property. Sitting about ten miles outside of Coram, it was perfectly placed for his work and nestled in amidst stunning beauty. However, he really bought the ranch because of the barn.

It was an older structure, painted the typical barn red and very well taken care of by the previous owner. The main floor of the barn was home to six over sized stalls. The floor was clean, swept every day after Baby was brushed and put away. Gentry liked to think the floor was so clean you could eat off of it, but he realized he would be the only one who would think that. Still, it was a nice place; one you wouldn't mind showing off. Having the extra stalls was nice as he was able to store hay in a couple of them and that saved him from having to constantly bring bails down from the loft, where the bulk of the hay was kept.

The smell of the old barn was always a welcome treat for him. The scent of stacked hay mixed with leather took him back to his years growing up in Idaho. He'd always loved horses and spent every minute he could riding, grooming and loving the horses he'd grown up with.

Baby neighed softly as he approached and stomped her foot in anticipation.

"Hey beautiful! How's my girl?" he said, rubbing her forehead and stroking her neck with his other hand. He leaned his head against hers and she nuzzled him with her velvety nose. It was a love affair for sure.

Baby went everywhere he went, warned him when danger approached and possessed the agility and surefootedness to get him into any area of the park. He referred to her often as his girl, his *best* girl, a Mustang of amazing reddish brown coloring with long lashes and a soft nose that she delighted in burrowing into his neck whenever she stood beside him. She was with him whenever he was out checking remote areas of the park and following up on problems in those areas.

Baby had a small white moon on her forehead, just like her mother, but her mother's was much larger. For this reason, she was aptly named Baby Moon, but Gentry called her Baby.

The ranger station had a two stall lean-to where he kept Baby during the day. He'd bring her into the park in the horse trailer, but between rides, she stayed in the lean-to. Not the little piece of heaven her barns stall was, but it would do in a pinch.

Gentry trained in law enforcement, like his brother Greyson. However, unlike Greyson, Gentry was also a retired military sniper. He used guns very "effectively" as his commanding officer noted in his referral letter to the National Parks Service. That type of training was highly valued in many government agencies, including the FBI and CIA. He'd looked into that line of work, but longed to be out of doors, *way* out of doors. That's how he'd ended up in Glacier National Park, never feeling the need to try something new.

However, on this day he would bring his sniper rifle with him. From what Greyson told him, he felt like it might be needed under the circumstances. Probably a bit over the top, but one never knew in cases like this.

The cowboy in him preferred a horse for transportation over pretty much any other kind. He relished the squeak of the leather as he climbed into the saddle and the warm, musty smell of Baby as she carried him along trails and into the forests.

Today Gentry was heading deep into West Glacier, checking out reports of drug use and wild parties. His assigned area of patrol was the Southwest section of the park, bordered on the west by Flathead River and included the Grinnel Glacier hiking trail and Going-to-the-Sun Road. He'd most likely be gone two or three days. He'd packed for that the night before, included his satphone and camping equipment with food and water in his saddlebags. He tied his bedroll to the back of his saddle along with a small two man tent for sleeping. Had the trip been a longer one, he would have brought Handsome, the pack mule that carried equipment and more food than he'd use on a short trip like this.

To all who entered Glacier National Park, it was clear the entire park was filled with beauty, but to Gentry, this section was his favorite. Snowcapped mountains thrusting skyward, thick forests and blue, blue Montana skies. There wasn't a place on the earth he enjoyed more, especially on horseback. Summer made for beautiful warm days, brightly colored wildflowers everywhere you looked and an easy, laid back atmosphere that was perfect for a few days on a horse. The steady footfall of Baby's hooves and the feel of the sun on his back made him want to head north and just keep going, but he had a job to do, so he stayed alert and kept vigilant. As he rode through the thickly forested area around Lake McDonald he watched for signs of campsites not vacated properly, campfires left unattended, anything that might need his attention.

Today all was quiet, but once in a while there was a rescue needed for some poor soul who'd gotten himself caught on a ledge, ill prepared to get off the side of the mountain. Worse were the hikers that had mis-stepped and either slid down the side of a rock wall or fallen off completely. These poor souls died very quickly, and by the time they were found the only way to identify their remains was in a high tech forensics lab. For the most part, however, the summer days were spent checking the park and fielding questions from hikers and campers he happened upon. Hopefully there wouldn't be too many distress or body retrieval calls this season. Those were the hardest part of the job.

He'd been riding for several hours and was ready to break for the day. He could tell by the sun what time of day it was, and by the growling in his stomach. He was ready to eat. He kept an eye out for a good place to stop for the night. He'd know it when he saw it.

Before too long, he found a small clearing with a nice flat looking area for his tent. There were plenty of wildflowers, trees all around and a nice looking spot for a campfire. Yup, it was the right spot and he dismounted. He pulled off his bedroll, tent and saddlebags he needed to set up camp.

He tied off a line for Baby, removed the saddle and set her near a good grazing spot with enough lead that she could munch to her heart's content. Not too far away he found a good place for a tent. He longed to sleep under the stars, but it wasn't safe to do that with bears around. A tent wasn't much safety, but would allow him time to grab a gun and protect himself before the animal was upon him. Baby would sound off before the animal ever reached the tent, for that matter.

When traveling alone, Gentry didn't cook his meals but relied on dried meats and fruits to alleviate any confrontation with hungry wildlife. Although they could smell the dried food if they were close enough, the scent of cooking food traveled much further. He also kept his food in a sealed container which he placed in a net and hung from a tree for safekeeping.

On this star-filled night, Gentry lay outside his tent, by the campfire, his head resting comfortably on Baby's saddle and chewed on beef jerky and dried apples, drinking in the beauty and majesty of the night sky. On nights like this, it was just good to be alive. He neither needed nor wanted anything else in life; this was enough.

He'd just relaxed with his hands behind his head when his satphone went off. He sighed and got up, walking to the tent. It was quite dark by now and he'd not thought to bring his flashlight in with him, so he fumbled around in the dark before finding the ringing phone buried under his sleeping bag.

"Beauchene."

Gentry listened carefully as his assistant spoke quickly and anxiously.

"Hey, Joe, hold up," he said, "slow down and tell me again. I only caught about half of that."

"Some hikers have found a casket not far from your location, maybe five to eight miles. They're pretty freaked out and don't plan to stay there for the night, but I did get the coordinates they called from. How do you want me to proceed?"

Gentry thought for a moment before answering.

"You still there, Gentry?"

"Yes, Joe, I'm here. You're going to be up late tonight making calls I'm afraid. You'll need to call the FBI office in Seattle and let them know what's been found. I'll make my way to the area tomorrow, just give me the coordinates and I'll triangulate from my position."

"Okay," said Joe, haltingly. "Then what?"

"Then I want you to calm down. You sound like a heifer in hard labor. I need you to keep your head. Can you do that?"

Joe Jackson was new to the station, but a good ranger. He was about four years younger than Gentry, without the military background, and had never worked a murder in the park before. This was going to take some patience on Gentry's part.

"Yeah, I can. Sorry."

"No worries, Joe, just listen up now because there's a whole list of things you're going to need to do for me."

Chapter Two

Gentry began the list of phone calls he'd need Joe to make, including rousing the staff to get food packed and large tents and supplies together. Next call would be to the chopper pilot, Cy Smithson. Cy's first name was actually Bernard, but he didn't like the sound of Bernard Smithson, for whatever the reason, so, for most of his adult life he'd been Cy. He was a good friend to Gentry and a very good pilot.

Gentry told Joe to have Cy fly the supplies up at first light, unless he heard from the FBI. If they're able to get their investigators in town and ready to chopper up by ten a.m., then Cy was to wait for them.

"Be sure and tell him, if he gets to the crime scene before I do, if he's without FBI, to stay back from the evidence and wait until I get there to start anything. He can go ahead and unload the chopper, but he's to stay put until I get there. You got that?" Gentry waited for Joe to answer.

"Yeah, yeah, I got that. He waits until you get there."

"Now, once you've let the FBI know what we suspect we've got up here and the supplies are at the helipad for transport in the morning, *and* you've talked with Smithy so he knows what we need, you should be good. Do you have any questions for me?"

"Nope. I've got it all down on paper." Joe was clearly proud of his listening skills.

"Good job. Guess I'm going to hit the hay and try to be up and on the trail by first light. I'll keep my satphone on through the night. If you need me for anything, call me."

"Will do."

Gentry ended the call thinking it would probably have been a good thing for him to bring one of the assistants up here with him. He was fairly certain the killer was gone, but with the information he'd gotten earlier in the day from Greyson, he wondered if he was safe out here on his own. However, he had Baby, and she wouldn't let anything get past her; she would be his backup, just like always.

***

The plane flew south, headed for the wide-open spaces of Montana.

"I'm late…I'll never get my rhythm back now."

Walter Bantus was frustrated and angry. He blamed one Ranger Greyson Beauchene for all of it, every bit. Beauchene shot him in the shoulder and the recovery time he'd just taken ruined everything. Twenty-seven days! He needed every kill to be twenty-seven days apart. His injury already cost him more than two months, making him miss the deadline, and that only served to fuel his fury. Then, of course, there was the misdirection.

He could have sworn he headed north that night…north, and further away from anyone who might recognize him or his wound. However, in his searing pain from the gunshot wound, and his subsequent fevered stupor, he'd gone south. He couldn't figure out when that happened, how he'd gotten so turned around.

He clenched his fist and set his jaw, trying to hide his displeasure. Beauchene, it was all his fault and somehow, he would pay.

How he hated the name Beauchene. He'd wanted to kill both Greyson and Aspen, should have done it early on, but he wanted to play with them first. He wanted some…company. Yes, company that was all. He'd only wanted to visit. Now, Aspen, *there* was a conversationalist. He'd seen how much she cared for him, how she asked about him and about his likes and dislikes. Maybe she was a little irritating, but for the most part, he was certain she was an admirer.

What was it Greyson said before he pulled the trigger? He'd made a point of saying Aspen never liked Walter anyway.

Walter sniggered at this, scoffed openly. She wanted him, he knew she did. She was just putting on a show for Beauchene. Oh, well, it worked out just fine in the end.

All was not lost, for in the belly of the plane was a casket, one he'd made himself. Inside was the body of his dearly departed 'wife'. The torn fabric of his life was slowly coming back together, stitched so no one would ever know it was once torn.

He chuckled softly to himself at the sadness displayed by the airline cargo manager. How easily he'd been persuaded to forgo the paperwork necessary to transport a body. He'd been fascinated by the fact that Walter made the casket. He talked at some length about wanting to do that himself, maybe make his own casket and store it away. He could see the craftsmanship, the 'love' that Walter had for his 'spouse'. When it came time to present the paperwork, he'd simply waved him on, even shook his hand.

Walter simply nodded for most of the conversation. Yes, sad she'd died so young, certainly a tragedy, what a sad loss of life. The man seriously droned *on and on*. Walter patiently portrayed his heavy sadness and loss, but it was all for show. She'd died just like he knew she would and in just the way he'd wanted.

Prior to killing her, he laid low and allowed himself to be pampered by this sweet, young Janae. She'd nursed him back to health, thrilled with each wad of cash he'd given her to buy groceries and set up their apartment. It was like playing house, and she loved her role.

Walter lucked out after he was treated for his wound when he lifted a wallet from a tourist. He'd bumped him with his healing shoulder, made a big deal of it while the guy apologized and offered to help, ushering him to a bench and fussing over him completely unaware Walter had already lifted his wallet. It took only seconds. Once the tourist was gone, he opened the wallet and gasped at his major score. Thirty-five hundred dollars in cash! That was more than Walter had seen in months. The funds supported them while he healed, fed them, housed them and paid for plane tickets for his 'wife's' burial. It couldn't have been more perfect. The guy *had* to be on vacation or something because everyone knew carrying that much cash on your person was just plain stupid. Walter was happy to have been the one to teach him about never carrying large amounts of cash, anywhere, ever.

They were beginning their descent into the airport in Kalispell and Walter grinned. He turned and the man next to him was studying him with a look of distaste. Walter's grin turned to pure evil, his eyes filled with darkness as he thought of killing and displaying his dead. The man's jaw dropped and his eyes widened as he looked quickly away, and Walter's smile deepened. People were so easily frightened. The passenger couldn't get off the plane fast enough.

***

Gentry didn't sleep well, which made it a long night. Usually when he was out in the park for an overnighter, he slept like a log, but every noise hit his ears like a parade. Baby was quiet all night, which kept him from getting up and checking the sounds. If it was something unusual, she would have let him know. Still, it irritated him that he was so edgy.

First light was just barely breaking over the park when he decided to get up, have some breakfast and head out. Once he finished rolling his bedroll and crawled out of the tent Baby greeted him with a morning nod and stomp. Before he did another thing he walked to where she was tethered and visited with her for a minute.

"There's my girl," he said stroking her neck and standing with her head resting over his shoulder. He gave her a hug and patted her sleek neck. "Hope you slept better than I did last night. I don't see any bags under those eyes, though, so you're probably ready to go. How about I eat breakfast in the saddle?"

He quickly broke down the tent and rolled it up, placing it in the bag and stowing it. The supplies coming up would include a bigger tent and more tarp. He wouldn't need this one. He saddled Baby and placed his hat on his head as she gazed back at him and neighed.

"You never did like this hat, but I do and since I'm not asking you to wear it, you can just keep your opinions to yourself. And yes," he said, reaching back into the other saddlebag, "I'm eating breakfast, see?" He held a strip of jerky up so she could see it. She neighed softly and turned her head back around, stamping her foot.

Gentry stuck the jerky in his mouth, grabbed a piece of dried pear and climbed into the saddle.

"Ready girl?"

Touching her sides softly with his heels they started out.

It was going to be another beautiful day, at least until he got to the crime scene. He referred to his satphone and GPS coordinates he'd entered there to guide him to his destination.

As the light of the day grew brighter around him, he watched for footprints or broken branches, anything that would be signs of an inexperienced hiker. It was useless, though, as these trails were used by many backwoods hikers, and expecting to find a specific print was ludicrous. He pulled at some high grass and chewed on the stem of one of the pieces as he scanned the trail ahead.

About three miles into the ride he spotted some hikers camped off the path. He turned into their camp and found them just sitting down to a breakfast much like his. They turned as he rode in.

"Hey gentlemen," he said nodding. "How are you this fine morning?"

"We've been better," said a small man, thin and wiry. He looked like a runner.

"You wouldn't by chance be the men that found the scene up the trail a ways, are you?" Gentry didn't want to give out too much information, in case they weren't the right men.

"That's us, and I have to say, that was more than creepy, it was disgusting. What is something like that doing up here anyway?" The wiry man seemed angry, his companion nodding in agreement.

"I'm sorry," said Gentry, "sorry you had to find that. I'm on my way there now. About how much further do you think it is?"

"Probably five miles or so. We wanted to get more space between us and that thing, but it got too dark. Good luck with it."

Gentry gave them a nod and turned Baby. They continued on up the way, and when he found the crime scene, he knew what the man was talking about. It was like nothing he'd ever seen before. As he stood staring at the casket, he could hear the chopper coming up over the ridge. That was a good thing. He had no idea what kept this crime scene from being desecrated by wildlife. Sitting in the center of the casket lid was a severed head, the eyes staring blankly out at the trees.

Chapter Three

Gentry untied the bedroll from his saddle and removed the tarp. He strode quickly to the casket and threw it lightly over the top covering both the casket and its accompanying appendage.

The chopper roared into the sky over the crime scene and landed gently in the clearing. Once it was down, engines cut and rotors slowed, the hustle and bustle began. The assistant to Gentry, Dylan Sandusky, came off first and jogged head down away from the moving blades. He hurried to where Gentry was standing.

"We're loaded to the hilt in there Gentry," he said, combing his fingers through brown hair, brushing it back from his face. "Everything went smoothly and we have supplies for a week's stay. We weren't sure how long we'd need to be up here. I'll stay and cook if that works for you."

Dylan was possessed with the rare blue eyes that looked like he wore colored contact lenses. Gentry delighted in teasing him about this.

"Thanks, Dylan. I'll help unload and setup," he said, as he started for the chopper. He stopped suddenly and turned back to Dylan. "Oh and…" he moved closer staring into his friends left eye, "yeah, just as I thought. Your left contact is slipping."

"Will you zip it?" he said as Gentry laughed and jogged toward the landing area.

The two men worked alongside the FBI Agent and pilot, Cy Packer, to get the supplies unloaded and placed in the appropriate area for setup. Once it was finished, the helicopter lifted off, heading back down to the ranger station.

A nicely formed brunette headed toward Gentry, sticking her hand out as she approached him.

"Hi, I'm Lauren Porcelli, Special Agent with the FBI. You must be Ranger Beauchene."

"In the flesh. You can call me Gentry," he said with a warm grin and firm handshake. "Dylan and I would be happy to help you get your tent up and gear stowed."

"Thanks so much," she said, looking at the grand view surrounding her. "It certainly is amazing up here. Chilly, but really amazing."

Her brown eyes came to rest on him, and he couldn't help but feel he'd just been sized up.

"Yeah, it can get cold even this time of year when it's sweltering everywhere else. We get the cool weather up here in the high country."

There was an awkward silence and Dylan cut in.

"How about we get started on that set up?"

Lauren's eyes were now on the reason for her trip into the park.

"Mind if we take a look at the crime scene first? CSI is on their way, but it will be at least a couple more hours before they can get transport to Kalispell and then up here. They have a lot of equipment that's got to come with them."

She reached into a backpack she carried off one shoulder.

"Dylan, can you get started on the unloading? I'm sure Cy would help you out."

"Will do, boss," he said, heading in the direction of the chopper.

"It looks like this crime scene may be a bit different from the others," said Lauren, scrutinizing the gruesome spectacle before her. "Unless I'm mistaken, that lump on the top of the casket is probably a human head." She pulled out a camera, never taking her eyes from the tarp.

"Wow. You're dead on," said Gentry, turning back to Lauren apologetically. "Sorry…that was obviously a poor choice of words. I covered it because I didn't want it just out in the open like it was. I have no idea how something like that wasn't completely destroyed by animals. Which reminds me, I need to make a call down to the station."

"No problem. I'll just go have a look," she said masking a grin. "Oh, and by the way…I'm perfectly fine with you assisting me on the investigation if you're willing. No sense in bringing more feet up here to get in the way."

"Happy to help," he said. Then calling to his assistant he said, "Hey, Dylan, would you help Lauren remove that tarp?"

He tipped his hat at her and hurried to Baby, now tied to a tree. Reaching down to his belt, he pulled his satphone from its holster.

"Jackson."

"Hey Joe, there are some hikers up here, the men that found the body. I came across them when I was heading in and need you to do an intercept. I'm going to send you a description so you can identify them, possibly have Cy do a fly over today and see if he can find them."

"Okay, what do you want with them?"

"They told me the site was disgusting. I need to know what they meant by that. Have them describe what they saw. I should have done that myself, but didn't think much about it until I actually saw the scene. I need to know what they saw right away. It could tell us if the killer is still in the park."

He gave Joe all the information on the hikers he had, including a detailed description of the man he spoke with.

"Read it back to me," he said.

Joe read the information he'd written back to Gentry.

"Anything else?" he asked.

"Nope that'll be it," said Gentry, "and make it a priority."

"Consider it done."

"Thanks, Joe."

Gentry ended the call, hoping they were still in the park and making their way down rather than already gone. He needed to know if they saw a severed head on top of the casket, or if they were just saying the casket itself was disgusting. If there was no head when they saw it, then the killer was still in the area, and possibly watching them now. He didn't want to go off hunting in the woods if there was no one out there.

"Hey Baby," he said stroking her neck and talking softly. "You keep a sharp eye out, you hear? If you see anything, just let me know."

Gentry pulled a carrot out of the pack he carried for Baby. She took it and began munching. The muffled crunch of her chewing the carrot always made him grin.

"There's my girl," he said running his hand down her soft mane.

He turned and headed into the camp area to find Lauren grinning at him.

"I used to have a horse. She was my best friend, and we went everywhere together," she said wistfully.

"What happened to her?"

"She got old and we had to put her down," she said looking down at the ground and moving the dirt with her foot. "That was the hardest day of my life…it's only been recently I could get another one, and he has a warrior's heart. But I will always miss my Cookie girl. I think that first love is the strongest, don't you?"

She looked up as she blinked back tears.

"You're probably right. What's your boy's name?"

Lauren gazed over at Baby and chuckled softly.

"I had a real hard time trying to find a name for him. He's a very strong horse, an Arabian. He can be a handful, and I'm still training him, but he's beautiful and gentle when I stroke him the way you just did. I actually didn't know I'd miss him so much. I call him Shadow. What did you name your Mustang?"

"Ah, I see you know horses. She's called Baby Moon, but I just call her Baby. She has the same moon shape on her forehead as her mother, but smaller. She's the gentlest horse I've ever owned."

They stared at Baby for a few seconds, Lauren was glad to be reminded of her own friend, Gentry happy he had Baby along with him.

He cleared his throat.

"Guess we better get to the task at hand, eh?"

"Yes, yes we should. I'll wait to open the casket until CSI gets here, but we can at least inspect the scene. I just heard from them while you were on the phone, they're heading up in about thirty minutes."

"Oh, good," sighed Gentry. "We need to clear this area as quickly as we can. I'm trying to determine if the killer is still up here. I can't help but think if that head was on the casket all night, animals would have been all over it. But it wasn't touched, which makes me wonder if it was placed there this morning. If it was, he's hanging around here somewhere. I've got a call into my station to have them look for the campers that found the casket and ask them what they saw."

They walked over to the scene, and Gentry was still disgusted by the young age of the victim.

"What happens in someone's life that makes them turn into a monster? This was a child, someone's daughter. It just..." Gentry looked away.

"Well, that's apparently this killers MO. I read the profile by Aspen Beauchene... Beauchene...isn't that your last name?"

"Yes, she's my sister-in-law," he said.

"Oh, I heard she'd gotten married, which was kind of surprising. He's got to have the patience of a saint," she said walking around the casket as she slipped into exam gloves.

Realizing how rude she'd just sounded she stopped abruptly and stared wide eyed at Gentry.

"Oh, my gosh, I'm so sorry. That sounded just catty," she said, blushing.

"No worries. You should hear their story; it makes me laugh to hear Greyson tell it. The whole thing is quite entertaining, to say the least. Well, at any other time it would be entertaining."

"Well, I was saying I'd read her profile and the Evergreen Killer is partial to young girls, runaways or homeless. It's sad, really, because he must exploit their need for a male figure in their lives. Pretty cruel if you ask me." She continued around the casket, examining the head without touching it.

"Hmmm...interesting," she said, muttering to herself. "This head was severed post mortem, which is a blessing for the poor girl. The interesting part is it's completely clean. No blood visible anywhere. Even her hair has been washed and *styled*."

The thought brought anger boiling up inside him. Gentry viewed death before, this part wasn't new to him, it was the idea of the deceased being a child. He made a mental note to never marry, never have children.

"What's the point of that?" she mused softly.

"I'm sorry...what?" he asked, thinking he'd somehow spoken his last sentence out loud.

"Oh, nothing, just talking to myself. I was wondering why he would wash the hair and clean up the head, I'm going to have to call Aspen on this one. This is definitely new to this killer."

Lauren excused herself and went to place the call.

"Well, at least she's not psychic," he thought to himself.

Gentry turned to see what Dylan was doing. As requested, he was setting up the tents and working on getting the campsite organized.

"Every park ranger should have a Dylan," he thought to himself, smiling. Dylan worked independently; making sure the jobs that needed to get done did get done. This was incredibly helpful to Gentry, especially at times like this when there was so much to do.

Gentry took the opportunity to study the area surrounding the crime scene. He checked for footprints, beyond those of his and Lauren's. There were areas where the grass was stomped down, and he could see impressions. He would do what he could to keep from messing with those areas until CSI could get a good look.

Lauren was making her way back to where he stood.

"Well," she called out. "Aspen has some kind of a flu bug and can't make it up here. She was pretty chapped about that, but she's sending a guy she's worked with before. I've worked with him as well, he's an older gentleman, Todd Fairfield, very nice and very thorough, *and* he lives in Kalispell, so with the help of your pilot, he could be here fairly quickly."

"I'll get right on that. Any more word on when CSI will be here? Maybe we could coordinate the flight and get them all up here at the same time."

"I'll check on that, you check on the pilot."

She started punching numbers into her phone while Gentry pulled his phone from the holster at his waist and began making the call to the station. As he waited for Joe to pick up, his eye caught sight of something dripping from a corner of the casket. Apparently, Lauren saw the drip the same time and with phones to their ears they walked slowly toward the 'leak' and stared.

It was blood, dripping slowly onto the ground from inside the casket.

Chapter Four

"What the-"

Gentry stared at the blood as Joe picked up the phone.

"Jackson."

"Uh, Joe, I need you to make arrangements for another flight up. We need that CSI team up here ASAP and there'll be another passenger. His name is Todd Fairfield. He's an FBI Profiler and we need him flown up with the CSI's. It's urgent, Joe, make this a top priority for your morning and do nothing else until those people are on their way up. Make sure Cy is notified first so we get the chopper reserved."

"I'm on it. Oh, and Gentry?"

"Yeah?"

"I've talked with the campers and they said there was just a coffin there, emphasizing they felt it was gross that such a thing was so "flagrantly displayed" in a National Park. Like *we* could do anything about that."

"Yeah, right. You're going to want to make law enforcement aware of our situation up here right away. Tell them the killer is still in the park. Have them close off all entrances and exits and distribute a picture of the perp so they know who they're looking for. We'll do what we can to keep it safe in camp."

Gentry glanced at Lauren, who was madly dialing another number.

"Hey," she said, with urgency. "We've got a situation and we're going to need that CSI team as fast as they can get here, the Profiler as well. It's extremely urgent they are here within the hour. I don't know what you need to do to make that happen, but make it happen. We've got what appears to be blood seeping out of the casket, and that can't be a good thing."

She listened for a minute and checked her watch.

"That's good news, but make sure they wait for Todd. I want them all up here right away."

She ended the call and stared at the sight. Gentry saw the concern on her face.

"How can I help?" he asked.

"CSI is already at the helipad. They're waiting for Todd, and he'll be there momentarily. Is there a bucket or something we can put under that drip?"

"Dylan," called Gentry, can you bring a pan or bucket to catch this blood?"

Dylan hurried over with a large bucket. He placed it under the slow stream of blood and stepped back.

"Thanks Dylan," said Gentry.

Lauren continued studying the dripping blood.

"I've never seen anything like that. I don't even know what to do myself. If we open the casket, we could destroy evidence, valuable evidence. I'm betting the killer wants us to do just that. So, we wait."

"Okay, I'm good with that," he said with a sigh of relief. "Let's do some scouting until the chopper gets here. We should check out the surrounding area, see if we can find anything that might help us out. Make sure everyone coming up here brings weapons and they wear them the whole time they're here. We could have a killer still out there."

Lauren turned and stared at Baby.

"Will she be happy with two riders? We could cover a lot more ground with Baby than we could on foot."

"Yeah, she'll do fine. I'll saddle her up and we can start looking. Dylan can handle the remaining set up. I do have one concern though."

She gazed at him, waiting for him to explain.

"I don't want you staying in a tent by yourself until we know Walter Bantus is no longer in the park. You'll need to stay in the tent with Dylan and I. It's a two room, and can be sectioned off, so you would at least have some privacy."

Lauren looked down and grinned.

"Well, I'd have to say," she said, looking back up at Gentry, her green eyes soft and teasing. "I've had a few invites from men in my day, but that's just about the single most romantic invitation I've ever had."

She laughed and Gentry reached up and adjusted the brim of his hat. He grinned mischievously.

"Well, I can be even more romantic than that, when necessary."

"Hey Dylan," Gentry called to his friend, "We're going to go have a look around, I'll have my phone on if you need anything." He motioned to his side arm and then to Dylan. Dylan nodded that he understood.

"I've heard of reasons to get pretty girls into the woods, but you're shameless, Beauchene. Truly shameless," he said shouting back and pointing directly at Gentry. He then waved them off with a laugh and returned to the job at hand.

Gentry shook his head at Dylan's comment as he and Lauren strode to where Baby was tethered. Baby watched as they approached and moved toward Gentry giving him a gentle shove against his chest with her forehead.

"Not you, too. You and Dylan are making me look bad, you know. Are you *jealous*? Now really, Baby, you'll always be my best girl, you know that." He was looking into her eyes and rubbing her under the chin.

Baby tossed her head and whinnied softly.

"I don't think she believes you," laughed Lauren, "not even a little."

Gentry snickered and began talking softly to Baby as he stroked her neck, running his hand down her back and over her rump, patting it softly. He walked a couple steps to where the saddle lay on the soft grass and pulled the saddle blanket out from under it.

"Here you go, beautiful," he said, tossing the blanket over her back and positioning it just below her withers. He patted her through the blanket. The saddle was next and he picked it up with both arms, tossing it onto the blanket and adjusting its placement. Gentry stroked her neck again, still muttering softly to her as he cinched the saddle into place and then ran his fingers through her mane.

"I think you love your horse almost as much as I do mine," said Lauren, admiring his gentle manner. "Mind you, I said, almost."

"Oh, I don't know about that. She's got my back, pretty much anywhere--"

Baby suddenly lurched backward and tossed her head, whinnying loudly. Her eyes were wide and wild as she searched the forest, continuing to toss her chin skyward.

"Whoa, girl, whoa. I've got you, whoa. It's okay, Baby, take it easy." Gentry studied the wooded area where Baby continued to stare and prance back and forth. "Good girl, good girl. Easy…easy."

"There's someone out there," he said softly to Lauren.

The hairs on the back of his neck stood up and he knew they were being watched. He put his foot into the stirrup and slid easily into the saddle, then offered his hand down to Lauren. She took a step back and grabbing his arm jumped easily up behind him with one fluid movement.

"Ah, you've done this before," he said, watching the forest for movement.

"A few times," she said, wrapping her arms around his waist. She scanned the woods as well. "Nice abs, if you don't mind my saying so."

Gentry smiled softly, holding a piece of grass in his teeth.

"Well, I like to do what I can, you know?"

Lauren giggled and they started off.

It was getting close to eleven a.m. as they headed to the trail.

"I think we'll do a small circle around the camp, head into the woods from the trail and see what we can see."

"Sounds good to me." Lauren was still studying the shadows.

The wind picked up just a bit, sending a soft sigh through the treetops. The mountains surrounding their camp were snowcapped and stood in stark contrast to the deep blue of the sky. Small wildflowers grew in bunches along the trail as the sun peeked through the thick canopy of trees on either side of them.

About fifty yards from camp, Gentry turned Baby off the path and into the woods. Both riders kept their gun hand free and at the ready. They studied the ground below them for foot prints, zigzagging back and forth checking the ground and surrounding bushes.

"Hold up," said Lauren, sliding off the side of the horse. "I think I see something."

"I'll go with you. Which way?"

She pointed to their direct left, treading softly through the underbrush. Gentry quickly tied Baby to a bush, pulled his side arm and followed behind Lauren. Lauren checked a thorny bush and found a piece of red fabric. She struggled into exam gloves before pulling the fabric free and placing it in an evidence bag. She squatted down and touched the mud.

"Someone was here. This footprint is fresh. If I've read my profile correctly, it's Walter Bantus' print. They move off in that direction." She pointed north, away from the crime scene.

"You know his *footprint*?" Gentry was amazed.

"Yup, it's all in the profile." She stood and looked around. Gentry watched her as she studied the area. He was beginning to think there was more to this woman than FBI and horses. She was smart, easy on the eyes and good at her job. Yes, she just might be a force to be reckoned with, and he was ready for some reckoning.

She looked at him, familiar with the look in his eye and smiled.

"Simmer down cowboy; we've got work to do first."

He laughed softly and headed back to Baby. The fact that she was calmly waiting at the bush where he'd tied her made him think Bantus was long gone.

They continued on, circling around the campsite and crime scene. There were no more footprints, but there was enough in the first find to let them know he'd been there, and probably hadn't left yet.

Gentry walked Baby around in a circle from where Lauren found the fabric scrap and noted more footprints.

"Over here, Lauren."

The two of them followed the footprints to a section of forest tramped down from a small tent or sleeping bag.

They walked around the site looking for any evidence he may have left behind.

"He slept here last night," said Gentry, still watching the surrounding woods.

"Looks like it," agreed Lauren. "We better post a guard for the night; this could get ugly…as if it's not already."

Gentry had Baby's reins wrapped tightly around his hand in case she got spooked.

Suddenly there was a high-pitched laugh like a giggle of insanity ringing through the forest. Baby's eyes were wild once again, and she stomped the ground, pulling at the reins. Gentry lifted his gun, but had no idea where to aim. Lauren did the same thing, but with the same result. Back to back they stood with guns drawn, Gentry's other hand still holding tightly to Baby.

There was just the one peal of laughter and then nothing. Gentry wanted to take off after the sound, but it seemed to come from every direction. There was no way to know where to go.

"Come on," he said, touching her arm, "let's get back to camp. He wanted to spook us, and I'd say he did that very well."

They hurried to the horse and after holstering their weapons, Gentry lifted himself into the saddle, pulling Lauren up right after him. Before they'd gone two lengths, the wildly insane laughter started again. No words, just laughter.

"This killer has become a little more creative in his approach and, unless I'm mistaken, he'll be much more devious than this." Lauren was talking softly into Gentry's ear as she rode behind him, her arms snuggly around his waist. If they weren't both feeling the level of anxiety they were, it would have been a very hot moment. As it was, he decided it was a very hot moment anyway.

"He's upped his ante in this game, Lauren," he whispered back to her. "He's out for as much blood as he can get, and from whomever he can get it. Greyson and Aspen warned me about this. He's angry with them for messing with his mojo, and he wants his revenge. I think we need to be very careful. Oh, and…FYI, you can whisper in my ear anytime you want to."

Chapter Five

Lauren laughed. "I'm pretty good at multi-tasking. I'll see what I can do."

Once on the trail they broke Baby into a soft trot and headed the short distance back to camp. Gentry was amazed Bantus would be so brazen as to do something like this in broad daylight. He could hear Dylan calling for him as they approached.

"Gentry! What was that? Did you hear it?"

Gentry held his finger to his lips, quieting his friend, fearing Bantus may be within earshot.

"Yeah, we heard it, it was nothing. Some kid playing a joke. Are you all done with the setup?"

"Just finished," he said, nodding his understanding.

The sound of a chopper was heard coming up over the rise.

"There's the CSI team and Profiler. Let's see what they can find out."

While they waited for the chopper to land, Lauren turned to Gentry. She studied his face, searching his eyes, his lips, and the light brown hair peeking out from under his hat. Gentry shifted just a bit, looking down and feeling like she'd inspected every skin cell. The movement of his body forced her out of her reverie and she turned away, not realizing she'd been staring.

"Oh, sorry, I'm afraid I stare when I'm thinking. Didn't mean to make you feel uncomfortable." Then continuing on she said, "You know...I think I'd like to enlist the help of anyone that has some free time up here. If CSI has to wait for the Profiler to examine the crime scene, maybe they would be willing to help in a search of the woods."

"Why?" asked Gentry, trying to still his emotions from her penetrating stare. "What are we looking for?"

"I've been thinking," she said, *not* looking at Gentry. "This killer has a thing about recordings. I'm willing to bet if we got some help searching we'd find two recording devices out there with laughter recorded on them, and possibly some small, but powerful speakers. He may have rigged them so movement would trigger the device, or they could be on some kind of a timer. This guy is no dummy."

"We'll get some help and check it out." Gentry raised his voice to be heard over the sound of the landing helicopter.

Once it set down, he ran to the chopper with one hand holding his hat in place. He opened the door, helping the occupants exit, and then began unloading equipment. Cy cut the engine right away and set about helping with the unloading.

The CSI team leader strode to Gentry and held out his hand.

"Monte Philpot," he said with a broad grin. His dark eyes smiled when he did, with genuine warmth indicating instant friendship. His wild and curly dark hair stuck out from under a baseball cap. He looked to be in his mid-forties. "Let me introduce to you the team."

He motioned for the CSI members to come over and they stood next to him.

"This is Amber James. She'll be your go-to for questions and updates."

Amber stuck out her hand and shook Gentry's hand firmly.

"Nice to meet you, Ranger Beauchene," she said with a broad smile.

"You, too," he said, appreciating her firm grip, "you can call me Gentry."

She smiled and placed a CSI ball cap over her short cropped black hair.

"This is Lance Anselman," continued Monte. "He takes care of all the evidence tagging."

The thirty-something young man shook his hand and smiled.

"I'm really the brains of this outfit, but they don't want you to know that."

He chuckled as he patted Gentry on the shoulder, picked up a black case and started in the direction of the crime scene.

"And last but not least," smiled Monte, "is our second in command, Sandy Stiffle."

"Don't listen to Anselman. He's the baby of the group. I've been with the CSI for ten years next month. He's just jealous."

She shook his hand, running the fingers of her other hand through thick brown hair. Then with both hands she grabbed the long strands and quickly putting them in a ponytail. As she headed to the crime scene, she winked at Gentry. "We'll be out of your hair before you know it."

"Don't go messing with my crime scene," called out a white haired gentleman exiting the chopper. He strode quickly to Gentry, shook his hand and grinned.

"Todd Fairfield," he said, "Profiler Extraordinaire."

He turned to the CSI's and called to them again.

"You guys get back here and help unload this equipment," he said, playfully, pointing to the chopper. The team stopped in their tracks and turned back to the helicopter.

"Oh, yeah, sorry. We were just focused on getting this body back down to civilization," said Monte. "Come on guys, let's get unloaded."

When they'd finished getting the supplies and equipment off the helicopter, Gentry made a general announcement for any who would be willing to help with the search.

"We've had a situation up here and we could sure use your help if you would be so obliged. I know Todd has to take some time going over the crime scene first, so maybe the rest of you would be available to help while you wait."

Everyone nodded and stood in a half circle around Gentry.

Gentry, Lauren, and Dylan plus the four CSIs made seven people available to assist in the search. Gentry knew the killer had knowledge of flying helicopters and suggested Cy stay with the chopper. Todd, the profiler, headed to where the coffin stood to begin his inspection.

"Here's how we're going to do this," Gentry began, "we'll walk in a straight line formation about five to six feet apart. We're looking for a small recording device, and it could be tiny so you'll have to move slowly and check everything. Also, the devices may be on the ground under a bush or affixed to a tree or branch. Check everything. This is going to take some time. Lauren will hand out evidence bags, and we'll all wear exam gloves. If you find something, let Lauren have a look at it before you disturb it. She'll need to photograph it before it's bagged and tagged.

Everyone nodded their agreement.

They started at the tree line bordering the clearing where they set up camp. Moving very slowly they carefully moved foliage and checked each tree trunk and branch, squatting down to examine beneath each bush. Gentry's assessment was correct, it was very slow going, but eventually they heard a call out for Lauren. It was Monte. Lauren hurried to where he stood pulling the camera from her backpack as she went. Everyone stopped where they were and waited until the go ahead was given to proceed.

"Yup, just as I thought," she announced, "he recorded that laughter we heard. Let's keep looking; there's at least one more."

Lauren photographed the device and scrutinized it once it was bagged. She identified the timer on it but saw it had malfunctioned and didn't go off as it should have.

"Hey everyone, there may be more than we thought. This one didn't go off, so we're looking for at least two more." She placed the bag in a pocket on her pack and returned to her place in the line and called go to being searching again. It wasn't ten minutes before two other people called out, then shortly after, one more called out. Lauren rushed to their positions, checking the devices one by one. When she came to the last unit, she quickly called out a warning.

"Get back, everyone. We need to clear the general area. Let's get everyone back to camp. This one is different, and I don't think it's a recording device."

She moved softly toward the unit and bent over, inspecting the casing without touching it, and checking it for a timer.

She stepped back immediately.

"Gentry, we need a bomb squad up here ASAP."

"Dylan, go back and let Cy know to get the chopper going. We're going to need him to head back to the station for another pick up. I'll call the station and get the bomb squad rolling. Okay everyone; let's get out of the woods until we can better understand what we're looking at."

The group moved carefully out of the woods, retracing their steps. Once safely out of danger Gentry pulled his satphone from its holster.

"Hey, Joe," he said, when his assistant answered. "I need a bomb squad up here immediately. I'll need you to contact Law Enforcement and get their squad together. Have them waiting at the helipad for Cy, he's heading down now. Also, get supplies and tents together for however many are coming. Get the rest of the staff to help you; you're going to have to pull this together quickly."

"On it," he said, "anything else?"

"Nope," chuckled Gentry. "If you can get this done as fast as I need it up here, you deserve a cape and a big red 'S' plastered on your chest. Good luck."

He ended the call and turned around to hear concern growing within the group of searchers.

"What's up?" he asked, strolling up to Lauren.

"Amber's missing, Amber James. She didn't come out of the woods with the others," she was searching the woods with her eyes as she spoke. Lauren started toward the wooded area and Gentry grabbed her arm and turned her to face him.

"What do you mean 'missing'?" he asked. "And where do you think you're going?"

"Amber didn't come out when we called to clear the woods and *someone* has to find her. She's probably hurt and obviously unconscious or she'd be calling out for help."

"No, I'm afraid you're not going in there, Lauren. We just called for a *bomb* squad, remember? It's not safe in there."

Lauren looked at his hand on her arm and he quickly withdrew it.

"I'm…sorry. I can't let you go back in, Lauren, you have no idea what's in there."

"Yes, I do have an idea. There's at least one possible bomb in there, and one human being in need of assistance. I'm a trained FBI Special Agent. I can handle this, I *will* handle this. I'm going to go find her."

She turned and jogged into the forest.

"Well, you're not going by yourself, I'm right behind you," said Gentry pulling his gun. "You get blown up…I get blown up. How's that for romantic."

Lauren snickered.

Gentry stopped momentarily and turned, addressing the concerned group.

"Everyone stay put. We'll be right back; we're going to see if we can find Amber. Dylan, how about you get some lunch together for everyone?"

Gentry didn't want anyone else in the woods unless absolutely necessary.

The sun was high in the sky as they walked into the forest. It was a little easier to see, but not by much. There were streams of sunlight coming down through the openings in the forest canopy.

Gentry and Lauren followed the steps they'd taken when the group first lined up.

"Okay, we can be fairly certain there are no devices from the edge of the woods to where the first device was found."

Lauren was assessing the fastest way to find Amber.

"I believe if we follow her position in the line straight to where we stopped, we'll find her. She wasn't ahead of us, so she fell somewhere between this starting line and where we stopped."

"Be careful," warned Gentry. "The group could have missed one."

They walked single file through the searched area. Gentry saw Amber and called out to Lauren.

"There. She's over here!"

Lying unconscious between two bushes was Amber, her mouth and nose covered with a white powdery substance.

Chapter Six

Lauren gasped and knelt down beside Amber. Gentry moved in behind her to get a better look.

Her legs were still bent as if she'd been close to the ground looking at the device that sprayed her. Since no one heard her cry out, she must have gone down immediately and gone down hard, possibly unconscious before she even hit the ground.

"We've got to get her to Monte, he's a doctor."

Gentry came around the bush, facing Lauren.

"I can carry her out. She's not injured, so it won't hurt to move her and we don't have to risk anyone else coming in here."

Lauren gingerly lifted the bush and saw a small device that had been set up to shoot the substance out when the branch was lifted.

"I'm not moving that until I get some pictures. Let's get her out of here now; we can come back with the camera." Lauren stood back so Gentry could pick Amber up and they walked quickly out of the woods.

Lauren came out first calling for the CSI team leader.

"Monte! We need you over here quick. Bring your medical bag."

Monte ran to the supplies they'd brought up and grabbed an old black case.

"Someone get a blanket to lay her on," he said as Gentry exited the woods.

Dylan quickly brought a blanket and spread it out on the ground. Gentry laid Amber on it and stepped back so Monte could have room to work.

He checked her eyes and mouth. Listened to her heart, checked her pulse and sighed.

"She's asleep," he said, relieved. "I'm going to bet this is a ground up sleep agent of some kind, and a pretty strong dose from the look of it. I'd lay odds on Rohypnol. That's incredibly dangerous stuff. Rohypnol could've killed her if the dose is too high for her weight. Her heart sounds good, though, so whoever did this knew what he was doing. He obviously planned on a weight range and worked his dosage off of that."

"Will she be okay then?" asked Lauren.

"We'll monitor her every half hour, see how she's doing, but I think she'll be fine. Depending on the dosage, we may not hear anything from her for the rest of the day. We'll just have to wait and see." Monte glanced to the casket.

"It looks like Todd is about done over there. He's going to want to see what's under the lid of that casket. Do you have anyone that could sit with Amber?" Monte looked up at Lauren and Gentry.

"I can stay with her," said Dylan. "I'd be happy to do that."

"Thanks."

Monte turned to the crime scene. "I'm more curious now than I was when we got here, and I was plenty curious then." He turned to the other team members. "Let's go have a look, shall we?"

Lauren glanced at Gentry.

"I need to get pictures of that device before we move it. Are you up for another walk in the woods?" she grinned slightly.

Gentry wasn't happy about going back in there before the bomb squad arrived, but they'd already been in once with no mishaps.

"After you, M'Lady," he said with a wave of his arm.

She grinned at him and headed into the brush. He followed her, enjoying the view from behind.

"Stop staring at my butt," she said with a smile to her tone.

"Well, I'd have to say it's the best looking thing I've seen all day," he grinned, lifting his hat and scratching his head.

"You say that to *all* the girls. Sounds like you have a few you like bringing into the woods according to Dylan," she teased.

"Yeah, don't believe everything you hear from him. He's just mad cause I tease him about his blue eyes."

"What's wrong with blue eyes?" she asked.

"Really? Have you *seen* his eyes? They make the sky look dull. They're girlie eyes, too blue for a man and I have to remind him of that every now and again." Gentry scoffed.

They reached the bush where the device lay hidden. Lauren reached into her bag for her camera.

"You hold the bush out of the way and I'll get some shots of it before we disconnect it. You better wear these."

She held out a pair of goggles and a facemask.

"Serious?" he said, staring at her.

"Of course. You want to find out if it all sprayed out and get a mouth full yourself? Better safe than sorry I always say." She placed the goggles snuggly over her eyes and the mask over her face. Gentry did the same and soon the smell of menthol permeated his sinuses.

"Whoa, what's with the stinky stuff?" he asked holding up the bush with watering eyes.

"You'll be happy to have that *stinky stuff* when we look at the contents of the casket. Trust me."

Lauren snapped a few pictures and gingerly lifted the device, unhooking it from the branch as she went. It appeared the small cartridge had emptied with the initial blast received by Amber. She inspected it a bit more before placing it in an evidence bag and labeling the bag.

"Bagged and tagged," she said, removing her goggles and mask. This was the first time she got a good look at Gentry, completely decked out in his Stetson hat, goggles and facemask. She couldn't help herself and started laughing.

"Do you *ever* remove that hat? It does sort of complete the ensemble, I guess."

Gentry removed the mask and goggles, handing them back to Lauren.

"As a matter of fact, I do. I take it off when I sleep, but usually it's covering my face at that point."

She laughed again as she took the goggles from him.

"You may want to hang onto that mask. They probably have the casket opened by now."

Gentry and Lauren headed back to the campsite just as the lid came off the pine box. Something was wrong.

The CSI team jumped back from the box and Todd leaned carefully over it, holding the mask to his face with his hand. He straightened and stepped back.

Lauren put the bagged evidence from the woods in her pack, along with both pairs of goggles and placed the mask over her mouth and nose. Gentry followed suit and they approached the scene. What they saw made everyone in the group want to wretch. Even the CSIs, who'd seen many gruesome crime scenes, were weak in the stomach.

Peering over the side, Gentry saw blood, lots of blood, like a soup. Floating in the blood were arms, legs, pieces of hair and another head. There was more than one body in this casket and from what they could see, all of the bodies had been surgically dismembered.

He stepped back and breathed in the menthol from the face mask. It seemed to help his stomach as much as disguise the wretched smell that infiltrated the area. He'd never experienced anything like this, and hoped he'd never have to again.

The cover was quickly replaced and the CSIs began to bring over large ice chests. They put on gloves that went up to their shoulders and full body gowns. They began readying the chests to receive the body parts. Larger evidence bags were brought out for the torsos and boxes for the heads.

Gentry turned and headed to where he'd tethered Baby. He removed his facemask as he walked and let it fall to the ground. At this moment in time, he needed to hold something living, something that breathed, that wasn't unconscious or cut up into little pieces. As he approached, Baby neighed softly, sensing his need and responding to it.

She strode to him, the familiar clomp, clomp of her feet already easing his stress.

"Hey Baby," he said softly, letting her drop her head over his shoulder. "How's my girl, huh?" He slowly stroked her neck, feeling the living flesh beneath his hand, sensing her heartbeat. He leaned his head into her and patted her again.

Lauren, approaching from behind him, walked around where he stood and turned to face him.

"I know things like this are tough. This is the worst I've ever seen, if that's any comfort."

She reached out and squeezed his arm.

"You need to feel life, right now, to feel something living in your arms. I know exactly how you feel. You're doing the right thing, you really are, and your feelings are normal."

Gentry dropped his arm from under Baby's neck and reached for Lauren. He swept her into him, pressing his lips against hers, feeling his heart pulse through him. She responded to his kiss, softly at first, then placing her hands on either side of his face she pressed against him, moving her arms around his neck and pulling him as close as she could.

It was exactly what he needed, but he pulled away from her, ashamed of his actions.

"I'm sorry, I didn't mean to use you like that. I…I just was in…"

"Shock," she said softly. "You weren't using me any more than I was using you. We're human beings, Gentry, we laugh, we cry, we *feel,* we need." She reached up and put her hand on his chest. "Feeling a living heart beating beneath the skin can bring us back to reality after viewing something like that. It's what makes us human beings."

He smiled slyly at her.

"Do you mind if I try that?" he said grinning slightly.

"Not at all," she said picking up his hand and placing it over his chest where her hand had been.

Gentry laughed softly.

"That isn't *exactly* what I had in mind," he said chuckling.

"Yeah, I know," she smiled knowingly. She lowered her hand and smacked his arm gently. "I know."

Gentry turned to Baby who nuzzled him with her soft nose.

"Thanks, girl." He patted her chest. Then turning to Lauren he said, "See? Baby doesn't mind."

"Yeah, yeah," she grinned, "let's get back to work."

The CSIs were still emptying the casket of body parts, bagging them and putting them in ice chests. It was grizzly work, but they were learning some things about the scene. As Lauren approached, Monte looked up.

"Well, Lauren," he said with a sigh, "this is most likely the blood from several bodies. It looks like we have two young girls, which is the killer's usual MO, but far more blood than could be drawn from only two bodies. Clearly the evidence at this scene differs drastically from the previous scenes. It appears they were embalmed prior to dismemberment. Mixing the blood of both victims, and from where ever he got the rest of it, will contaminate DNA, rendering it useless as evidence. We'll be hard pressed to chalk these murders up to the Evergreen killer. There was no sapling that we could find, but we haven't removed the torso's as yet. Without that sapling, this could just be a copycat murder. This crime scene is a mess, nowhere near the way the other scenes have been laid out. The other team that's worked these scenes has left us volumes of evidence to compare, so we'll be comparing our evidence with theirs. We'll see what the torso gives us when we finally get to it."

Gentry watched Lauren's face. He couldn't help but wonder how she managed to keep her sanity with all the ugliness she must see each day. He saw some of it in his line of work, but nothing like this. Lauren was listening intently, her face a mask of concentration. Not even a hint of the repulsion he felt.

Gazing from the gruesome crime scene before him to his horse serenely grazing on the opposite side of the site was like experiencing two different worlds. The passion he felt when he held Lauren in his arms, her body against his, that was real, that was *human*. This crime scene, it was, animal…no not animal, animals didn't kill for the joy of killing. Animals killed to survive. These killings were not done by anyone with even a shred of humanity in them. They were done by a monster. Somehow, it helped him understand the difference between the two worlds.

He refused to call the killer an animal and demean the beauty that thrived in the animal kingdom. He refused to call him human, and lessen the dignity of the men and women that walked this world. The only word for him was monster.

Just as the reconciling of his worlds was beginning to make sense, a loud fit of laughter emanated from the woods. It appeared the nocturnal animals would be setting off the motion sensors on the remaining devices. This would be a long night.

Chapter Seven

Dylan was prepping for dinner as the team wound down their part of the investigation. Amber was beginning to come around, slowly, and with a massive headache that kept her from wanting anything in her stomach. Sitting upright seemed to make the pain worse, so Monte made the decision to have her on a gurney for the flight back to the station. Gentry supplied one from the first aid kit he had with his gear. It was compact and fit inside the kit, but telescoped out to a full sized gurney.

After discussing the situation with Gentry, it was decided the CSI would take all the blood with them in extra containers and dispose of it at the station. It was dangerous to leave that amount of blood in the woods where animals could get aggressive with anyone found near it, including the campers.

They poured large amounts of water over the spot where the blood dripped from inside the casket to dilute the scent as much as possible. It was a lot of work and required each person to take turns hauling buckets of water up from a stream a hundred yards from the site, but it was a good precautionary measure.

The tents were set up; one large one and a small one close by it. The campfire was a safe distance from the tents but close enough to keep it cozy. On the opposite side of the campfire from the tents, Dylan set up the kitchen and was busy preparing barbecued hamburgers for dinner. The air smelled of dinner cooking and it made the group hungry.

"We've got a tent set up for you, Todd, if you need to stay another night. We've got plenty of food, and as you can see an excellent cook." Gentry waited for the profiler to answer.

"I think I'll head down with the others. I need to get this addendum to the current profile typed up and off to the FBI in Seattle. It's valuable information and needs to be included ASAP. Thanks for the invite, though."

"No problem. We'll eat some burgers and you can be on your way then," he said, motioning to the seats around the campfire.

Everyone gathered in the kitchen area and enjoyed the early dinner. The conversation led to campouts from their childhoods, and once one person told a story, someone else added theirs and around the group it went.

"I remember one time when my dad took his new truck camping for the first time," Gentry leaned back and enjoyed the memory. "He wasn't an animal person back then, well, a small animal person and my mom had this miniature dachshund she wanted to take camping with us. Well, she won out and the dog wasn't allowed at the beach, so we put her in the back of the truck with all the windows open when we went down to swim. When we got back to camp my dad about killed that dog. She'd torn every screen out of every window in the canopy on the back of his new truck."

"I remember camping with my grandpa," said Lauren, a wistful smile gracing her lips. "It was the best trip ever and we laughed and told stories around the campfire that night. We played games and ate popcorn until we couldn't eat another thing. We finally went to bed and broke camp in the morning. My grandpa died at his house the night they got home. They said it was a massive heart attack, but I'll always have that last campout and remember him laughing and having such a good time."

There were more stories, some happy, some sad, but all good solid memories. Memories that brought them all back to a simpler time when decisions weren't quite so hard and life wasn't nearly as ugly as it could get in their line of work.

When they finished eating, light was waning and the group prepared to head back down to the station.

They all worked together cleaning up dinner and getting the food put away. The casket was loaded onto the chopper first, followed by the CSI equipment, then Amber's gurney and finally everyone else. The helicopter rose slowly and sped quickly away once it was airborne.

Gentry, Dylan and Lauren were the only occupants of the campsite for the night. Gentry wasn't convinced Walter Bantus was out of the park. The bomb squad would be coming up the next day to scour the woods and before darkness set in the three campers went about masking off around the area where they thought the recording devices to be.

As they settled around the campfire for the night, darkness closed in around them. It was a beautiful starlit evening, the full moon sat motionless in a sea of stars.

"It certainly is amazing up here," sighed Lauren. "I'm thinking I should bring Shadow up here and camp. It would have to be next year; he needs a little more behavioral training, I think."

"Well, come on up anyway," smiled Gentry, "I can get a horse for you. It's a great time of year to come to Glacier, which reminds me, I need to make a call."

"Still shameless," chuckled Dylan. "I don't care what color my eyes are, you're still shameless."

"What are you going on about, blue eyes?" Gentry teased him back. "That was a flagrant ploy to get a beautiful woman to notice your girlie eyes. Now who's being shameless, hmm?"

Dylan snickered and Lauren giggled at his discomfort.

Gentry pulled his satphone from the holster on his belt. He dialed the station number and waited for Joe to pick up.

"Jackson."

"Hey, Joe," said Gentry, "I'm going to need Handsome brought up here with two more horses."

"To the campsite?" he asked.

"Yeah, I'll need them here with tack and more supplies. Make sure there's extra rope and shovels."

"Shovels?" Joe sounded confused.

"Yeah, I don't know. Just make sure they're included. This guy we're looking for is crazy-weird, and we need to be prepared. Oh, and make sure you schedule a chopper pick up for whoever you get to bring Handsome and two more horses up. They'll need a way to get back down."

"Done."

"Oh, Joe?" Gentry remembered one more item of business.

"Yeah?"

"How soon will the bomb squad be up here? We need to get on Bantus' trail before he's gone."

"They told me it would be sometime before noon tomorrow."

"Thanks."

Gentry ended the call and stuffed the satphone back in its holster.

***

Lauren laughed at the banter between the two men. She could tell they were good friends and after the day they'd had, it was good to see the interaction between them and enjoy a laugh or two. Somehow, it helped her relax.

As she watched and listened to them, she reflected on her own life and how her priorities had changed over the years. From as early as she could remember she'd wanted to be an FBI Special Agent. She had no idea where that came from. Her parents weren't agents; no one she knew was affiliated in any way with the FBI. It's like the idea was imprinted on her at birth. Maybe her mother's gynecologist was an undercover G-man. She giggled at the thought.

She'd worked hard in her career to get where she was. Making a name for yourself at the Bureau wasn't an easy thing to do as a woman, but she'd done it, and here she was, working the highest profile case out there. Still, it wasn't all she'd hoped it would be, or maybe it didn't make her feel the way she thought it would.

She gazed across the fire pit at Gentry, laughing and having a good time with his friend. He'd done it right, by all appearances. He'd made friends along the way to get where he was. Lauren realized she'd made connections, and that was a far cry from friends.

Maybe that's what made her take a second look at this man. Well, the first look was how he worked with his horse. Clearly he had a gentle heart, and that heart spoke to her in ways she'd not known before. Better said, it was in ways she'd never allowed herself to know before.

She'd dated, but never seriously. There was little time for that in her line of work. What was it about this man that made her rethink how she used her time? Lauren was sure she'd done life correctly, at least until Gentry Beauchene stepped into view.

Well, she had to stop this line of thinking right now. He was no different from any man she'd ever dated. He had one thing on his mind and one thing alone. Okay, two things. Women and his horse. Right?

No, she wasn't right and she knew it. This man was the genuine article, the real deal. He had integrity, grit and an incredible amount of sex appeal. Nice. What was she supposed to do with this man?

***

"You're being awfully quiet over there," Gentry said, his smile soft and inviting. "What are you thinking so hard about?"

"Oh, you know, just reviewing the case, going over what we know so far."

Lauren stared at the fire, watching the flames dance around the logs snapping and popping small embers into the air as it burned.

"Well, cough it up," chuckled Gentry. "What do we know so far?"

He was beginning to notice things about her, how her mouth turned down just a tiny bit at the corners when she was thinking. How her eyebrows would furrow when she was focused on a conversation, devouring information she needed to remember. There was something she did with her hands, too. She 'talked' with her hands a lot. They were very expressive, with long fingers and well manicured nails. They'd felt really good resting on his chest when he'd kissed her earlier in the day.

Gentry could still taste her mouth on his, he remembered how she'd accepted his kiss, not just kissing back, but almost like she was giving herself permission to kiss him back. He wondered how he could possibly know that, but there was a hesitancy in the beginning of the kiss, and then that wonderful sense of…yes…*allowing* herself to give back. This was a woman that worked too hard in her lifetime and needed to relax, a woman that needed him, because he was just the man to help her do that.

"Well," she began, her mouth forming that amazing pout. "We have a lot of assumptions, but no proof of anything, really. We assume Bantus is still in the park and he's toying with us, almost like he wants to be caught, in my humble opinion. He's far more into the game then he's been before, and that could be good or bad. He could get sloppy, or he could get more aggressive."

She thought for a moment and Gentry didn't stop her. He was beginning to enjoy her thoughtful moments.

"If he's still here, he's playing a dangerous game. He should have learned from his encounter in Denali that sticking around a crime scene is like playing with fire, and he got burned last time. So why is he still here? What is he thinking? This is where I wish I'd done a more thorough study of profiling."

Dylan rose and grabbed the coffee pot, refilling everyone's cup before setting it back down and returning to his seat.

"How many vacations have you had in your career, Miss Porcelli?" he asked her as he slid into his chair. He leaned back and took a sip of his drink.

"Hmm? Me? Call me Lauren." she looked startled. "Well, I did go on a cruise once, but I went by myself and totally decided never to do that again. The ship was filled with families and couples and I felt like the odd one out everywhere I went. Other than that, none, really."

"Serious?" Gentry eyed her skeptically. "You've had one vacation? How does Shadow feel about that?"

"He's new on the scene. I've only had him about eight months. But Cookie, now, I think she noticed, and that's my biggest regret. I wish I'd spent more time with her." She smiled wistfully into the flames.

"Well, it's never too late, you know." Gentry smiled a warm, sexy, inviting smile. "There's a lot to see up here, and a lot to explore."

He'd wanted to add, 'me included' to the 'explore' part of his comment, but thought better of it.

Lauren raised her eyes from the fire and stared at Gentry.

"I guess I've just never had a lot of time to spend playing."

"Oh, now, there's where you're thinking is skewed." Gentry's soft blue-green eyes stared right back at her. "You're just not playing enough."

"Hey Dylan," he said turning to his friend. "We're going to have to show the lady how we play in Montana, eh?"

Dylan grinned and sat back in his seat.

"Pretty much like this, isn't it? A good fire, good company and a beautiful night? Pretty much like this, I'd say."

Baby neighed softly, nervously. Her tether was about twenty feet from where the group sat and Gentry was keeping an eye on her throughout the conversation. She was his first line of defense.

"What is it, girl?" he said, calling to her.

She neighed again, this time moving her feet slightly and staring into the woods as she lifted her head.

Gentry's voice got low as he looked around the campfire.

"You have your gun on you, Dylan?" he said softly.

"Yup, I do."

"I have mine, as well," muttered Lauren.

Gentry stood and walked to where Baby was tethered.

"There's my good girl," he said, rubbing her forehead and patting her neck. "You just keep an eye out, you hear? That's my girl."

He grabbed her brush out of his saddlebag and started slowly brushing her down, glancing into the woods now and then without actually *looking* like he was looking. The brushing seemed to help calm Baby.

"Hey Dylan," called Gentry, "come help me move her line closer to the tents. I meant to do that earlier and forgot."

He patted her rump and began untying one end of her line. Dylan joined him, loosening the other end and they carried the rope to a couple of trees on the opposite side of the campsite and nearer the tent.

Gentry walked back to his saddle and put the brush back in the bag. He picked up the saddle and looked at Lauren.

"You're sleeping with us tonight, right? And I mean that in the most innocent of ways."

There was that grin again. He could tell she liked his grin.

"I'll take first watch," said Dylan. "I'll come and get you in about three hours, so you better get some sleep in there."

Lauren and Gentry stood and he stretched before heading into the tent.

"You coming?" he said smiling.

Chapter Eight

Once in the tent, Lauren turned on the battery powered lamp and started to the back of the tent. She headed into the separate room where she would sleep. She'd taken only a couple steps when she felt a gentle hand on her arm as Gentry pulled her to him.

"Where do you think you're going?" he said grinning.

"I'm going to bed…alone, Mr. Beauchene. You'd best do the same," she said smiling back up at him.

She grabbed the brim of his hat and pulled the hat down over his forehead. Setting the lamp on the floor, she wrapped her arms around his neck and stared into his eyes.

"You get one kiss, Mister, and that's it."

There was that permission thing again. She was going to take a great amount of loosening up.

Gentry released her waist and took her face in his hands. He stroked her cheeks with his thumbs and gazed softly into her eyes.

"I'm going to have to teach you how to relax, Ms. Porcelli."

With that he softly, and briefly, touched her lips to his, holding her there for a short few seconds. He stepped back and smiled at her, leaving a very weak-kneed Special Agent to stumble into her room and close the partition.

It was four a.m. when Dylan entered the tent and softly shook Gentry awake.

"Man! Already? I don't think I'd even closed my eyes yet!" Gentry sat up and ran his hands over his face.

"I actually let you sleep a couple of extra hours," he grinned. "Mostly cause I didn't want to sleep for two hours and get up again. Have at it; it's been quiet all night.

"I'm on it. Sleep well, Dylan."

He stood up and having slept in his clothes, slipped into his boots, pulled on his coat and placed his hat on his head. He stretched and headed out the tent door, and gazed up at a blanket of stars that always made him gasp just a little in wonder.

He checked around the side of the tent where Baby was sleeping. She must have smelled him because she turned her head and whinnied softly. Gentry grabbed a carrot from the cooler and after stuffing it in his pocket, strolled to where she stood.

"Hey, girl," he whispered, stroking her neck and scratching her forehead. "How's my best lady, eh?"

Gentry had his hand in his pocket and Baby nudged his arm, trying to reveal the hidden treat.

"You've got me pegged, don't you now?" he said with a soft chuckle.

He pulled his hand from his pocket revealing the juicy carrot, which he promptly gave to her. She chomped on the vegetable with satisfaction, bringing a smile to Gentry's face.

"Go back to sleep, girl. Not daylight yet."

He walked back around the front of the tent and poured himself a cup of hot coffee. He stoked the fire, added a couple logs and sat down in one of the camping chairs, keeping his back to the front of the tent.

The night was nothing short of stunning. Realizing there was a beautiful woman sleeping right behind him made him wonder why he'd never shared this view with a woman before. He figured it was because he'd never found anyone he'd cared to share it with. He didn't know enough about her, really, except that she loved horses. That was a definite plus.

However, this was business, and that didn't leave a lot of time for personal talk. In reality, he didn't know how she actually felt about anything. Maybe she just liked to kiss guys. She was certainly good at it.

He smiled again at the thought, remembering the feeling of her mouth on his. Yup, she was really quite good at it.

He took a sip of the hot coffee and scanned the campsite and surrounding area. The coffee slid easily down his throat and as he swallowed there came a deep, low moan from the woods in front of him. The batteries on the remaining devices were wearing down, giving off a much creepier sound than the original laughter. It sounded like one of those scary clown movies where the clown started moving in slow motion, laughing slowly and menacingly as its voice gets deeper and deeper.

"*Okay,*" he thought to himself, "*now I'm creeping myself out.*"

Occasionally there was a large snap of a twig or small branch. Gentry was familiar with the nocturnal animal life of his park, but just the same the sound made him jump. Without knowing for sure if Bantus was in the park, there was always an uneasy feeling when one of those sounds jumped out of the brush at him, raising the hairs on the back of his neck at least temporarily.

The movement of night animals continued to set the recorders off a couple times an hour. He was glad they'd discovered them earlier and expected that eerie sound. Between it and the snapping branches he would already have been to the other tent, grabbed his night scope from its protective case and been searching the woods. As it was, he did that anyway, just to make sure what he'd heard was forest critters.

Returning to his chair, he picked up his cup from the small table beside him, took a careful drink of the dark hot liquid and slowly scanned the forest with the night scope. All was quiet as he took another sip of coffee and set the cup back on the table. He lowered his scope and laid it across his lap, drinking in the beauty of this pre-dawn hour.

Suddenly Baby snapped to attention, rearing up and whinnying loudly. Gentry grabbed his scope and jumped to his feet. He ran to her side, pulling down on her lead rope.

"Whoa, girl," he said as he tugged gently at the rope, "whoa, now. What'd you hear out there, huh?"

Gentry raised the scope to his eye and searched the woods.

"Looks like whatever it was is long gone," he said patting her neck and running his hand down her back. "Good job, as usual, Baby. Good job."

He scanned the foliage one more time, but was certain the problem was gone, as Baby was calm and once again munching on grass. Gentry strolled to the spare tent and grabbed a couple handfuls of hay from the bale brought up in the last chopper load. He returned to where she stood and dropped the handfuls on the ground in front of her. She neighed softly and chewed contentedly on the hay.

Gentry turned to go back to sit down and saw Lauren standing beside the tent.

"Did she wake you?" he asked, happy for the company. "Sorry."

"It's fine," she said smiling at him. "Didn't see anything out there?"

"Nope. But *she* sure did, or at least she heard something. I'll check out the area tomorrow and see if I can find any footprints," he glanced at Lauren and nervously glanced up to the sky.

"Ever see such a night sky?"

"No, I haven't," she said, "It's absolutely stunning."

"You should go back to bed. We've got a big day ahead."

"No, I think I'm up for good at this point. But it's so beautiful, I don't mind."

"Well," he said pointing to the east, "the sun is going to be coming up over that ridge in about an hour. It's definitely worth staying up for."

Gentry got another cup and poured some coffee for Lauren. She pulled a chair up to the tent next to Gentry and sat down, wrapping her coat around her. He handed her the cup and sat down next to her.

"You know," he said, smiling, "we haven't actually had much opportunity to talk. I don't know very much about you at all. Do you have brothers? Sisters?"

"Yes, I do, two sisters actually," she replied. "I don't get to see them that often, and I miss them a lot. How about you?"

"I have two brothers, all Park Rangers and two sisters, one is a profiler for the Wyoming State Police and one is a Doctor. My mom and dad still live in Idaho, where we grew up."

"Ah, that explains the horses. Though, I guess not all people that grew up in Idaho had horses, right?"

They laughed and Gentry adjusted his hat.

"Where are you from? Where did you grow up?" he tipped his head forward and watched her face as she thought about home.

"Oh, I grew up in the Mid-West, a little town in Iowa. It was a farming community and I loved every minute of it. Small school, small town, friends that last a lifetime, it was perfection."

Gentry grinned and leaned back.

"I can relate to that. Growing up in a small town is awesome. Someday, if I can get past what I've seen these last two days, I'm going to have a ranch where my kids can grow up without fearing for their lives. I mean, I'm sure big city kids don't all fear for their lives, it's just that I prefer small country towns. It's all about roots, I guess, you know, where you come from."

Lauren smiled.

"I've never thought about having kids. It seems my brain has been quite 'tunnel visioned'. All I've ever wanted in life was to be an FBI agent. Having a family seems to conflict with that lifestyle. Not much time to really settle down or raise a family. An agent is constantly called out at all hours of the day or night. It's not like your normal nine to five job, it's…very demanding."

"So," smiled Gentry, "it sounds like it's not all you'd hoped it would be."

"Oh, it is. It's just that, it's probably a little *more* than I'd hoped. You know, it's more time consuming than I ever thought it would be. But it's also incredibly interesting. I've met or worked with such a variety of people, and the cases are always fascinating."

"I hope they're not all as gruesome as this one." Gentry took a sip of his coffee, winced, and dumped it on the ground, pouring himself a fresh cup.

"Well, they're either gruesome, heartbreaking or rewarding, but the majority are rewarding. It's not an incredibly positive lifestyle. I have to work every day to protect my attitude. It's easy to become cynical in this line of work."

"I think you need to look into the National Parks System. Yes, as you can see, we have a bit of the gruesome, but you only need raise your eyes and beauty explodes right in front of you."

Gentry stood and grabbed the lantern, preparing to walk the perimeter of the camp, checking into the forest with his night scope.

"Mind if I tag along?" she asked, standing.

"Not at all," he said, starting out, "You can carry the lantern. Feels good to move around a little bit rather than spend the whole time in a chair. He carried his cup of coffee in one hand and his scope in the other.

"How long have you been a park ranger?" she asked as they strolled through the dew covered grass. The air was crisp and she held her coat closed around her with her free arm.

"Hmm," he said, trying to remember, "I guess it's been about seven years now."

"Good grief! When did you graduate? When you were ten?"

Gentry laughed and peered down at her.

"No, I was actually just out of the service and a good solid twenty-three."

"Do you enjoy it?" she asked him.

"Can't think of a single thing I'd rather do," he said, smiling down at her.

"What about you? How long have you been with the bureau?"

"About five years," she said pensively.

"And do *you* enjoy it?"

"Most of the time. It can be very difficult, but it's always very rewarding."

They walked the remaining perimeter, Gentry pausing now and again to check the forest. Their conversation never stopped. He was happy to have chosen the park system over the FBI. Still, it was fascinating to hear her stories. It was even more fascinating to hear her *tell* them. She was really quite stunning to watch, and quite animated in her delivery.

They arrived back at the tent and after checking on Baby they sat back down in their chairs. It wasn't but just a few minutes and Gentry pointed to the east and the rising sun. A thin layer of clouds shone with incredible pinks and yellows as the sun burst over the snow covered peak.

He set down his cup and stood.

"I've always wanted to do this," he said, taking her cup and putting it on the table.

"What-"

"Shhh…" he said, pulling her to her feet and placing his finger softly over her mouth.

He pulled her to him, pointed to the rising sun. He watched her take in the gorgeous colors of the new day, the sounds of birds bursting into song in the tops of the trees. He lifted her chin and placed his mouth over hers, drinking in the warmth of her body in his arms.

He felt Lauren merge into him and acknowledged her response. His hands explored her back, bringing her close enough to feel their hearts beating between them. Gentry held her tightly, his tongue exploring her mouth, their passion rising with the morning sun.

Chapter Nine

The sound of someone loudly clearing their throat broke the reverie of the moment. Gentry jumped back, Lauren straightened her shirt, both trying to look far too nonchalant for the moment.

"A little late for that, don't you think?" grinned Dylan. "How long was that kiss anyway? It's almost high noon."

"Very funny," snorted Gentry. "We were just getting to know each other, you know, so we can work together…like professionals."

Dylan's laughter could be heard for miles as he stumbled from the tent.

"I think you're about a mile and a half past the 'getting to know you' phase, and the professional piece just went right out the window."

Dylan moved past them toward the campfire. "I'll stoke what's left of the fire and get some breakfast going. You better *never* give me grief about my eyes again, Gentry, because *man*, have I got the goods on you. I mean, getting it on with an FBI Special Agent. Oh…this is good stuff."

The laughter continued as he went about getting breakfast.

Gentry, head partially down, lifted the brim of his hat and peered up at Lauren, who was looking a little pale. When she saw his glance, combined with the pained wince he gave her, she started laughing as well. Gentry grinned and headed to where Baby was standing, having watched the whole exchange.

"Hey, Baby Moon," he said rubbing her forehead. "I'm going to go have a look in the woods. You stay here and guard these two trouble makers, you hear?"

Baby raised her head and stared at him. Her demeanor made him glad horses couldn't talk. The body language was more than enough.

"Dylan," he called out, "I'm going to go see if I can figure out what spooked Baby this morning."

"Okay, Casanova. I'll be here, cooking your breakfast." He was chuckling before he even finished his sentence.

Lauren hurried over to Gentry.

"I'm going with you."

"Sure you want to risk your professionalism?" he grinned.

"Oh shut up and move," she said, disgusted, but still smiling.

That exchange started a whole new round of laughter from Dylan.

Gentry and Lauren wove through the woods, watching the ground for tracks of any kind. They'd only gone about fifteen yards into the woods when Gentry heard Lauren call to him.

"Over here."

He moved to her location and knelt down. The tracks were Bobcat, and they were the only tracks in the moist dirt.

"Well, that's a relief," sighed Gentry, standing. "At least she wasn't spooked by Bantus."

"Yeah, for sure," agreed Lauren. "Still, I feel strange about him right now. Something's up, but I can't figure out what."

"And you would know this…how?" queried Gentry.

"My gut…and my gut never lies."

Without looking at him she headed back to camp, deep in thought.

Gentry followed behind her, watching the ground for any other signs of intruders. It appeared their friendly Bobcat was the only one that ventured into their general area. It didn't stop him from taking a quick look around, however. He felt a little nervous about this killer, too.

Breakfast was beginning to smell really good. Dylan was busy frying hash browns in the drippings from the bacon. The cookware he used was a huge frying pan, set on a grill over the open fire pit. The pan was big enough to fry bacon, eggs and potatoes, each food having its own section of the huge fryer. The smell of the different foods made Gentry's mouth water, in spite of his nervous stomach.

"Great looking breakfast, Dylan, as usual. Did any of that blue stuff you put in your eyes drip into the cooking, because, that could really ruin the flavor." Gentry stood beside the fire pit with his hands on his hips gazing over the deliciousness.

"Well, I think I managed to keep it all where it belonged, unlike your mouth, lover boy. Think you can keep that to yourself long enough to eat…because breakfast is *ready*."

He handed a plate to Lauren, then dished one for Gentry and for himself. They sat together around the campfire in the chilly morning air enjoying the delicious meal.

"Hey, you got any chow left?" A familiar voice boomed up from the trail.

Riding slowly into camp, followed by two horses and a pack mule, was Charlie, with no last name. No one was sure if he really didn't have a last name or if he'd simply forgotten it, but ask him what it was and he pointedly told you it didn't matter.

Charlie helped with odd jobs around the station often taking care of errands into the park. He was a mountain man of sorts. Getting messages to him was difficult because he didn't have a phone or electricity at his cabin, even plumbing or a bathroom, for that matter. Unless you wanted to spend two days getting to the cabin, the only way to get a hold of Charlie was by carrier pigeon, and apparently, that's exactly what Joe had done. They kept a set of pigeons at the station just for communications with Charlie. It was effective and worked for when they needed a job done right away.

Charlie lifted his old Stetson hat off his head and moved the wild mass of gray hair out of his face, setting the hat back down to hold it all in place. It barely worked. His full beard held tell-tale signs of younger days when his hair was black, and when his teeth were still present in his wide and welcoming smile.

"Hey Charlie!" called Gentry, surprised to see the man this soon. "How'd you get up here so fast?"

"Oh, you know, the usual," he said, stopping his small procession. "Left early yesterday, got about three quarters of the way here and camped about four miles from here last night. But I'm mighty hungry if you've got any leftovers."

"We've got plenty," smiled Dylan. "More can be made if you need it."

"I just might, if it's any good," said Charlie as he dismounted and stretched.

Gentry and Charlie tied the horses and mule to Baby's line. Gentry brought out the opened bale of hay and spread it out for them to eat. Charlie brought his own horse, so there was no need to call for the chopper. Not to mention…this was Charlie…and there was no way he'd ride in a chopper.

Once the animals were fed and secured the group returned to the campfire. Their unique, and odiferous guest sat down next to Lauren.

"And who's this pretty little thing?" he asked, his nearly toothless grin spreading across his face.

Lauren maintained very well, actually appearing to enjoy the grizzled man despite the old horse, old tobacco and musty clothing smells emanating from his person. She grinned warmly and stuck out her hand.

"Why, thanks Charlie. My name is Lauren and I'm a Special Agent with the FBI."

Charlie's grin widened even further.

"Well, that makes you even *nicer* lookin'. You can probably shoot better'n these two yahoo's, eh?"

"Yeah, I'm betting I can," she laughed.

"Hey, not so fast," teased Gentry. "I'm a military trained sniper, you know."

Charlie waived him away with his hand.

"Aww…that don't mean nuthin'."

It obviously meant something to Lauren because she looked at him with renewed respect, raising an eyebrow and checking him out again, head to toe. It was like she hadn't even seen him before.

"Well, I can see I should have led out with that little tidbit of information," he thought smugly to himself. He folded his hands across his stomach and leaned back, offering her his most charming smile.

"Pathetic," moaned Dylan.

Lauren laughed at the two of them.

Charlie ate his breakfast and the group visited together. Once he was finished cleaning out the frying pan of any uneaten contents, he handed his plate to Dylan.

"Yup, have to agree with the young 'un on that one," teased Charlie. Turning to Lauren he continued as he rose to go. "You watch out for that boy. He's a tricky fella."

"Hey," complained Gentry, "just what do you mean by 'tricky'?"

He grinned at Gentry, his lips falling into the empty spaces in his gums.

He walked to the line and untied his horse. Slipping easily into the saddle he turned his mare and walked her to the campfire.

"You watch yerself, young lady. I'm jus' sayin'. Oh, and your mare's name is Gladys, very gentle, an easy ride. And your girl," he said to Dylan, "is Knuckles. Be nice to her…she bites if you're mean."

'That said, he rode out onto the trail and headed back to his cabin.

"Knuckles? What kind of a name is Knuckles for a *mare*?" Dylan shook his head as he watched Charlie ride out of sight.

"She's Charlie's mare, that's what kind of a name it is. That's fairly tame when you consider what he could have named her." Gentry laughed and kicked at the fire pit.

The group worked together cleaning and packing up the campsite and stowing the gear on Handsome. He was a very gentle mule with warm eyes and a sweet disposition. Handsome could haul just about anything for just about as far as it needed hauling. Dylan packed some sandwiches and chips with bottled water for lunches later in the day and stowed them in the saddlebags on each horse.

"Hey Handsome," said Gentry, greeting the mule and patting his back. "We haven't been on the trail for some time, eh? Good to be working together again."

The mule tossed his head, as if acknowledging the greeting and turned back to the hay.

Gladys and Knuckles were saddled and ready to go. The smaller tent was rolled up and stowed in its pack on Baby, while the larger one with the sleeping bags went with the pack mule. Gentry took his own bedroll and tied it to the back of Baby's saddle.

Once finished with his own packing, he quietly watched Lauren meet Gladys for the first time. She strolled up to the mare and slowly raised her hand, running it down the sleek neck. She spoke softly, rubbing the mare's nose and offered her a carrot she'd stolen from Dylan. Gladys munched the carrot and tossed her head lightly in acknowledgement.

Dylan walked to Knuckles and immediately apologized to her for the name she was given. She turned and stared at him, waiting for her carrot. He reached in his pocket while he stroked her forehead and told her she was really too pretty to be called Knuckles. He handed her the carrot and she contentedly crunched the crisp treat, apparently already having come to terms with the name.

They returned to the campfire and sat down in the chairs that weren't packed yet. Within minutes the sound of the chopper was heard coming up over the ridge. The bomb squad had arrived.

Chapter Ten

The chopper set down and Gentry jogged out to meet it. He ran under the blades, holding his Stetson and opened the door for the bomb squad members.

Cy cut the engine and exited the chopper, standing beside Gentry and helping his passengers onto the grassy clearing.

Three men stepped off the chopper, followed by a very large German Shepherd the men lovingly referred to as Pepper.

"My name is Thomas, I'm the lead blower upper," he said smiling at Gentry and shaking his hand. "These guys behind me are Chuck and Jasper."

"Gentry Beauchene," he said, shaking Thomas' hand.

Both men nodded silently and began picking up bags of equipment.

Lauren stepped forward and displayed her badge for them to see.

"I'm Lauren Porcelli, FBI Special Agent. Thanks for getting here so quickly."

"Happy to help," he said, still smiling.

"And who's this?" said Lauren bending over and scratching the top of Pepper's head.

"That's Pepper, she's our head bomb sniffer, and she's the best at what she does. She's saved a lot of lives by finding a device before one of us stepped on it. Pepper's pretty amazing."

"Well, how do you do, Pepper?" Lauren stood up.

"Pepper, shake," said Thomas.

Pepper raised her paw and Lauren giggled as she shook it gently.

"Point us in the direction of that bomb and we'll get started," said Thomas.

Lauren pointed to the taped off area.

"I wish I could tell you exactly where they are or if there's more than one. I can take you to the one I found, but there could be more out there."

"No worries. Pepper will find any that are out there. Don't need you in there, you could get hurt. We'll just suit up and head in. Shouldn't take too long."

"Thanks, again," said Lauren, "We'll be over by the campfire pit when you're finished."

"Roger that," said Thomas, already pulling his suit out of the chopper.

Cy stayed with the chopper, per previous instruction, and Lauren and Gentry strode back to the chairs and sat down. Dylan, already sitting and having watched everyone at the chopper, stood and stretched.

"I'm going to take a walk, get some fresh air," he said.

"Oh," laughed Gentry, "like the air up the trail is going to be fresher than the air here?"

"You never know," he grinned. "It could be."

As Dylan set out on the trail, Lauren and Gentry watched the men finish putting the suits on, checking each other's helmet, neck, wrist and ankle seals. Once everyone was ready, they disappeared into the woods.

"What's his point?" asked Gentry, turning to Lauren.

"What do you mean?" she asked.

"Well, why put a bunch of recording devices, along with at least one explosive device, and nothing hidden in or around the casket itself?"

"Because he *wants* us to find the casket. He gives us easy access, and just to make himself feel that he's got the upper hand, he places these devices because he thinks it's going to throw us off our game," Lauren was studying the trees as she spoke. "He manages to throw us for a little bit, but not for long. To me, it seems like a lot of work for a small payoff, but maybe that's all he needs."

Lauren's satphone rang and she quickly answered it.

"Porcelli."

She listened to the conversation, occasionally adding an 'okay' or an "uh-huh" here and there. While she was engaged in her conversation, Gentry's satphone went off, as well, and he hurried away from Lauren to keep from disturbing her conversation.

"Beauchene."

"Hey Gentry, it's Joe. Here's what I have so far from law enforcement. There has been no evidence Bantus ever left the park. He's got to still be in the park somewhere, and if he's traveling on foot, which apparently he is, he can't have gotten too far, unless he's an expert hiker and climber, which I doubt."

"I don't put anything past this guy," mused Gentry, "he seems to know at least *something* about a lot of different things."

"Yeah, well I thought you should know what I'd heard so far."

"Appreciate it, Joe. Thanks for letting me know."

Gentry ended the call and returned to his chair by the fire pit. Lauren was finished with her conversation and filled him in.

"So," she began, "it appears Mr. Bantus' fingerprints were everywhere on the evidence. Todd's opinion is he'd planned on making this killing different from the others, but wanted to make sure he got credit for it. That's fine because it's much easier for us that way."

Gentry was studying Lauren as she spoke. She really was beautiful, her expressive hands, her full lips, her short hair that accented her high cheekbones. But what was really intriguing about her was the level of intelligence she possessed, the calm investigative demeanor, and her ability to handle death with dignity and professionalism.

Gentry wasn't a mousy person by any means, but even *he'd* had a difficult time with that crime scene. Lauren seemed to take it all in stride, even helping him sort through it.

"What?" asked Lauren with a smirk.

"Oh, sorry," grinned Gentry. "I was just thinking how amazing you are."

"Is this another ploy to get me into your tent?" she chuckled.

"No, really, I mean, I've watched the way you've handled yourself around this crime scene. And it's not just that, it's how careful you are with everyone else…like you understand how hard this is on everyone's psyche and you make sure they're okay. I just think that takes a pretty special human being, that's all."

Lauren smiled and stared at her shoes for a moment, raising her eyes and scanning the camp as she responded to his comment.

"It's just that we're used to seeing the ugly side of life, but not everyone is. Even the CSI can be affected by something this gruesome." She was blushing slightly at his compliment.

Gentry changed the subject.

"I think we need to make some plans for where we're going to look from here," he began. "This is a big place, and he could be anywhere. I'm trying to think where he'd go from here, but I'm not the trained FBI Special Agent." He sat back in his chair and waited for her response.

"Well," Lauren began, "let's wait until Dylan gets back. I hate repeating myself."

"Yeah, I agree with that," said Gentry, "maybe we should go for a walk as well. Those guys are going to be in there for at least the rest of the hour, you think?"

Lauren shrugged and stared into the forest, trying to see where the men were.

"We could do that," she said, teasing him, "but the question then arises, can I trust you?"

In his best southern drawl, Gentry replied, "Why ma'am, I'm highly insulted you would question my integrity in such a fashion."

Lauren threw her head back and laughed. Gentry grinned and they both strolled to the trail, wondering which way to go.

"Dylan went that way," said Gentry pointing north, "I say we go south."

"Sounds like a plan," smiled Lauren.

They headed down the trail with the sun streaming through the trees. They spoke a little more about growing up, about horses and whose horse was smartest. Gentry enjoyed the conversation, enjoyed being able to talk with a woman who had a brain *and* a personality.

Suddenly he stopped in the middle of the trail, turned sideways and checked up and down the trail. Seeing no one coming he wrapped his arms around Lauren and pulled her to him, feeling his heart beating against his chest.

"And just what do you think you're doing?" she grinned.

"What any red-blooded male would do when confronted with a situation such as this," he said smiling down at her. "I'm going to kiss you."

"Oh really," she said wrapping her arms around his neck. "What 'situation' would you be talking about? I didn't notice any 'situation'. This was an innocent walk, that's all. Some good conversa-"

Gentry covered her mouth with his and drank in the wonder that was Lauren Porcelli. Lauren responded in kind, stroking the back of his head with her long, slender fingers, weaving them gently through his hair and moving his hat until it fell to the ground. Their breathing became heavy, and Gentry found himself wishing they'd not broken camp so early. He could use a tent right about now.

Lauren held his face gently in her hands as she pulled away and looked up at him. Her green eyes sparkled in the sunlight coming through the trees.

"Has anyone ever told you how beautiful you are?" he asked her.

"No one that mattered," she grinned, "are you telling me I'm beautiful?"

"Only if I matter," he said searching her eyes, her face and her mouth.

"You matter," she said softly.

"I was hoping you'd say that," he said, pulling her to him once again, unable to get close enough or hold her tight enough. He thought for sure he'd squeeze the life right out of her, but she kept giving him more reason to hold on, and hold on he did. He kissed her with all the passion he could and still remain upright. She was fire in his arms, burning him from the inside out and still he couldn't get enough of her.

The kiss ended and the couple stayed in the embrace, forgetting there was a world of life around them, staring into each other's eyes.

"Let's just stay right here," whispered Gentry, hugging her to him and breathing the words softly into her ear. "Let's never leave this moment."

"I'm fine with that," smiled Lauren, kissing his face. "I'm taking a mental picture as we speak."

"Want me to grab a camera? I've got one in my backpack."

Dylan was standing not ten feet from them, grinning his "I've got the goods on you *again*" grin.

"Go away, Dylan," smirked Gentry, his eyes never leaving Lauren's face. "I'll take my own pictures, thank-you."

"Wow," said Dylan, turning back toward camp. "Offer to do a good deed and you get shut down. That's harsh, Gentry, really, really harsh…" His words faded as he walked away.

"How would you feel about hanging out with a cowboy?" he said studying the contour of her lips, the gentle slope of her nose and her amazing green eyes.

"Is that what you call this?" she smiled.

They reluctantly released each other and turned to head back to camp. Gentry bent down and picked up his hat.

"You got my hat dirty," he said with a sly smile as he brushed the dirt off the brim.

"Your fault, not mine. You started it," she giggled.

Suddenly, from the direction of the woods came a loud explosion that echoed through the treetops.

Lauren gasped and ran as fast as she could toward the campsite with Gentry right behind her.

Chapter Eleven

They ran into camp in time to see two of the squad carrying a third out of the woods. He appeared unconscious.

"What happened?" called out Gentry.

"We detonated the device using a containment chamber, and it worked great. But a second later Chuck backed into the tree behind us and another one went off to his left. It was all bark, though, but still had enough of a punch to knock us all on our cans. I think he'll be okay, it looks like he hit his head when he fell."

The men were removing their suits as he spoke, and Chuck let out a low moan as he started coming around. Pepper trotted over and lay down beside Chuck, laying her head on his stomach.

"Oh, yeah," grinned Thomas, brushing Chuck's strawberry blond hair off his forehead. "He hit his head alright. Check out that lump."

A nice egg sized mound was protruding out of his right temple. Thomas checked his eyes for dilation and everything appeared normal.

"He'll be fine, just needs to relax a bit. Good thing for Pepper she was checking out an area to the north of us. She could have been hurt."

Thomas turned and looked at Lauren.

"You're a lucky lady. If you'd moved that bush even an inch further we wouldn't be having this conversation. It was rigged to look like a timer was on it, but the detonator was actually connected to the bush. You were right to call us."

Lauren tried to hide her grimace, nodding her head and looking down. Gentry knew she was thinking the same thing he was…how close she'd come to getting killed. The thought ignited feelings in him, feelings he'd never had before. He was certain he'd feel this way about *any* human being having endured such a close call. It was ludicrous to think he cared specifically for Lauren…he barely knew her. Just enjoying someone's company doesn't mean anything. And is that what he was doing? Enjoying her company?

"Are you okay, Gentry?" Lauren touched his arm as she spoke, concern filling her eyes.

"Oh, yeah, yeah, I'm fine. I was just thinking…you know…"

His voice trailed off. He glanced into her eyes and quickly turned away.

"Well you sure paled all of a sudden. You're sure you're okay?"

"Yeah, I'm good," he said, turning to Thomas. "How can we help you?"

"As soon as Chuck is up for it, we'll finish combing the search area and make sure there are no bombs or other devices. It will take us another hour, at least."

Dylan stood with his arms folded across his chest.

"Let's have a seat and wait. It appears that's all we can do."

Gentry and Lauren both nodded and followed Dylan out of the woods to the fire pit.

Once they were seated, Gentry glanced from Dylan to Lauren.

"We need a plan. If we're going to find this maniac, then we need to figure out which is the most logical way out of the park from here, what route he would take to get there and how long it would take him."

"Well," mused Dylan, "I believe that would be Kalispell. But if he were hiking out from here he would have to head Southwest out of the park."

Gentry jumped from his chair and strode quickly to Baby. He untied a long tubular case from the back of the saddle and hurried back to Dylan and Lauren. Pulling a map from the case all three dropped to the ground as Gentry unrolled the map.

"The footprints out of the woods went North. I think he was playing us with that. I'll bet he headed west to Whitefish and from there south to Kalispell." Gentry was pointing out the towns on the map, drawing lines with his finger from one point to the other.

"It's pretty rough country, but if you're by yourself you could probably make it in four or five days. What do you think?"

Dylan spoke as he studied the map.

"That seems like the only likely scenario," agreed Lauren. "From what we know, Bantus is quite grandiose in his thinking. It would be like him to think he could easily make it out on foot, but I don't believe he's the mountain man he considers himself to be. There's nothing in his profile to lead me to believe he's had much experience with rough terrain. He could have gotten himself into some trouble with the route he's taking. We've got to get moving, now. It might be our best chance of finding him."

"Dylan," Gentry spoke firmly, but quickly. "You're going to stay here and wait for the information from the bomb squad. Then you'll see them safely off the mountain via chopper. We're going to head southeast and you can catch up to us once they're finished. Are you good with that?"

"I'm good," said Dylan, "you two go ahead. I'll see you in a while."

Gentry rolled the map back up as he called out instructions to Dylan.

"You keep Handsome with you. Call me on your satphone when you're heading out and I'll give you our coordinates."

"Go, go. I'll find you. I'll keep my satphone on."

Gentry and Lauren hurried to their mounts and started out of the campsite. Gentry's head was a mass of confusion. He couldn't keep a clear thought in his head if he tried. He had to clean out his head, think straight, be organized. However, every time he tried, the picture of a beautiful woman, one Lauren Porcelli, floated into his head and his clear thinking was history.

He realized if he allowed his feelings for Lauren to cloud his judgment he wasn't going to be very effective at his job. That was all he needed to know. He was on the trail of a killer, and he would find him and end this.

The trail followed the path of an old ice flow, now a meadow, cut through the forest. There was at least twenty-five feet of grass and wildflowers on either side of them as they headed southwest. The fragrance of the blossoms warmed by the sun filled the air. Mountain peaks rose majestically on either side of them, in front and behind them. The sky stood out in stark contrast to the snowcapped peaks.

They rode along in silence, both immersed in their own thoughts, until Gentry called out to Lauren.

"I believe this is where we turn off for Whitefish. It's not a well-traveled trail, but that's why I think he may have chosen it."

"Right behind you, cowboy," said Lauren with a laugh.

Gentry leaned down and pulled at some tall grass growing along the trail. He picked out one blade that looked fresh and thick with juice and dropped the others. Holding the one blade between his teeth he responded to Lauren.

"If you keep talking like that, we'll never get anything accomplished." He grinned as his blue-green eyes scanned the trial ahead.

"You're right. Get your butt moving, Ranger Man. We've got a killer to catch."

She was even sexy when she was bossy. Her comment hadn't helped a bit.

Clearing his head once again, he began studying the trail looking for signs of recent travel. It was a good trail to hide on, one not often used. Which meant it was also going to help them out as they tracked their prey.

Gentry motioned for Lauren to stop, as he studied the trail ahead. Slipping out of the saddle, he stood beside Baby.

"There's a campfire up there," he said softly, "about five hundred feet ahead of us."

Lauren dismounted as well and stared ahead.

"I see that," she said. "We need to tie off the horses and hike in. We can't let him hear us coming."

"Agreed."

They walked into the woods and found a place to tie off Baby and Gladys. From there they headed straight toward the campfire. It was only a short hike and before they even came close to the camp they heard voices and music playing. This wasn't Bantus' camp.

"Let's go back and get the horses. We don't want innocent campers to think we're sneaking up on them." Gentry turned to go back and bumped into Lauren who was lost in thought and not paying attention.

"Uh, hello?" he said grinning down at her. "I believe *back* is that way."

He pointed to the path behind her and she blushed.

"Yeah, sorry, just thinking about the...case."

They both turned and Gentry grinned.

"Which case," he chuckled, "you and me or this guy that's killing people?"

"Cute. Really cute," she said, trying to sound annoyed.

Baby and Gladys were right where they'd left them, contentedly grazing on the sweet tender shoots of grass. Untying their reins, they climbed into the saddles and headed back out to the trail, the horses clomping leisurely along.

It was just a few minutes before they reached the camp and found two couples enjoying a lazy morning around the fire.

"Good morning," smiled Gentry, "my name is Ranger Beauchene. I hope you're enjoying your stay in the park."

One dark haired man spoke up.

"Yes, we are. It's a beautiful park."

"We like to think so," agreed Gentry. "Where are you from?"

They chatted with the two couples for a few minutes and Gentry pulled a printed copy of Bantus' photo from his inside jacket pocket.

"Have any of you seen this man?" he asked, handing the picture down to the dark haired camper.

"Hey, Roger," he called out, "isn't this the guy who came by yesterday and asked if this was the way to Whitefish?"

Roger came over and checked out the photo.

"Yup, that's him. Weird little guy."

"How's that?" asked Gentry, taking the photo back.

"I don't know," said Roger, "it's just…he was…kinda jumpy."

He glanced to his friend for confirmation and he nodded in agreement.

"Yeah, he just seemed in a big hurry to get there, but no horse, no supplies, not even a backpack. I can't imagine he'd make it that far without supplies of some kind, and without a horse. It would take days to hike that far."

"How did he look? Was he in good shape? Clean clothes? Did he look dressed for the hike?" Lauren was asking the questions now.

"Oh, yeah. He was clean, clothes were dry. Didn't look like he'd shaved in a few days, but maybe that's just his style, you know? He was very nice, very polite."

"Thanks for the information. You've been very helpful," said Gentry, slowly turning Baby to go. He touched the brim of his hat as he went.

"What did he do?" asked the first man.

"Oh, we just got word he might be lost, is all. His family contacted the ranger station to see if we'd heard anything. He's only a couple days late, but we want to make sure he didn't get into any trouble with animals, or accidents. We're trying to figure out which way he went. Thanks again for your help."

They rode back out to the trail and got enough distance between them and the campers before they spoke.

"Looks like we're going in the right direction," said Lauren, when they were out of earshot.

"Yup. There's a campground about four or five miles up this trail. It's actually accessed from another road, but we'll cross that road and head a little more south into the campground. We'll check around there and see if anyone in that group has seen anything."

Gentry's eyes searched the trail, brush and forest. He was on Bantus' scent now, and his gut was telling him things were going to get rough from here.

Chapter Twelve

They continued on down the trail, watching for signs of Bantus, asking campers along the way if they'd seen him. A few had interacted with him, mostly giving him directions to Whitefish, but there were others who hadn't seen him even pass by.

That little piece of information bothered Gentry. He wondered if they'd lost his trail. However, the campers could easily have missed a lone hiker walking by, but Bantus could also have kept to the woods so people wouldn't see him. If he was keeping to the woods, he and Lauren might miss him completely. He figured as long as people were seeing him, they were on the right trail.

It was well past lunchtime and Gentry's stomach was telling him it was time to eat.

"Hey, Lauren," he called back to her, "you okay to stop for some lunch?"

"I thought you'd never ask," she said. "I'm starving."

Gentry turned Baby off the trail to a nice clearing where she and Gladys could graze while he and Lauren ate some lunch. Once the horses were tied to a grazing line, the two riders took their lunch from the saddlebags and sat down, leaning against a couple of trees.

"Oh," moaned Lauren with her first bite of sandwich. "This is wonderful."

"Yeah, Dylan makes a mean tuna and pickle," he said, biting into his sandwich. He pulled out the individual bag of chips, Sour Cream and Onion…his favorite and crunched quietly.

The sun was warm coming through the trees and there was enough of a breeze that it was neither too hot nor too cold.

"We've only got about three more miles to the campground. Maybe we should stay the night there and let Dylan catch up with us." Gentry took another bite of his sandwich.

"How long do we have before dark?" asked Lauren, crunching contentedly on a potato chip.

Gentry took a drink of water and checked the sun's placement in the sky.

"We've probably got about five more hours of good daylight. We could go on past the campsite until we lose daylight, I just don't want to set up camp in the dark. You never know what you're going to be sleeping on when you do that."

"As long as whatever I'm sleeping on stays put, I'm good with it." Lauren smiled that gorgeous broad, white toothed, smooth lipped smile.

"You know, I'm just sitting here wondering why you couldn't have been a pain in the butt, with a lousy personality. Now, is that too much to ask?"

Gentry leaned over and softly kissed her neck.

"Dang, Lauren. I mean, you could have been missing teeth or even had raunchy breath," he said, making his way to her chin line and talking in a breathy whisper, "but ooohhh noooo…you had to be perfect…in every way. *Perfect*… Thanks a lot."

Lauren smiled as Gentry's lips made their way along her jaw line. She pushed him back, and covered his mouth with one hand. Composing herself, she took a deep breath and released him, then turned, sitting forward with her arms on her bent knees.

"You know, there are very few women who think they're beautiful on this planet. We all think we're homely and unappealing. Too fat, too thin, too dark, too pale, too tall, too short. It's incredible how hard a woman can be on herself. And yet, a man thinks he can suck in his gut, throw his shoulders back and act like a Jackass and women will fall all over him. Most men with zero personality have got the tiniest clue that they *have* zero personality. Women are painfully aware of every one of their shortcomings. What's up with that?"

"I'll have you know, I don't have to suck in my stomach-"

"Ohhh, this I know. I copped a feel on horseback the other day, remember?"

Now it was Gentry's turn to laugh.

"I don't think I've ever heard that from a woman's lips before," he laughed, adjusting his hat.

He stood up and brushed off his backside. Lauren stood also and started brushing herself off as well.

"Need any help with that?" grinned Gentry.

"Now, see? Did I ask *you* that?" she said, more of a statement than a question.

"You're just jealous you didn't think of it first."

Lauren reached over and slapped his arm.

"C'mon cowboy, we've got a trail to hit."

"That's '*MR.* Cowboy' to you," he said rubbing his arm.

They stowed their trash back in the saddlebags and continued on their way. They hadn't been on the trail very long when the sound of someone singing, and not very well, came from behind them.

"Dylan, please spare us your vocal repertoire. I already have a headache."

"Now, Ranger Beauchene, that's just rude. I don't think I can take much more of these put downs. I may have to find a new line of work, like, singing…in a cantina somewhere." Dylan was grinning as he slowly trotted Knuckles up in line behind Lauren with Handsome bringing up the rear.

"That would work, if it was far enough away." Gentry chuckled and grabbed another blade of grass, sticking it in his mouth.

"If you can stop being rude long enough, maybe you could fill me in on what you've found so far?" Dylan slowed Knuckles in step with Gladys and Baby.

"You first," said Gentry. "Did Cy and the bomb squad head back down?"

"Yup," he said, "they didn't find any more explosives than the two, but they did find two more recording devices and they're sending them into the lab with the explosives."

Gentry explained what they'd heard so far with Lauren filling in a few holes. He told Dylan they were stopping at the campground ahead to question the campers and see if anyone talked with or saw Bantus going through.

"Thanks for the sandwiches, Dylan," said Lauren, "they really hit the spot."

"Well, I'm flattered that at least *someone* noticed my hard work. You're entirely welcome."

Gentry was chewing his blade of grass, his eyes constantly searching the surrounding area.

"Dylan, you're *such* a girl."

"Well! I slave all day over a hot stove…"

Gentry chuckled and shook his head. "*Such* a girl."

They continued their course for the next few hours, with Dylan's comedy monologue breaking up the day. The group arrived at the campground and after questioning the campers found that Bantus spent the previous night there. This gave them a time frame to work with. Since they didn't know the time he left their campsite, it was impossible to know how long it took him to get this far, but they were informed he'd left early in the morning, so they could at least know from this point on.

"We still have a good two hours of daylight," mused Gentry. "I vote we move on for at least another hour. We're definitely getting further on horseback than he is on foot. I'd hate to burn that much daylight sitting in a campground."

"I agree," said Lauren. "I'm all for moving on."

They mounted up and started back down the trail they'd followed most of the day. Every so often Gentry would dismount and walk the perimeter of an area slowly, stopping every now and then to inspect the ground.

"See anything new?" asked Lauren as she followed him on foot.

Dylan stayed in the saddle and held onto the other two horses and Handsome.

"No," replied Gentry, contemplating the area. "It's just this stupid feeling I have, like we're missing something…something really obvious. I've had it all day and it's making me crazy. We're *missing* something."

They mounted their horses again and continued on down the trail. Whatever it was, Gentry wasn't seeing it. Baby wasn't giving any clues either, and if Bantus was close he was fairly certain she'd let him know. However, they continued on for the next hour with Gentry at full alert, making both Lauren and Dylan nervous as well.

The daylight was waning and the three began keeping eyes peeled for a good spot to set up camp for the night. Once found, they began unloading the camping gear and getting the campsite set up. They set up one tent and kept Handsome and the horses tethered close by. The fire pit was set up close to the tent, far enough away to avoid sparks from the fire, but close enough so no one would be alone at any time.

Gentry wasn't taking any chances with this killer. He was certain Bantus hadn't left the park yet, and though he was glad for the opportunity to catch him, knowing he was out there somewhere made his skin crawl.

Dylan set about fixing dinner as soon as the cookware and food was unloaded. Gentry finished removing the load from Handsome and brushed him down. Baby and Knuckles would be next. Lauren enjoyed brushing Gladys and chose to do that herself.

"Hey Baby," said Gentry, approaching the horse after he'd finished with Handsome. "You did good today, girl."

He started at her head with the brush and using long even strokes, brushed under her mane and then down her back and sides. She neighed softly letting Gentry know it was her favorite part of the day, right along with his.

"Good girl," he said, stopping the brushing long enough to stroke her nose and cradle her chin in his hand. "That's my Baby."

Lauren was watching him as she brushed Gladys. He caught her staring out of the corner of his eye.

"She's a beautiful horse," said Gentry as he stood back and admired Baby. "I just have to make sure she knows I know that."

"You're very good with her," said Lauren. "I enjoy watching you."

"If you two are done over there, dinner is served," called Dylan.

It smelled wonderful and Gentry was starving. From the look on her face, so was Lauren. They sat down together under cover of a million stars. The fire was warm and added a soft glow to the campsite and the surrounding trees. It'd been a beautiful day, and the brilliantly lit sky made the night just as amazing.

They were just beginning to clean up from dinner when they heard that same maniacal laugh from their previous campsite.

"That's not possible…" said Gentry.

The other's hadn't heard it yet, soft and muffled.

"What…what do you hear?" asked Lauren turning toward Gentry.

The sound was growing, coming from their tent.

"What- there's no way," said Lauren, shocked. "There's no way he could find us and plant something like that without us seeing it. There's just no way."

Dylan stopped what he was doing when he finally heard it.

"What the-" He set the frying pan down against the rocks they'd used to confine the campfire. "Where's it coming from?"

Gentry pulled his gun from the holster, pulled out his small flashlight from his Jacket pocket and started for the tent. The laughter stopped and he continued on into the tent, Lauren was right behind him with her gun drawn. When they went through the flaps he pointed his gun left and she went right, following the flashlight beams around the tent until they knew it was clear.

Heading back outside, the laughter started again and Gentry walked back to the campfire. Thinking again, he turned and strode around the outside of the tent, checking the woods behind it. Lauren was still with him. He walked past where the saddles were stowed, on the ground next to the tent and froze, listening intently. The sound was coming from the *saddles*.

He turned and nodded to Lauren. Understanding his nod, she covered him, keeping her gun pointed and scanning the area around the tent. The darkness was thick, making the sound even more menacing and evil.

Holstering his gun he quickly knelt down and started emptying saddlebags, his first. He didn't have to go very far before the laughter started up again as he pulled a tiny recording device from the bottom of his bag. Gentry was angry.

Chapter Thirteen

"Don't touch it!" cried Lauren, worried about the fingerprints.

Gentry froze with his fingers already covering most of the device. Lauren reached into her saddlebags and pulled out a small evidence bag. She opened it up and using the edge of it like a glove, switched the irritating sound off. She then held it under Gentry's hand watching him drop it in.

"No worries anyway," she said shrugging, "there never are any prints. Sorry to freak, I guess I wasn't thinking that through very well."

"I figured as much, but didn't want to spoil your moment."

He smiled as he stood up, but his face quickly went back to a scowl.

"He's playing us, Lauren and it's really starting to tick me off. Who *is* this guy? I'm getting tired of the game, really tired. I need some face to face time with this loser so I can-"

"Whoa, there," said Lauren laying her hand gently on his arm. "Let's get one thing clear right now." She stared hard into his eyes, not flinching, not asking a question, only stating her terms.

"I'm the FBI agent, and this guy goes down on *my* command," she said. "Are we clear on that? I need to be certain you're clear with where I stand on this point."

Gentry's eyes flashed anger as he responded to her demand.

"I get it," he said, pulling his arm away. "You're the boss, I'm just the ranger."

"Gentry, you know that's not what I meant," she said, struggling for the right words. "You don't like a woman calling the shots. I'm used to that, but it's important to lay down ground rules. You don't do anything from here on out without my knowledge and direct approval."

"Yes, ma'am," he said, his mouth in a tight frown. "Yes, *ma'am.*"

He turned and strode angrily to the fire pit and sat down, staring at the flames.

Lauren turned and tore open the tent flaps, stomping into the tent and making sure the flaps closed behind her.

"Come on, Gentry," said Dylan softly. "You know she's right. She's always been lead on this. *She's FBI* for crying out loud."

"I know," replied Gentry tersely. "I get that, but what's infuriating is…how do I protect someone who's calling the shots?"

"Did it ever occur to you that she's not the one that needs protecting?" Dylan was squatted down, moving the pan of fried potatoes from the grate over the fire.

Gentry knew immediately what his friend was saying, and he felt like he needed to pick his chin up off the ground.

It was Greyson who shot Bantus, and it was Aspen who profiled him, was kidnapped and held hostage with his brother. Greyson and Aspen were then rescued by a swat team from Fairbanks. Bantus now had an ax to grind with his family; Gentry was the one now who needed to watch his back and the fact that Lauren should be in charge was appropriate, if for no other reason than that very connection.

Suddenly he felt incredibly foolish. He was stupid to question her authority, she was right to establish the chain of command. He knew that from his time in the service, and he should have known that from the start of this investigation.

"Now, would you get your butt in there and apologize before this delicious dinner is ruined?" Dylan stood and brushed the dirt off his knees.

Gentry sighed. How he hated being the fool and then having to apologize for it. But Dylan was right. He stood and glanced back at the tent. Facing the fire pit he sighed again and turned, walking slowly to the tent.

As he entered the tent there was a soft glow from the battery powered lantern. Lauren set the lantern on a table in the back section, where she was sitting in a chair. She looked up as Gentry walked in and looked back down again, staring at nothing.

He moved softly to where she sat and taking her arm, pulled her to him.

"I'm sorry, Lauren," he whispered in her ear as he hugged her. "You're absolutely right. You're the one running point on this investigation. I'm here to back you up. I guess those lines got crossed somewhere."

Lauren placed her hands on his chest, gazed up into his face.

"They got crossed when we started being this familiar with each other. It's wrong. I have a job to do and it's selfish of me to think of anything but those girls who have died, and will die if we don't stop this man. I didn't make my position on the team clear from the start like I should have. I'm sorry for that, Gentry, but I'm making it clear now. I'm FBI, and I have no emotional attachments at this point."

She looked up at him, no anger on her face, no malice, just matter of fact.

"I knew you were right when you first said it," he began, "I just let my ego get in the way and got my manly feathers ruffled. I will, of course, respect your leadership of this team. I apologize for my behavior."

Lauren turned and took a few steps away, pivoting back to face him.

"This last recorder makes me wonder if Bantus has an apprentice, an assistant, if you will, someone he's manipulating to do his work. It's part of his profile. I should have noticed this before. I can't imagine he's hanging around this close to us, planting this stuff and moving along with us, out of our eyesight. It's too big a chance to take, even for him. I don't know for sure, really, it's a suspicion I have at this point, that's all."

"Well, we can think about that later. Dylan says dinners on, if you're hungry, and you better be or I'm in big trouble with his inner she wolf."

"I'm starving," she giggled, and headed for the door.

They walked to the campfire and Dylan handed each of them a plate. Gentry took his and sat down, still working to wrap his head around this new 'policy'. There was nothing wrong with it, exactly. He knew the dynamic of the team had changed. It would take some getting used to simply because he'd always felt like he and Lauren were equals in the investigation. He now would relinquish command to her, which he should have done in the beginning.

He decided he would concentrate on the innocents whose lives were taken as much as he could. When he did, it changed his focus entirely. He could do this and *would* do this, but heaven help this woman if she tried to fly away home when this investigation was over. They had some things to discuss when the timing was right.

Dinner was delicious, salmon, baked over the fire and fried potatoes. Dylan grinned at the moans coming from Lauren as she gushed over how delicious the meal was. The three of them settled back in their chairs and enjoyed some laughter and good food. Gentry continued to tease Dylan about his 'girlie' blue eyes, at which point Lauren mocked offense about blue eyes being girlie. Dylan poked pretty hard at Gentry about his love affair with his horse, and how no woman could ever hope to compete with *that* relationship. They had a good time throwing each other's dysfunction back and forth over the fire.

They cleaned up dinner and after a few minutes around the fire to allow the food to settle, they hit the hay, hoping to be awake at first light. This time of year that could be as early as four a.m., and they would eat a quick breakfast and load up.

Gentry lay in bed for a long time before sleep overtook him. He focused on where they would travel the next day and how they would transport Bantus once they found him. He thought about the girls this man so callously killed, remembering the vacant stare from the eyes of the young woman Bantus heartlessly displayed atop the casket. He thought of the parents of that girl, and how hard it would be for them to have a closed casket funeral for their daughter because she was in pieces. How do parents deal with that kind of heartbreak?

He closed his eyes, breathed deeply and let sleep overtake him. His last thoughts were of the warmth of loving and inviting arms around his neck, amazing green eyes gazing into his, and the smell of soft brown hair.

***

The morning dawned a bit chilly, with clouds overhead threatening rain. They ate a breakfast of dried fruit and jerky on the trail as they continued their search for Bantus.

The conversations were quiet, they rode side by side as the trail widened and discussed the plan for the day together. They would continue to interview campers along the way, and by the end of the day they would stop at the next campground and camp there, spending the evening interviewing that set of campers or anyone who may have seen Bantus.

"Okay," said Dylan, "shouldn't we be about on top of him by now? He's on foot…how far could he get on his own?"

"Well, you have to realize how many days advance he has on us. How long was the casket there? Definitely leaving the crime scene the way he did makes me wonder if he's close, but that could have been the work of his apprentice as easily as it was Bantus himself. We're on the right path; we're finding signs of him as we go. He's not a fool. We won't find him unless he trips up somewhere along the way, or unless he wants us to find him."

Lauren and Gentry scanned the trail. Both of them squinted at something ahead of them. They saw a small wood post on the side of the trail, pounded into the ground with what looked like an envelope tacked to it. Lauren rode ahead and dismounted to examine it more closely. Reaching into her saddlebags she pulled out a pair of exam gloves and wiggled into them, never taking her eyes from the letter. Gentry and Dylan rode up behind her and stopped.

"It looks like you've got a letter, Gentry," she said, still examining the post. Once her gloves were on, she pulled the note off, and inspected the envelope, front and back. It looked fairly benign, except that it was a sure bet it was penned by Walter Bantus.

After handing a pair of gloves to Gentry and watching him pull them on, she handed the letter to him. He dismounted and stared at the handwriting.

"This could be from a camper, you know," he said, opening the note with care.

"And this camper would know you were coming this way, how?" asked Lauren, hands on her hips. "It's Bantus, alright; we've got a sample of his handwriting in his profile."

"Yeah, I suppose you're right. But if it is, then it means he may be watching us, just keeping far enough ahead of us to follow our movements and know what we're doing."

The outside of the envelope read, "For Ranger Beauchene, Park Business". Gentry carefully unfolded the letter and read it aloud.

"Dear Ranger Beauchene;

What a fine job you're doing tracking me. It's quite impressive. I'm leaving a little peace offering for you ahead. I hope you like it. I'll be out of the park and long gone before you ever find my little gift to you, but just know I was only thinking of you."

There was no signature at the end of the note, but there didn't need to be. It was clear Bantus was toying with them again.

"This doesn't make me feel very warm and fuzzy," said Gentry, handing the letter to Lauren and studying the trail ahead.

"I know what you're saying," nodded Lauren, studying the letter. "This raises all kinds of questions now…like…is his revenge still directed at you? Is his 'gift' the revenge or should we expect more? Did an accomplice leave the note? Is he still keeping his twenty-seven day rhythm? Depending on what we hear from the campers and hikers today, we'll hopefully get some answers to these questions. Stay alert; we may have a stalker with us."

They found a few individual campers along the trail and stopped to talk to them. No one saw Bantus, at least not from looking at the picture. This gave further credence to Lauren's feeling that an accomplice was now running the show, but each camper made it clear that, with the exception of the three of them, no one had come down the trail since they'd made camp.

Gentry, Dylan and Lauren stayed together, still riding side by side and watching the forest. The three riders continued to follow the ancient ice flow, scanning as much as they could as they rode along. Occasionally Gentry would pull his binoculars out of his saddlebag and attempt to search the woods. The canopy was so thick overhead there was no way he could see anything.

It was still early morning, they'd been on the trail since five a.m. and Gentry glanced at his watch. It was nearly seven a.m.

A scream suddenly pierced the air, apparently coming from the campground up ahead.

"Dylan," yelled Lauren, "stay with Handsome and follow us in. We're going on ahead."

They were already at a full gallop as the scream turned to a tortured wail. The hair on the back of Gentry's neck snapped to attention. They were only a few hundred feet from the campground, but it felt like they'd never get there.

Chapter Fourteen

Both Lauren and Gentry galloped into the campground at full speed, skidding their mounts to a stop. Gentry was already out of the saddle and dropping to the ground before Baby came to a stop.

A woman ran to him, with a man right behind her. Gentry knew right away the anguished sounds they'd heard came from this same woman now pleading with him.

"My daughter! He took my daughter! You have to find her and bring her back to us. He took her this morning…please…find her…she's all we have in the world!"

The man came up behind the distraught mother and took her in his arms.

"Who do we call? Can you help us?"

There were tears in his eyes and his voice choked up as he laid his head against his wife's hair. They sobbed, heartbroken and frightened.

"My name is Ranger Beauchene, this is FBI Special Agent, Lauren Porcelli. We'll find your daughter."

"How d…did you kn…know?" sobbed the woman. "How dd…did you get here so fast?"

"Is there a place where we can talk? Can we go to your campsite?"

The husband nodded and still holding his wife he led them to their campsite. As luck would have it, it was a large fifth wheel, which would allow them some privacy.

It was late in the day; most of the campers were finished with dinner

They entered the camper and sat down. Lauren took the lead and spoke quietly and slowly, gently holding the woman's hand. She pulled a picture of Walter Bantus from her inside Jacket pocket.

"Is this the man who took your daughter?" she asked.

"Yes! Yes, that's him," she was sobbing again, barely able to contain her emotions.

"Who is he? Why are you looking for him?" the man's level of concern rose instantly.

"How about we start at the beginning," smiled Lauren, not wanting to address the question just yet.

"Lauren," Gentry softly touched her shoulder. "I'm going to go get Dylan and get a search organized."

***

Lauren nodded and turned back to the husband and wife.

"Tell me your names. You already know I'm Lauren Porcelli. Please call me Lauren."

"We're the Thompson's, I'm Jack and this is Rose. Our daughter is Emma." Jack choked again on his words as he bowed his head, his shoulders shaking, tears falling onto his lap.

"Jack? Rose? I need you to look at me. Can you do that? Look at me." Lauren continued to talk softly as the couple, dazed and exhausted, peered up at her.

"We were lucky to come upon your camp so quickly," said Lauren. "Because of that, there's a good chance we'll find her soon, but I'll need you to do your best to focus. I need every detail of when you realized Emma was gone and when you think he may have taken her."

Rose glanced at her husband.

"We were cleaning up the breakfast dishes."

He nodded in agreement.

***

The fire was crackling as Jack and Rose Thompson went into the trailer for bed. It was late, probably close to ten p.m. Walter Bantus sat beside the warm fire and grinned at his new friend.

Emma stared at the fire, tucking her long dark hair behind her ear. At sixteen years old, Emma was a force to be reckoned with. Active in about every sport she could get into and an award winning gymnast, she loved the outdoors. She'd studied Karate for the last four years and was the proud wearer of a brown belt. She was also captain of her soccer team, pitcher for her baseball team and lead scorer on her basketball team. But her real love was camping; spending time camping with her parents.

She'd had a brother, an older brother who'd passed away when he was five and she was just a baby. Her mom and brother, Danny, were in a parking lot of a grocery store; Danny was seated in the shopping cart while their mom unloaded groceries. A large diesel truck backed quickly out of a parking spot across from where they were parked. The driver was young, didn't realize he was going as fast as he was and didn't see the shopping cart. He ran right into the cart, crushing it against the back of the car next to theirs before he even knew what was happening. Danny was still in the cart and died instantly. Emma was glad she was too young to have experienced the loss.

"This is the best part of camping, I think," she said grinning at their guest. "Mom and Dad always go to bed too early. They miss out on the cold, crisp air and cozy fire."

She glanced to where the tent was set up next to the fifth wheel.

"I hope you'll be warm enough in the tent. It's the one my friends and I always put up in the backyard when I have a sleep over. Dad brought it because sometimes I like to sleep in the tent so I can hear the animals and the birds."

According to what Bantus learned from her parents, Emma was a good kid, excellent grades and very respectful to her parents. They knew she loved them, and their love for her made for a close knit family.

Walter got most of the pertinent information from Jack and Rose when he arrived. Listening to them dote and brag over their daughter was almost more than he could take. Still, it was necessary information, and he could look as interested as the next guy.

They were from Seattle, been camping in Glacier for about a week, heading home in a couple more weeks. Jack sold insurance and Rose was a homemaker, yada, yada, yada. He wanted to gag at the syrupy sweetness.

He was aware this girl would be useless to him, at least as one of 'his', but he still thought he could use her. She'd make a very nice decoy, and possibly give him some time to get out of the park without the ever present Beauchene and company getting in his way.

What was it about these Beauchene boys? They were always trouble, yet, he felt drawn to them somehow, seeking out their parks since his first encounter with Greyson. Each encounter left unfinished business, forcing him to research and find another Beauchene. What would he do when he ran out of brothers? His mind was forced back to the present.

"It's a beautiful night," smiled Walter. "I usually go for a walk before I hit the hay. Wanna walk with me?"

"No, I better not. I'm not quite ready for bed, so I'll just sit here by the fire."

"Aw, c'mon," he said with a little added charm, "I'm not going to bite. Just a walk around the main road of the camp, we'll make a loop and come right back."

Emma eyed him skeptically. He wasn't exactly a stranger, but he 'felt' strange to her.

"No, thanks. I'll wait."

Walter put on his best grin and headed out for his walk. There had to be a way to get her away from her parents. He'd only need a moment. When he returned from his walk, Emma wasn't in her chair. He glanced around the campsite and figured she must have gone to bed.

"Tomorrow's another day," he said, his eyes filling with evil, "another day."

Walter woke the next morning to breakfast on the table. It was a bit cloudy and cool, but still the forest was alive with birds and chipmunks crying out to each other. He dressed and walked out to the table.

"How can I help? I feel like I'm taking advantage," he said, oozing with confidence.

"No problem," smiled Jack. "We were just getting ready to sit down. Why don't you have a seat by Emma."

Emma didn't hear the conversation. She was in another land, another world, enveloped in a story that whisked her away to dangerous adventures.

"Emma," said her dad, clearing his throat.

"Hmm?" she asked glancing up. "Oh…sorry."

"Let's put away the book," he said, "we've got company at the table."

"Sure, sorry, didn't see you come out," she grinned.

They ate a delicious breakfast of perfectly crisped hash browns, eggs over easy and bacon. The air was filled with the smell and the food tasted even better in the outdoors than in a house somewhere. They ate and visited over the meal.

"Where are you headed, Walter," asked Rose.

"I'm on my way to Colorado, and then to California. I worked for the last fifteen years, saving money for a trip across the western United States." This was not true, but they would never know that. "I figured if I walked it, I would see far more than I could driving a car."

"What kind of work do you do?" asked Jack.

"Oh, mostly odd jobs, really," smiled Walter, "You know, putting myself through school for a while, and then I decided to work a full time job and put school off for a while so I could see the country while I was young enough to do that. I did work one job for the last five years, as journalist for the local newspaper."

"That's very interesting. Is that something you'll go back to once you've seen the country?" Rose was enjoying the conversation and smiled as she asked her question.

"No, I did enjoy it, but I'm thinking I'll head back to med school," he said, lying through his teeth, "I think I really want to be a surgeon."

Jack smiled and Rose glanced at her daughter.

"Emma, maybe you and Walter could bring us some water. The faucet is just over there. Would you mind Walter?" Rose peered at their guest.

"Not at all," he smiled, standing to go.

Emma wrinkled her nose, but grinned at her parents and headed to get the famous family water bucket, used for heating dishwater.

Rose grinned at her daughter.

"We could take the dishes into the fifth wheel for washing, but I like the idea of being out of doors when we camp, you know? I want the whole experience of tent camping, but the safety of a locked door."

"I understand that concept," Walter said, smiling, "why be in a kitchen when you can be here." He spread his arms out, scanning the campsite as he spoke.

Emma returned with the bucket and she and Walter headed through the brush to the other side of the campsite.

"Oh, I know this area," said Walter. "Come 'ere. I want to show you something, it's just over there."

"My mom and dad will worry; we better get the water and head back." Emma bent over the water spigot and turned it on, holding the bucket below it. Slowly into her field of vision came a small black box with a blinking light. She stood up, curious about the box and looked at a man who was no longer the kind, sweet guest he'd originally appeared to be. She dropped the bucket and turned to go, but Walter grabbed her arm and pulled her back.

"Make the smallest noise and your mommy and daddy go boom." He said, his eyes filled with evil. "We're going this way, and you're going to act like my best friend. Do you understand what I'm saying?"

Emma shook her head weakly, pulling away from the hateful face staring back at her. She could hear her mother calling her and Bantus put his finger to his lips, holding the little black box with the blinking light to clarify his intentions.

They walked for what felt like over an hour until they came to the place he'd apparently tried to take her to the night before. It looked like some kind of a cellar dug into the ground with a wood plank door over the opening. Lots of fresh dirt was scattered about the area in an effort to mask the dig.

"Welcome to your new home. They'll be so busy looking for you they won't have time to look for me."

"Who are you?" she asked, staring into the darkness of his eyes.

"My name is Walter, just like I told you. Now be a good girl and open the door."

"I'm not going in there," she said firmly.

"Oh, but you are," satisfaction oozing through his whole being. "You're going in there and so am I. When I'm done with you, you'll be sorry you ever met me. And don't forget, I still have this." He held up the black box.

"I'm already sorry I met you. But, you're not going to be very happy about meeting me, either," she said. She turned quickly and using her best Karate form, struck with a lightning fast punch to his throat. The black box flew from his hand as he grunted and returned with a kick of his own.

Emma jumped back, barely avoiding his strike and kicked his knee with the ball of her foot. Bantus cried out in pain, his eyes alight like burning oil. He went for her face, found flesh and with one stroke her world went black.

***

Dylan was met by Gentry as he approached the campground. Gentry waited for him with the satphone to his ear, calling out instructions for Joe. He ended the call and stared at Dylan as he rode into the group camping area.

"What's going on? What's happened?"

Gentry steered Baby to where Dylan was standing and dismounted. He spoke softly, keeping the conversation private.

"Bantus took a young girl from the campground. He'd been here a day or so; I don't have all the facts, yet. Lauren is interviewing the parents now. It looks like she's been gone since just after breakfast this morning. He has a few hours on us, if that's the case."

"What do you want me to do? How can I help?"

"Looks like, at the very least, we'll be spending the night here. It would be very helpful if you would set up a command post. Check out the group campsite. If there's room, it would be a good place to put it. Put up all the tents we have, then call down to Joe and find out how many are going to be coming up here and figure out supplies and accommodations for that number. You got it?"

"I'm on it. I'll go have a look."

Gentry headed back to the Thompson's campsite. His stomach gnawed at him, but he knew it wasn't hunger. He wasn't sure he'd ever be hungry again.

Knocking softly on their door he heard "come in". The mood in the camper was solemn and heavy. The couple spoke softly to Lauren, explaining about the last time they saw their daughter.

"They walked off into the brush with the bucket in her hand. We found the bucket sitting under the spigot a few minutes later, and our Emma was nowhere to be seen." Jack took his wife's hand and squeezed it.

Lauren glanced to Gentry and back to the distraught couple.

"The good news is, he doesn't have that much of a head start on us. Will you excuse us?"

Lauren motioned to Gentry to step outside. They exited the fifth wheel and went to the opposite end from where the parents were sitting inside.

"What have you got for me?" she asked quickly.

"I've called my assistant at the station and he's calling your office to fill them in. The local LEO's are organizing searchers on horseback and will have them heading out in the next hour. Dylan is setting up a command post and getting more supplies and tents for the searchers that are coming."

Lauren glanced up at the camper.

"This could get ugly," she sighed. "Really, really ugly."

Chapter Fifteen

Emma moaned softly and tried to open her eyes. The room spun, a complete blur and she lifted her hands to her head in an effort to stop the movement. It didn't help, so she lay still and waited for everything to focus. Eventually the spinning stopped and she carefully moved only her eyes, and very slowly inspected what she could see.

The ceiling was low; she probably wouldn't be able to stand completely. The wall and ceiling were wood planks. It smelled moist, but the wood was still new and masked most of the smell.

She raised her hand and felt her head. It hurt, like a raging volcano was inside trying to burn it's way out. The light was dim, but as she moved her hand away she saw blood on her fingers. He'd hit her, but she had no memory of it.

Laying her hand back down, she realized she was on a thin mattress, with a pillow under her head. *Where am I?*

Very carefully she raised herself up on one arm, but the pain shot through her head and forced her back down before she could get a look. The room swam once again and faded to black.

***

Gentry hurried to the group camping area, happy to see their tents were the only ones there. They would cordon off the group area and reserve it for the searchers, once they arrived. He began helping Dylan get things arranged, using their big two-room tent for the main command center.

Lauren arrived a few minutes later.

"How are they holding up?" Gentry could tell from the haggard look on her face, they weren't doing well.

"I guess as good as anyone in their situation could be. They're encouraged that we happened to ride in at the moment we did," she studied the ground at her feet. "Gentry, we can't wait for searchers to arrive. We have to try and pick up a trail if we can. Are you willing?"

"Absolutely," he said firmly. "Let's go."

Gentry called to Dylan to let him know they were heading out to investigate and to keep putting the campsite together.

"And Dylan," he said, "would you call Joe and get me an updated ETA for the search party?"

"Will do," he said waving them off.

"Let's walk the path they took before we use the horses," said Lauren.

"Agreed."

Gentry watched as Lauren went to Gladys' saddlebags and pulled out her camera.

"We'll be back, girl. I'm gonna need you on this big time." She patted her neck and nuzzled her face. Gentry knew the need to feel the warmth of the horse, the life that warmth represented. He went to where Baby was tethered and put both arms around her neck.

"I won't be far, girl. Keep sharp, you hear?"

Gentry checked his phone holster, making sure the satphone was still there. It was.

The two headed to the Thompson's campsite. Jack and Rose were apparently inside the camper and Lauren didn't want to disturb them. She moved immediately into the brush and headed in the direction of the water faucet as Jack explained it to them earlier.

They found the footprints right away and Lauren removed some yellow crime scene tape from her Jacket pocket, quickly sealing off the area so the prints wouldn't be disturbed.

"I hope people will honor this tape and go around on their own until we can get some guards up here to keep them back," she said as she and Gentry tied off the last strip.

"Well, we can't stand around here and watch it ourselves, that's for sure," said Gentry. "Let's keep going."

They continued in the direction of the watering area. Jack and Rose, while looking for Emma, removed the bucket and took it back to their campsite. There was nothing there that told them anything they didn't already know and plenty of campers used the water faucet between the time of the kidnapping and now. The road in front of the area was paved, but they saw on the opposite side of the paved roadway the double set of footprints began again.

Pulling the phone out, Gentry called Dylan.

"Sandusky."

"Hey Dylan, take a break from set up and find the camp hosts will you? We need them to stick around the path we've taped off between the Thompson's site, the water faucet and the trail across from it. Let me know when that's done, will you?

"I'll take care of that now."

Gentry ended the call as Lauren approached.

"Good idea," she said smiling, "ever think of joining the FBI?"

Gentry smiled and put his hand on her back, directing her toward the next set of prints.

"Yeah, once," he grinned, "for about thirty seconds."

They moved silently through the woods, watching for any signs of torn clothing, shoes and footprints, anything that would allow them to stay on the path of the killer and his captive.

There were footprints, and fortunately no one else had used the same path that day. Only two sets of prints lay in the damp earth on the trail. However, the trail was soon covered with pine needles, fallen leaves and small branches and it was impossible to know which way they'd gone.

Gentry stopped on the trail and looked in all directions, hunting for a sign, any sign at all telling them which way to go. Lauren did the same.

"This isn't going to do a bit of good," sighed Gentry. "We may as well go back to camp and wait for the searchers to arrive. We could get started on a grid search and be ready to make assignments when they get here."

"I just don't think I can sit there knowing what this girl could be going through," Lauren said, rubbing her forehead. "There has to be something we can do."

"There is," said Gentry, putting his arm around her shoulder and giving her a squeeze. "We can get started on a grid search, like I said. I understand what you're saying, Lauren, I really do, but it's either stop the search now and make up the grid, or wait for everyone to get here and *then* postpone searching while we wait for a grid to be done."

"Yeah, yeah, I know," she said, obvious frustration clouding her face. "I should be used to this, I shouldn't be so disoriented. I just can't seem to find my focus in this case. Why? What is there about it that makes focusing so difficult?"

"I don't know," said Gentry, walking a little further and squatting down into the dirt, looking at the tracks. "I think for me it's seeing that casket for the first time. I can't get that girl's face out of my head."

His phone rang and it was Dylan confirming the camp hosts were guarding the trail. He said Joe was still organizing the searchers and he'd let them know as soon as he had more information. Gentry thanked him and ended the call.

He stood up and faced Lauren. He squared his shoulders and strode quickly back to where she stood.

"We can't let this girl down, Lauren. We *have* to stay clearheaded for her. If that means putting the other crime scene out of my head, I'll do it. I have to do it, and so do you. We have to get a grip here, for Emma and for Jack and Rose. They need us to think this through and use the training we both have to find her, they're counting on us."

Lauren gazed at Gentry with renewed determination. Her eyes were narrowed, her mouth a thin line. She shook her head as if to clear it and peered up at Gentry.

"You're right. Let's get back to camp and get that grid search set up."

Without another word she turned and headed back the way they'd come. Gentry grinned and followed after her. She didn't have to think twice. Once her mind was made up, the outcome was a done deal. He could see it in her face…and oh…how he admired her spunk.

***

Emma awoke to the same piercing pain in her head. She didn't know if she was alone or if Walter was there with her. There was no indication he was there.

"I'm thirsty."

There was no answer.

She forced herself to sit up, very slowly. The room wasn't spinning anymore with her movement, though her head still felt like it might explode at the least provocation. She gazed slowly around the dimly lit room and saw the source of the light. It was a battery operated camping lantern, and there were two more lanterns sitting beside it on a small shelf across from where she lay. Spares? She wondered how long she'd been there, but had no way of knowing. She didn't know if it was day or night outside, and which way was outside?

She tried to stand but fell backwards onto…what? She looked down and realized she'd been lying on a bench or narrow bed, with a mattress covering it. How did she get on the bed? She just couldn't remember anything at all about the attack, but she knew she was bleeding.

The room was small, completely enclosed with thin wood boards. There was nothing in the room but the makeshift bed and…water? Was that bottles of water on the shelf beside the lanterns?

Emma wanted to go look, she really was thirsty, but standing wasn't going to work with her head feeling the way it did. Though only a few feet from her, it was just out of reach.

As she sat on the bed, she slowly looked up and saw a padded ceiling. Her head started spinning, making it hard to see what it was made of, but whatever it was, it would surely keep anyone from hearing her cries for help. Not that she could make any amount of noise in her condition; the thought of it sent pain soaring through her skull again.

Eventually she stood on wobbly legs, and realized there would be no standing up straight. The whole room appeared to be not more than three feet wide and possibly five to six feet long. Had she been any taller she wouldn't have been able to lie stretched out on the bed. As far as depth was concerned, it couldn't have been more than four to four and a half feet deep.

It wasn't particularly cold inside, but she saw a blanket on the bed should she need it.

Emma reached slowly toward the lantern, turning her head away to avoid direct eye contact with it. She felt the items on the shelf, picking up a bottle of water and whatever the cellophane package was beside it. Moving slowly she felt behind her until she was sure the bench or bed or whatever it was-

What had he said to her? Something about he was coming in here with her and she'd be sorry she'd ever met him... She gasped and quickly checked to make sure her clothing hadn't been removed. Emma could tell it hadn't, and she was certain she would know if she'd been raped.

It was then she remembered the solid kick she'd given to his knee cap. He wouldn't have been able to get down here with the crack she'd heard from his leg. So…how did *she* get down here? Looking around the room she realized he could have rolled her into the confined area and she'd have landed on the bed from any side of the door. He must have done that, because he certainly couldn't have carried her down.

She sat down on the bench and got her first good look at the cellophane bag. It was jerky. He hadn't meant for her to die down here, not right away anyway. She opened the water and drank slowly, then opened the jerky. Biting it wasn't going to work. It caused too much motion for her head to deal with, but she could suck on it until it was soft.

How long would it take someone to find her? *Could* anyone find her? She sat back against the wall and shut her eyes. The pain in her head was lessening at least a little bit. She wanted her mom and dad and wondered if she'd ever see them again. She worried for the first time about her parents and what they must be going through. The thought brought with it feelings of defeat, causing tears to form and begin their journey down her face, but she quickly wiped them away. NO! She wasn't going to let that happen. She *would* see her parents again.

Wiping the tears from her cheeks she scanned the room once more and decided no matter what, she'd find a way to make some noise. She *would* be heard.

Chapter Sixteen

"Do you think he's killed her?" Gentry asked the question not really wanting to know the answer.

"No, I don't think so," replied a preoccupied Lauren, her eyes studying the grid map before her.

She'd been so lost in thought Gentry wasn't sure she was answering his question, or a string of thinking that was floating through her head.

"No, I'd be willing to bet this was a ploy to keep us busy so he could be rid of us," she said, coming out of her stupor. "I've called the Bureau and they've got agents posted at all exits and entrances, but he could come out anywhere between those places."

"But, Emma is the right age, the right gender, why would he treat her any differently?"

Lauren thought for a minute before answering.

"Basically, because I believe she's the wrong segment of society. She's close to her parents, excels in school and sports, she definitely doesn't fit the profile. When I review what I know of him, he's most likely stashed her somewhere that will take us a while to find, giving him the time he needs to disappear again, and it just might work."

The searchers were approaching the command center tent, having just been dropped by the chopper. Joe talked with Gentry earlier and let him know an update on their arrival and that Charlie would be coming his way with several horses in tow ready for use in the search.

There were eight men and six women, not nearly enough, but better than just he and Lauren working the grids.

Lauren turned the team over to Gentry to explain the grid pattern and make the team assignments. Dylan was to man the command center and the rest were paired up as search teams. They each prepared their packs and readied their weapons while waiting for the horses to arrive.

The waiting was the most difficult part and it seemed like they did a lot of that. However, since Lauren and Gentry already had their horses, they took their grid map and started out. The others were encouraged to do a search of the park and then enlarge the search to one hundred yards around the campground perimeter, just in case he'd not gone as far as originally thought.

Before leaving the campground Gentry rode to the Thompsons campsite and spoke with Jack and Rose. They wanted to help in the search, but Gentry explained to them, should Emma show up at the campground, they needed to be there for her. They understood and agreed to stay put.

"Stay strong," Gentry said as he slid into his saddle. "Remember, she's as worried about you as you are about her. Be strong for each other and for Emma."

He turned Baby toward the entrance to the camp and nodded to Lauren. The two of them headed southeast into the brush where they believe Bantus took Emma. The search for them would be a short one, as daylight would be gone in a couple hours, but hopefully Charlie would have the mounts for the other searchers up by this evening or early tomorrow morning.

They'd only ridden a short way when Lauren shook her head.

"What's up? Something wrong?"

She was riding in front of him on the trail and he saw her shaking her head.

"I'm starving, and how in the world can I think of food at a time like this?"

"Your body is thinking about food because it needs fuel," said Gentry, pulling some jerky from his pack. "That doesn't make you a villain."

He handed her the jerky and reached back into the bag getting a piece for himself. He also pulled out a small bag of dried pears and handed some to Lauren.

"Here," he said with a smile, "these not only taste good, they're a great source of that fuel I was talking about."

Lauren took the fruit offering a half smile in return.

"You're pretty good at this trail stuff," she said as she chewed the piece of fruit.

"Yeah, well, that's just the tip of the iceberg. You should see me line dance."

Lauren chuckled weakly and gave Gladys a soft kick to move her off the trail.

"You search the right side, I'll search the left," she said, moving off to the left. Gentry started through the brush on his side.

They'd crisscrossed the grid for a good hour and found nothing. No footprints, no scraps of clothing left behind, nothing. There was no sign at all once the footprints were lost in the thick carpet of forest floor that anyone had even been through there and daylight was becoming scarce, as well.

"Hey," he called turning back to where they left the campground road. "We'd need to start heading back; it's going to get dark pretty quickly."

Lauren rode up behind him.

"I agree. It's just so hard to stop. Wish I had some night vision glasses."

"Yeah, well since they're back at the command center, we may as well call it a night."

They rode back and Lauren was once again lost in thought.

"Something on your mind?" he said, squinting in her direction.

"Other than picturing you line dancing?" she teased, "no, not really."

The two rode in silence out of the brush and to the road. The occasional heavy exhales of the horses and their footfalls on the soft earth were all that could be heard. The birds had gone to bed and the campers were calling to each other around their fires. Night had fallen.

They were greeted on the road that stretched around the camp by their friend, Charlie. He was coming up the trail with several horses following behind him, thirteen, to be exact.

"Charlie?" called Gentry, "Is that you?"

"Yup, it is," called a weary voice.

"How in the world did you manage that many horses and so fast? Did you have some help?"

Charlie yawned and stretched in the saddle.

"Naw," he said with a chuckle. "They were good boys and girls, but I'm sure they're ready to be on a line and enjoying some grazing. I'm just lucky I live halfway up here. Got a pigeon from your boy at the station telling me you needed horses. Now, about that grazing line, eh?"

"Follow me," smiled Gentry, shaking his head. "We've got a spot ready for them."

Once the horses were tied to the line, Charlie set about introducing each agent to his horse and telling them the strengths and weaknesses of each mount. He was in his element, and it usually made Gentry grin to watch him. However, on this night, it was a more somber mood that settled over the group.

Gentry and Lauren left Dylan to explain the grid and maps to the searchers and walked with heavy steps to the Thompson campsite. They were seated around their campfire staring at the flames as the two approached.

"Hey Jack, Rose," called Gentry. "May we join you?"

Several campers who'd heard what happened were also staying in the Thompson campsite, offering any support they could. Often, it wasn't what was said, it was just someone being there, and in this instance, that was the case.

"What have you heard?" pressed Rose, eager for any news of her daughter.

"I'm afraid it was too late to start the search by the time we got people and horses up here," said Lauren, "but we'll be heading out at first light."

Lauren continued as she sat down beside Rose.

"I know it's hard to wait, but if we send them out in the dark, we could search an area and miss something, something important."

"We understand," said Jack. "It's just…the waiting is unbearable."

"It's the worst part," agreed Gentry, "we feel that, too, but we'll find her. We will, and we want you to know that. Just hang in there with us, okay?"

"There's nothing else we can do," said Rose, a tear falling down her cheek. "We'll be fine. Our Emma is a strong girl, she'll hold her own. We know she will."

Lauren patted Rose's hand and stood.

"That's an excellent attitude to have. Hang onto that. I know sleeping will be hard to do, but you'll need to get some rest tonight. Tomorrow is a big day. Take care."

Gentry stood with Lauren and they both turned and strode from the camp.

"*That* never gets any easier," said Lauren. "Like my telling them to sleep is going to make it happen. I know I wouldn't be able to eat, sleep or think straight if it was my daughter out there. I guess the fact they know nothing about Walter Bantus helps."

"I like the way you think about the family, and what they're feeling," smiled Gentry. "You display a great amount of compassion and that's hard to find in your line of work."

"I don't know about that," sighed Lauren, "but I know I wouldn't want to be in their shoes. I can't even imagine what those shoes feel like, but from the looks on their faces, I'd say I'd rather be dead than endure it."

"It's good that you have that capacity to empathize with them," said Gentry, "I hope you never let the job change that. It's the best part of you."

He put his arm around her and squeezed her shoulders. She leaned into him as they continued to walk and he released her, worried he wouldn't be able to stop something if he started it. Now was neither the time nor the place, but when your world was in chaos, it sure seemed like the comfort of a warm body would help calm the nerves and relax the mind.

Gentry reached up and lifted his hat and softly scratched his head, then replaced the hat. He made himself think about Emma and where she was, if she was alive, and if she was then how was she doing? It cleared his mind of any other thoughts almost immediately, making him fairly certain he wouldn't be sleeping much tonight.

***

Emma's arms ached as she let the two by four drop to the floor. Partially bent over and shoving a board into the roof of her 'prison' for the last however long it'd been had taken its toll. She'd managed to pull one of the boards from the wall of her dungeon, but it was heavy and awkward, taking far more effort than she'd thought it would.

She'd hoped someone would hear the thud of the board hitting the ceiling, but she wasn't even sure anyone *could* hear it. The idea of going through all of that, possibly for nothing, made her weak in the knees and she collapsed onto the bed. With no idea of what time it was, she would try again when she woke, and hope it would be at a time someone would hear it. How could she know if she was even in an area where anyone was walking? What if she was so far into the woods no one ever came by? How much food and water did she have? Would it last long enough for her to be found? Was he going to come back? For all she knew, she could be pounding on the ceiling when everyone was sleeping and sleeping when everyone was looking for her.

She had to sleep though, she couldn't keep going. Her head ached, her arms ached, everything ached. Clearing her head, she knew they hadn't walked so far she would be isolated. Someone would hear her. She'd start again when she woke.

Chapter Seventeen

The next morning Gentry and Lauren looked like they hadn't slept at all. It was a rough night and Gentry was certain it was going to be a long day.

Opting to eat in the saddle, the two began their search back at the grid they'd searched the evening before.

"I just want to check something out," said Lauren. "Follow me; I thought I saw some earth that looked like it was freshly disturbed. It could have just been someone digging a fire pit, but I couldn't see that well at the time and it's been gnawing at me all night."

Gentry followed her through the brush. Within about thirty minutes Lauren stopped and dismounted, tying Gladys to a bush. Gentry did the same with Baby and followed Lauren to an area of woods that certainly did have disturbed earth, and far more than one would need to dig a fire pit.

"Where do you suppose all this came from?" Lauren was astounded.

"It's too new to be from any work done on the campground. And it looks as if someone was trying to hide it," said Gentry pointing to the surrounding bushes. "Look how it's so evenly distributed under those bushes-"

Gentry quickly held his hand out, stopping Lauren from moving forward. He froze in place.

"Wh-"

"Shhh," he said, his finger at his lips. "Did you hear that?"

They remained frozen in place and listened to a soft 'thump, thump, thump."

"I hear it!" said Lauren. "I hear it!"

They split up, each searching through the dirt on hands and knees, looking and listening for the place the sound was coming from. As the sun began to shine through the trees and down to the forest floor, Gentry caught a reflection of sunlight off of something in the ground… something metal.

"Lauren! Over here!" he cried out as he jumped to his feet and ran full speed to the object buried in the dirt.

The thumping was still soft, but was causing enough of a vibration in the fresh dirt that it had partially uncovered a padlock.

"Emma!" called Lauren, "Emma! Can you hear me?"

The thumping stopped and Lauren repeated her call.

"Emma! Can you hear me?"

A very soft, almost imperceptible call came back.

"Yes, I can hear you."

"Emma," yelled Lauren, "Stay where you are and get back from the door. My partner is going to get help. Do you understand? We're going to get you out."

"Yes," came the reply.

"Listen," urged Gentry, his eyes boring into her, "I know you know this, but I have to say it anyway. You keep your gun in your hand from this moment on. If you hear *anyone* coming toward you, you call out and make them identify themselves or be shot. I mean it, Lauren. You stay alert, stay safe. I'll hurry as fast as I can."

She understood his concern, and was already pulling her gun from the holster as he spoke.

"I'll be fine," she assured him. "Now *GO!*"

Gentry jumped to his feet and ran to Baby.

He grabbed her reins from the bush she'd been tied to and swung up into the saddle.

"Let's go girl," he said, "we found her!"

Riding into camp at a full gallop Gentry went directly to the command center.

"Dylan! We found her. Get these coordinates out to all the searchers and have them meet us there. We're going to start digging her out. She's alive, Dylan! She's alive!"

"I need two shovels, and something I can use to cut off a padlock. I'll use my first aid kit from Baby if she needs any tending to."

Dylan was gathering the needed items as fast as Gentry was calling them out.

"I need some time to find cutters, Gentry, I'll have to check with campers and see if anyone has some."

"As fast as you can, Dylan. I'm going to Thompson's campsite, run them down to me there as soon as you get them," he said as he spun Baby around and galloped off.

Jumping down before she'd come to a complete stop, Gentry raced to the camper and pounded on the door.

A startled Rose answered and saw Gentry grinning up at her.

"You found her?" she said, tears forming in her eyes. "You found my baby? Is she..is she…"

"She's alive," he said with relief, "she's alive and we'll be bringing her to you as soon as we can get to her. She's buried in some kind of a container, but she's alive and talking to us."

Rose fell into Gentry's arms as Jack stepped out of the fifth wheel.

"You found her? She's okay?"

"She appears to be fine. I have to get back and help, but please, stay here and we'll bring her to you as soon as we can."

Rose released him and clung to her husband, sobs of relief and thankfulness resounding through the campsite. Other campers who'd come to sit with them and comfort them were also in the trailer and rejoiced at the news, sending word throughout the camp that Emma was found.

Gentry turned as Dylan came running to the site and handed him the cutters. Gentry clapped his friend on the shoulder and grinned. He jumped deftly into the saddle, and holding the shovels and cutter across the front of him, he hurried back to where Lauren was still talking with Emma.

Other searchers were beginning to arrive along with men from the campground with shovels and picks. Gentry dismounted and tied off Baby, rushing to Lauren, and the lock, now completely exposed. Gentry cut the lock with a loud snap as others worked removing the three inches of dirt from the door.

Within minutes they opened the cellar like cover and saw Emma, the side of her head matted with blood, wincing in the sunlight, but smiling through tears of relief and exhaustion. Gentry reached down and pulled her out of the small chamber. She stumbled a little as her feet hit the ground and she turned to Lauren, hugging her tightly.

"I didn't know if anyone could even hear me, or if it was night or day. I just kept hitting the ceiling until you came," she said through her tears.

Gentry helped her to a fallen tree trunk and sat her down. She was unsteady on her feet and he could tell she was dizzy.

"How many fingers do you see?" he said holding up his first and second fingers.

"Two," she said firmly.

"Good girl. As soon as the medical gets here, they'll get you cleaned up a little bit. I'll just be over there, okay?" Gentry stood and watched her face.

"Please," she said, tears filling her eyes, "don't leave me. I don't want to be alone."

He sat back down immediately and put his arm around her shoulders.

"I can do that," he said with a smile. "I'd be honored to stay with you."

Within a very few minutes the medical team arrived and took over, working together to check out her wound and make sure there were no other injuries. The blood was dried, which meant she was no longer bleeding, and that was a good thing. They wiped the excess blood off of her face and called it good, knowing they'd have more time once they got her to camp and she'd seen her parents.

"We'll check the wound more thoroughly when we get back to camp," said the head medical technician. He nodded to Emma and stood.

"Let's get you back to your parents," said Lauren, "they're pretty anxious to see you. Can you ride a horse?"

Emma nodded in the affirmative and Lauren and Gentry helped her to the horses. They put her in the saddle on Gladys and Lauren slipped in behind the saddle, holding her arms around Emma and taking the reins.

"I can do that," smiled a determined Emma gazing hopefully at the reins, "if it's okay with you."

"You can do whatever you like," said Lauren returning the smile, "you are my hero, Emma."

Gentry rode beside Emma and Lauren, in case he needed to assist in keeping Emma in the saddle, but she did just fine on her own. He marveled that she could be that together after what she'd been through.

It was a short ride back to camp, the excitement to get Emma reunited with her parents practically leading the way. The bouncing didn't do anything for her headache, but the joy of freedom far outweighed the pain.

As they rode into camp, the cheers went up from the other campers amidst shouts of joy and clapping, laughter and tears. Emma guided the horse to her campsite and saw her mother and father standing anxiously at the edge of their site.

"Let me get down first, Emma," said Lauren, "and I'll help you down. You've got a nasty gash on your head and it could cause some dizziness."

"Yeah, I can feel it," said Emma, a little overwhelmed by all the attention.

Lauren slid off Gladys and gently helped Emma down. When she was sure Emma was standing on her own, she stepped out of the way and watched the glorious reunion.

More cheers ascended from the campers as Jack and Rose hugged their daughter for the first time since her abduction.

He dismounted and held onto the horses while Lauren helped Emma into the fifth wheel. In a very few minutes Lauren exited the camper and Gentry grabbed her with his free arm, pulling her to his side and gently squeezing her.

The two of them mounted their horses and headed for the command center. As they were leaving Jack, Rose and Emma called out as they exited the camper and approached them.

"Thank you for finding our daughter," said Jack, nearly unable to speak through his tears. "We'll never forget you; never forget what you did here today."

"It was good fortune that we got here when we did," said Lauren, "we're so happy we could help."

"We need to have our medical team get a better look at you, Emma," said Gentry, "we just want to have that gash checked out and see if you need stitches. They're coming over now, is that okay?"

Emma nodded and Lauren and Gentry mounted their horses.

Lauren turned Gladys to face the Thompson family.

"I know the first thing you're going to want to do is to get out of Dodge," she said, "but we'll need you to stay put for the time being, in case we have to get more information from you. Just know you're safe. He's not going to come back, there are too many FBI agents around, and we'll keep them around until you leave."

"We'll stay put," said Jack, hugging his wife and daughter standing on either side of him.

The medical team arrived so Gentry and Lauren left the family in their care. As they urged their horses in the direction of the command center Gentry put in a very relieved call to his assistant.

"Jackson."

"Hey Joe, we found her. She's okay. We need the CSI team back up here. He had her buried in a good sized cellar not far from the campground."

"When would he have time to dig a cellar?" Joe was astonished at the concept.

"That's not all. It was completely lined with two by fours. Now, tell me how he got those up here undetected? *And* it had a cellar door on it, soundproofed, somewhat, with hinges and a padlock." Gentry was really getting tired of Bantus, and it was showing.

"Who *is* this guy?"

"Joe, I want you to ask around. Find out if anyone filed for a work permit in the name of the park, the town, the state, anything that looks or feels funky. Check with the hardware stores in town, he had to buy those supplies somewhere. I want names, dates and where the permits were going to be used. I want copies of receipts you suspect might be Bantus. Get me anything you can, and get it fast."

"Done."

The call ended and the two dismounted, having arrived at the command center. Gentry felt numb, and tied off Baby without realizing he'd done it. He entered the tent and no one was there as Dylan was standing watch with other agents at the wooden cellar Emma was buried in. They would be there until the CSI team arrived. Gentry stood in the center of the tent with clenched fists. He didn't know why, he just stood there, frozen in time, wondering how anyone could do something like this to a living, breathing human being.

"Breathe, Ranger Beauchene," came a soft voice from behind him.

He turned to see Lauren gazing up at him, her amazing green eyes studying his face.

They were alone in the tent, and he wanted her more than he'd wanted anyone or anything in his life. He took her in his arms and kissed her, feeling the familiar beat of her heart, sensing the longing they both felt. All the tension, all the anxiety, all the fears of the last two days left him and he felt he'd collapse if he let go of her.

"Gentry, stop," she said pulling away. She was breathing heavily and couldn't look him in the eye. She stepped back and turned away, her arms folded in front of her. "I do want you, Gentry, I do. I need to feel your arms around me, know the touch of your hands, but I *refuse* to give this guy another *minute* of thinking he's not on our radar. I want him running for his life, so we can chase him into a corner and finish this. I want to watch him die."

Gentry removed his hat and ran his hand through his hair, setting the hat back on his head. His knees were still weak, his heart still pushing the blood through his veins at an unbelievable pace, but he knew she was right. If for no other reason, he wanted to kill the man for ruining his moment. However, he knew there would be others. There had to be, because now he knew she was a part of him and he could never live without her.

Chapter Eighteen

"I understand, Lauren," he replied, "and we *will* catch this freak of nature, and then you're going to feel my arms around you for a very long time. I promise you that."

Lauren tried to smile, but it was forced and brief.

Emma had to be debriefed; they still had no details of her abduction. Once the medical team radioed them with the all clear, Lauren and Gentry headed to the Thompson campsite again, this time on foot.

The family sat together at their dining table inside the camper.

"Jack, Rose," Gentry said kindly, "it's important we hear Emma's story now. She could give us some clues that may help us catch this man. Can we have a few minutes alone with her to ask some questions?"

"Are you okay with that, honey?" asked Rose, holding her daughters hand and standing.

Emma remained sitting. "Yeah, Mom, I'm fine. It might help me to get it all out."

"Okay, we'll be just outside," said her dad.

They both stepped out of the camper and closed the door behind them.

Emma sat back in her seat at the table; a large white bandage graced the left side of her forehead. Lauren and Gentry slid into the opposite side.

"How are you feeling?" asked Lauren. "Is your head okay?"

"Yeah, he hit me with something, but I don't remember any of that," began Emma. "It's not bad, but it was enough to knock me out for a while. I can't thank you enough for finding me. I'll do anything I can to help you find him."

"I'm sorry to have to ask you this," said Lauren, touching her arm, "but you're certain you weren't sexually assaulted?"

"I'm sure. When I came to, my clothes were still on me, undisturbed. I could tell he didn't…"

"Very good," said Lauren, "You did very well."

For the next hour Emma recited everything she remembered, right up until she heard his knee crack. Gentry was especially interested in the small black box with the red blinking light.

"Did he tell you, actually *say* it was a bomb?"

"No, he didn't, and that's why I thought he was bluffing. At first I thought it was real, but the more he flashed it in my face, the more I figured he was lying to get me to go with him. I figured if he was going to lock me in a box in the ground I'd make him wish he hadn't, so I took out his knee."

"You're sure about that knee?" asked Lauren.

"Positive. It was his left knee, I think, I heard a fairly loud crack and he screamed in pain. It felt good to hear him scream. I suppose that makes me a bad guy, but I can't help what I feel."

"No, that doesn't make you a bad guy, Emma," said Lauren, squeezing her hand across the table. "It makes you braver than any young lady I've ever met."

"Well, he told me he was going down into that box with me, and that I'd be sorry I ever met him. I knew if he couldn't climb up or down, he wouldn't be getting in the box. I wondered for a while if he would come back for me. He sure did a lot to keep me alive. He even had a blanket on the bed."

"You're a lucky girl," said Gentry, "and a smart one. You did everything right. If you hadn't been pounding on that door the way you did, I don't know if we'd ever have found you. Just to make sure he was bluffing, we'll check the rig for anything suspicious, but you were probably right about the bluff."

Lauren was taking notes as Emma spoke, writing down the important points that may be of use later. Once they finished with the interview, Lauren and Gentry rose to leave.

"Wait," said Emma, rising slowly.

She put her arms around both of them at once and hugged them tightly.

"Thank you for saving me." Her voice was a whisper.

"You're entirely welcome," smiled Lauren. "You were a big help, just remember that."

Gentry and Lauren spent the next half hour searching the Thompson's fifth wheel for any sign of a bomb, large or small. They found nothing, which is exactly what they thought they'd find. Emma's instincts were correct.

Gentry's phone rang again. It was Joe. He listened as Joe updated him on how the preparations were proceeding.

"Gotcha, thanks Joe. Good work."

He ended the call and relayed the conversation to Lauren.

"Joe has the CSI on their way to the helipad. You FBI types are fast."

"Well, as soon as you went to tell the family, I called the team in Seattle and let them know they would be needed. I needed them on their way ASAP."

The two left the camper for the last time and said their good-byes to the family. They walked back to the command tent and Dylan was busily taking the extra tents down along with the remaining equipment and stowing it all for pick up by the chopper.

He'd already fixed lunch and put it in the cooler for them when they were ready, and after the high tension day so far, they were ready. They sat down together and reviewed the events of the abduction while they ate.

"Bantus is injured, and it sounds fairly serious," Lauren sounded hopeful for the first time that day. "This could mean he's not actually out of the park yet, he may be holed up somewhere with a bad leg."

"Dylan," said Gentry, "have you packed the maps yet?"

"No, they're right over there," he said pointing to the small table, "underneath it in the rolls."

"Perfect," replied Gentry, standing and heading to the table.

"One of these…" he said unrolling the maps one at a time and rolling them back up until he found the one he needed. "Ah, this would be the one."

The others came to the table and gazed at the map lying open. Gentry was pointing to different areas on the map.

"So…if he was hurt, he couldn't have gone this route because of the river through there. No way he could cross it one-legged." Gentry took a bite of his sandwich.

Dylan pointed to another area.

"How about here? Once you're down from the mountain it's pretty smooth terrain…well, flat anyway."

"Or here," said Lauren pointing almost due south. "Check it out, the descent is more gradual and there's a bridge over the river. He may even have gotten a ride out of the park from there. But, surely someone would have checked passengers IDs when we have an active APB."

"It's happened before that someone made it through a checkpoint…wouldn't be unheard of." Gentry took another bite of his sandwich. "Good job on the sandwiches, Dylan. I had no idea I was this hungry."

"Well, you know what they say," he said smiling slyly. "It's the little things in life…"

"And *they* are absolutely right," Gentry replied, then turned back to the map, "I think you might be onto something, Lauren. I do believe that would be a much better route. It's been less than forty-eight hours since he took her. With the injuries he's sustained, maybe he's still in the park and hasn't made it to the bridge yet. I'm going to alert the guards at that exit and make sure they check every car. I could kiss you, you know."

"I believe you already have," grinned Dylan, glancing at both of them. "I saw it with my own eyes."

"Oh, well, then, perhaps I should kiss *you*," he said with a sly grin.

"Animal." Dylan backed up, just in case.

Gentry finished his lunch and hurried to the staging area outside the main tent where the saddles were kept. He needed fresh batteries from the saddlebag in his satphone, not wanting to risk a dead phone at this point in the investigation. There were only three saddles left, as the other horses were in the process of being returned to Charlie.

Baby whinnied softly and watched him approach.

"Hey, there's my girl," he said, strolling up to her and resting her head on his shoulder. He stroked her neck with both hands and talked quietly to her. "You did a good job in there, you know. Thanks for getting me where I needed to be. We found her, Baby. We found her and you helped. How does that feel, eh?"

Lauren came around the side of the tent and watched him talk to Baby. Gladys stood next to Baby chewing contentedly on some grass. Lauren walked to her saddle and pulled Gladys' brush from the saddlebag. Gentry watched her slowly move the brush over the mare's shiny coat.

"Gentry, I'm...I'm sorry about...when..."

"Don't worry about it, Lauren," he said, leaning down and pulling some batteries from the bags. "I get where you were coming from, and I know you understood where I was at. It's okay." Then he grinned his 'uh-oh, here it comes' grin. "However, if you should want to make it up to me any time soon..."

"Don't push it, Beauchene," she said with a laugh. "I could bring you up on charges of sexual harassment in the workplace."

"Well, if you're ever feeling a *need* to be sexually harassed, just let me know. I'll be your go to guy." He smiled at her and tipped his hat.

"You're hopeless, you know that?"

Lauren giggled and finished brushing Gladys. Once finished she walked back around the tent.

Gentry remembered his reason for coming out and quickly removed his satphone from his waist holster, dialing the station.

"Jackson."

"Hey Joe, I need you to call the guard station at the West Glacier entrance to the park. Tell them to be on the lookout for Bantus, we believe he's been injured and has a bad knee."

"Will do," replied Joe. "How's everything else going up there?"

"Good. It's nice to have a happy ending on this one."

"You sound tired," said Joe, "Dylan says you've been…busy with that FBI agent."

"Oh yeah?" laughed Gentry, "well I guess I'm going to have to have a talk with Dylan."

Joe chuckled.

"I'm working on the information about the building materials. I have a few leads and will be going into Kalispell for a face to face with the manager at a couple stores. I'll keep you posted."

Gentry thanked him and ended the call. He was still grinning from Joe's remark about how 'busy' he'd been. He shook his head as he replaced the phone on his belt and headed back into the tent, chuckling about two grown men were gossiping about his love life.

"Like a bunch of girls," he chuckled.

Chapter Nineteen

The next couple of days were a blur. Eight teams of two FBI agents were assigned to each city that bordered the park. Lauren was assigned as lead over all the search teams. Instead of requesting another agent to assist her, she requested Gentry Beauchene. He knew the area in and around the park better than anyone and having worked with him thus far, felt he would have her back as well as any Agent.

Gentry wasn't sure how he felt about leaving the park. He remembered questioning Greyson when he'd made the decision to work with Aspen. Now he understood far more than before why he'd do such a thing. The only way to protect these Bureau women was to stay with them. Yeah, he got it now. Although he knew Lauren would scoff at the idea of being 'protected', it made Gentry feel better keeping her close to him. He knew Lauren was more than capable of taking care of herself. With a half smile he realized she could probably do that better than he could.

Dylan was assigned to them, as well, since they'd been working together. He'd also been privy to decisions and information on the case and it made sense to keep him on the task force.

There were two or three person teams assigned to the different cities including Cut Bank, Conrad, Columbia Falls, Whitefish, Kalispell and Evergreen. The small towns bordering Flathead Lake were assigned to two teams. This was due in part to their locations, as they would require a lot of travel around the lake.

Lauren, Gentry and Dylan were assigned to the area around Kalispell, including Whitefish and Columbia Falls. This was the area Gentry was most familiar with. It was also the closest in proximity to the most likely exit Bantus may have taken.

Since the decision was made to keep them close to the park, and since Gentry's ranch just happened to be in their assigned search area, he offered his ranch as a place to stay for the three of them once they got back to the station. He had a regular housekeeper that kept the place dusted and swept even when he was gone, so he wasn't worried about inviting them to stay.

Gentry notified his housekeeper of the guests he would have with him when he came home and asked that she make up two of the rooms for them and have them ready. He also asked if she would be willing to do some cooking and shopping for them as well. She was agreeable to that. Gentry was a pretty good cook himself, but with the time restraints they had, he was pretty certain there wouldn't be a lot of time to play chef.

Gentry, Lauren and Dylan rode the horses down to the station where Charlie would pick them up. The trip down would be an overnight, unless you were Charlie, so they rode as far as they could for the day. They waited to leave until the extra tents and equipment were picked up by Cy and taken by chopper down to the station. Once that was finished, they loaded Handsome with their things and started out.

The day was beautiful, and it was about ten in the morning on their fourth day in the park before they left. Enjoying the feel of crisp clean air on his skin, Gentry lead the small party out of the campground and back onto their original trail. The birds were back in full force for the summer and they called to each other from the treetops. Angry squirrels cried out, occasionally jumping from tree to tree.

There was still a concern Bantus remained in the park. He'd not been found exiting from any park entrance and they knew he was injured, possibly severely. If he couldn't walk, Gentry thought they may find him and the thought brought a smile to his face. He figured he'd probably have to fight Lauren for the first crack at him, but he was willing to take his place in line. However, the thought of holding Lauren back so she wouldn't kill Bantus made his smile widen.

Without warning, the maniacal laughter from their crime scene camp filled the air. Gentry stopped Baby and jumped down, pulling his weapon and scanning the surrounding area. Lauren and Dylan did the same thing, everyone searching for the source of the sound, and at the same time, for the killer.

Eventually Gentry turned around and began pulling things out of his saddlebags. There, buried at the bottom of the bag was a small recorder, seemingly identical to the units they'd found in the woods. He reached in to pull it out, hoping to find a way to shut the thing off.

"Don't!" yelled Lauren. "Don't touch it. Fingerprints, remember?"

Gentry stepped back and Lauren reached into the bag, using an exam glove like a potholder. She wrapped the latex glove around the unit and pulled it out.

"Okay," she said over the laughter, "this one's different."

"How?" asked Gentry, looking over her shoulder. "How's it different?"

"Well, for one thing, it's got an on/off switch."

Lauren turned back to the bag and looked to make sure there was nothing else in there.

"So, who turned it on?" asked Lauren, never taking her eyes from the unit.

Both men knew it was a rhetorical question.

Dylan leaned over and inspected the small device.

"It could be on a timer of some sort as long as it's on," he said staring at it.

"Well," said Gentry, irritated by the continuous laughter. "Would it be okay to turn it *off*?"

"Oh, yeah, sorry," said Lauren, using a finger from the glove and silencing the device.

The forest sounds returned and the anxiety level of all three riders dropped. Interestingly, Baby never made a move and that spoke volumes to Gentry.

He turned to face her, walking around to stroke her nose.

"He's not here, is he girl," he said, staring into her eyes and slowly stroking her forehead and nose. Then speaking to the others he said, "I think we're safe for the time being, but we need to put our heads together and figure out when and who could have planted that. I think that's definite confirmation Bantus had an accomplice up here."

Gentry's satphone began ringing. He pulled it from his belt.

"Beauchene."

It was Joe and his voice was filled with a cross of anger and confusion.

"Slow down, Joe," said Gentry, straining to understand what he was hearing. "You got a *what*?"

Gentry bowed his head and began massaging his forehead, moving his hat up as he did.

"Have you left the station unlocked and unattended at any time?"

It was silent as Gentry listened to the answer.

"Okay, here's what I want you to do," he replied, "put the letter in an evidence bag and use some gloves with it from now on. Put it in the safe and I'll look at it tomorrow when we get down there, okay?"

Joe was still upset and the others could hear his voice, but couldn't make out any of the words.

"I know, I know, Joe," said Gentry, trying to calm his assistant down. "I have an FBI agent with me, you know that."

Joe obviously calmed down and Gentry ended the call warning Joe to keep the door locked even when he was there.

"Well," said Gentry, removing his hat and scratching his head. "Joe got a letter and opened it, thinking it was just station business, but it was actually for me. Supposedly from one Walter Bantus."

"What did it say?" asked Lauren, her face solemn and concerned.

"Basically that he wanted to see me dead and that I'd never find 'the girl' he planted in the park."

Dylan rubbed his chin. "Well, one out of two isn't bad," he said playfully.

Both Lauren and Gentry looked at him with a flat stare.

Dylan raised his palms in defense.

"Just sayin'," he said as he mounted Knuckles. "I mean, obviously that was written a while ago."

"Ya *think?*" said Gentry, shaking his head.

"Hey, whaddaya expect from a guy riding a mare called Knuckles."

Lauren and Gentry slid into their saddles, chuckling softly. In spite of it all, it always felt good to laugh, and he knew he could count on Dylan for the comic relief at the right time.

They rode on, stopping for a lunch packed by Dylan before they left. The horses were tied on a line, allowing them some grazing time while their three riders discussed options.

"We have another four to five hours of daylight," said Gentry glancing up to check the sun's location in the sky. "We would then be only about an hour away from the station. So, we could probably stop a little earlier, get a little more rest and still be able to make the station by early morning tomorrow. That letter isn't going anywhere and I already know what it says."

"That sounds good to me. I'm exhausted and ready for a break," said Lauren. "We know he's nowhere near us, and even if he was, he couldn't get to us very fast in his condition. But boy…I'd sure like him to try…" Her voice trailed off as she grinned at the thought.

Dylan and Gentry both laughed at her euphoria, which brought her out of it immediately.

"What?" she said defensively, "It's true, and you both feel the same way."

"Yeah, we do," laughed Gentry, "but we're not fantasizing about it on horseback."

They talked for a while about possible suspects for Bantus' accomplice. They reviewed each person that came for the search, what they knew of them and how long they'd been with the Bureau. Without personnel files, there was no way they'd ever get anywhere.

Lauren called her office and requested the files on all personnel involved in the search for Emma and subsequent assignments related to the case to be couriered to Gentry's home for review first thing in the morning. She gave them the address and ended the call.

"That should give us a starting place, at least," she said with satisfaction.

"Okay, well, I say for the rest of the evening we just chill," said Gentry. "We need a night before we get back into the blood and gore, and I say we take it."

"Agreed," said Dylan and Lauren in unison.

Continuing on for another hour and a half, Gentry found a nice open place to camp with room for a line for Baby, Gladys, Knuckles and Handsome. There was plenty of grazing area and a nice spot for a tent and campfire.

After tethering the horses the three set about getting the camp put together for the evening. With all of them working together, it took less than thirty minutes to get the tent set up and the fire pit done. In a very short time they were all seated around a crackling fire as the chill of the oncoming evening settled around them.

They visited together through the remainder of the afternoon and when the time came everyone pitched in and helped with dinner. They dined on the last of the trout that was brought up by the last chopper, potatoes baked in the coals and fresh green beans. It was delicious, and as always tasted far better around a campfire than a kitchen table. It was a good night spent under another starlit sky accented by a stark bright moon.

As the evening advanced, the air chilled even more and Lauren went into the tent for her coat. Gentry heard her rummaging around and then heard a shout of surprise.

"What the-"

Gentry jumped from his chair and rushed into the tent, his gun drawn.

"What? What is it?"

Lauren was seated on her rolled out sleeping bag with a look of disbelief on her face. On the bag lay an envelope and she hand held a flashlight beam on it, staring. The envelope had her name on it. She quickly reached into her pocket for a pair of gloves. Stretching them onto her hands, she picked up the envelope and held her flashlight over it again. She looked up as Gentry approached her and gently opened the envelope. She gingerly pulled the letter out and slowly unfolded it.

Gentry holstered his gun and sat down beside her, reading the words she read aloud.

"My dear FBI Agent;

I look forward to the day when I can plant a beautiful evergreen sapling in your chest cavity. You'll never find the Thompson girl because I plan to come back and keep her for myself, so I've made sure she can't be found. Don't bother yourselves with searching.

Until we meet face to face;

Walter Bantus

Chapter Twenty

"Okay, so now we know for sure these were planted by someone before we found Emma," said Gentry, trying to keep his anger at a minimum. "He's got an accomplice."

Lauren nodded and continued staring at the page. Her face was contemplative, not fearful or angry. The wheels were definitely turning.

"What are you thinking?" asked Gentry as Dylan came through the tent door and sat down on the other end of the sleeping bag.

"What is that?" asked Dylan, "What's happened?"

"Lauren got her own personal message from our friend Walter," Gentry replied.

"Nice."

Dylan walked over and stood behind her, reading the note over her shoulder.

"It says the same thing yours did, almost to the letter," He said, "guy's not very original, is he?"

"Well, you know," joked Gentry, "He's got a lot on his plate right now. He's got a young girl stashed underground that really isn't any more, he's got a bad leg…of course, he didn't know he'd have a bad leg when he wrote this one-"

"Guys," said Lauren, interrupting them, "this is wrong. There's something about this that's just wrong."

"How?" asked Gentry, "how is it wrong? What's wrong about it?"

"I…I don't know," replied Lauren, biting her lip and continuing to stare at the page. "I need to review that profile. NOW."

Lauren was standing as she spoke and hurried out of the tent to the saddlebag with her file in it. She pulled it out of the bag and walked swiftly back into the tent.

"Uh, let's go back out to the fire. It's warmer out there." She turned and walked to her chair by the fire.

Gentry watched her go and glanced at Dylan.

"Bad case of one track mind," he grinned, "care to place a bet as to whether she knows we're not sitting by her right now?"

"No way," chuckled Dylan.

They made their way out of the tent and to the chairs. Before sitting down, Gentry walked to the line and checked the horses. He stroked Baby softly and patted her neck, then returned to the fire.

Gentry waited patiently for Lauren to complete her review of the profile. She didn't look any different when she laid the papers in her lap than she did when she was reviewing them. The concern and confusion was still there.

"What has you so bothered about this, Lauren?" he asked her. He wasn't aware of anything on that page that was any different than what was in his letter. The signature looked the same, the wording as well as near as he could tell. He couldn't figure out what had her so stumped…though she was beautiful when she was stumped. That thought made him grin.

"Well," she said glancing up at him for the first time, then back down at the page. She did a swift double take. "What's so funny?"

"Funny? Oh…it's not…I wasn't…there's a…"

"Yeah, that's what I thought," she grinned, "eyes on the goal, Mr. Beauchene, eyes on the goal."

"Oh…" he said, studying the contours of her face, "they are…"

Her eyes went from his eyes to his lips and then quickly down to the paper.

"I mean it, Gentry."

"So do I," he said, rising and walking to the horses once again. As he walked away, Lauren continued on about the letter.

"Why would he not stop the delivery of these letters if he knew we'd found Emma? It doesn't track that he would be that careless. Could he really think we'd not find her? Walter Bantus would have a contingency for every eventuality. He would. The fact that number one, he doesn't know she's been found doesn't track with fact number two, he didn't have a plan for her being found. He had to at least have a *plan* that included her rescue. It appears he didn't, and that's the part that doesn't track. We can be fairly certain he doesn't know Emma's been found, which means he's nowhere near where we are. This isn't right."

Gentry continued over to Baby, her words rolling around in his head. A visit with Baby was the best way to get his thoughts in order.

"Hey Baby Moon," he said striding up to the mare, "you're looking kind of small compared to these other two ladies. Not intimidated, are you?"

Baby whinnied softly and tossed her head.

"Good girl," he said softly. "Now, take me for example. I don't let that lady over there by the fire intimidate me, either. Exactly. I just can't figure out why she matters, and yet I commit myself to her in my thinking and with my big fat mouth, but what if I don't really care like I think I do?"

Baby laid her head on his shoulder and nuzzled his neck.

"Yeah, I mean, you know what they say about people that get involved during a high tension encounter. Well, this encounter is pretty high tension, don't you think?"

Baby lifted her head and continued to chew on the grass, pieces of it sticking out either side of her mouth.

"You have it all together, don't you girl. Not a care in the world. Well, you just wait…one day you'll meet that special stud that will whisk you off your hooves and you'll be done for. Then you can come talk to me about it and I'll have all the answers because I'll have been there…except for the hooves part."

Gentry laughed and patted Baby's neck, running his hand along her back as he walked back to the fire.

Lauren was on her satphone when he sat down next to her.

"Okay, yeah…sounds good. Thanks."

She ended the call and peered at Gentry.

"They got the results of the autopsy on the girls in the casket. Haven't ID'd them yet, but it's Bantus alright. His fingerprints are everywhere, just like all the others. The 'soup' they were in is making time of death a little difficult to determine, so it will be a while on that, but it's him, alright."

"Well, we pretty much knew that," said Gentry leaning back in his chair.

"Yeah, it's nothing new, nothing we didn't already know."

Lauren's disappointment was keen. He could hear it in her voice and see it in her demeanor.

"We'll get him," said Gentry, "there's no doubt there. He can't go on forever. He's going to make a mistake at some point and we'll be ready when he does."

"I know," she sighed. "I just want him found before he can hurt anyone else. Bless Emma. She may have saved several lives if he's going to be laid up for a while."

"We've got APB's at all the local hospitals and clinics. We'll find him."

Lauren focused her deep green eyes on Gentry, thinking and staring at him before she spoke. This made his mind want to go places he promised he wouldn't and he forced himself to concentrate on the task at hand.

"You know, he's got this thing about having his killings twenty-seven days apart. Aspen made note of that in her profile. He was thrown off that cycle when he was shot. I believe that's why we found two bodies in that casket."

The memory made Gentry shiver.

"Now," she continued, "he's more than likely going to be thrown off again. It makes me wonder if he's keeping track of how many days out of his game plan he's gotten, and what this is going to do to his frame of mind. Which brings me to the question of who is our mole and how do we find him…or her."

"Well," replied Gentry thoughtfully, "first, we need a list of everyone who came up from the Bureau. Then we match it to the search team assignments and make sure we didn't have an extra 'helper'. If that matches up, then I think we should start by reviewing the personnel files you ordered. We'll be at the ranch tomorrow and we can start early."

"Agreed," said Lauren, firmly, "I'll need a shower first."

"Yeah, me too," he said grinning slyly. "We could-"

"No, we couldn't," she said, smiling back at him.

"There's nothing more you can do tonight. I say you put it away and enjoy our last evening in the park. Just look at that sky…it sucks the stress right out of you." Gentry chuckled as he took off his hat and laid his head against the back of his chair and stared up at the stars.

Lauren followed suit. It was the first time since dinner she'd had time to think about how full her stomach was and how beautiful the night sky was.

"It feels like night just kind of settles over the park," she sighed. "I mean, it nestles in all around you and smiles down on you through a canopy of stars."

"That's the beauty of Glacier Park, right there," smiled Gentry, still studying the sky. "You've described it perfectly."

They sat in silence for a minute before Dylan added his two cents worth.

"Just makes you wanna hold hands and sing all the verses of Kumbaya, you know?" he said, laughing at the two of them. "Seriously, you need to go find a nice quiet place and-"

"*Shut-up Dylan*," said Gentry and Lauren in unison.

"Just sayin'," said Dylan with a wide grin.

***

The next morning was cloudy and threatening rain. They kept their rain gear on the top inside their bags when they packed up, just in case they needed it. The remaining trail time would be under two hours for arrival at the station. Gentry knew if *he* was looking forward to some time at the house, he was sure Baby was thinking of a nice rest as well. He'd called Joe and told him to let Charlie know he could pick up Gladys and Knuckles at the station.

They stayed to the trail they'd been on, continuing to check for any signs of a wounded Bantus, but there were none. Gentry wondered as they rode along if they'd ever catch a break in this case. He knew enough about law enforcement that often cases like this were solved because someone saw something and called it in. He hoped this would be the case, but on a cloud covered dreary day like today, he wasn't sure they'd ever get this guy.

Time passed quickly on the trail, the three of them lost in their own thoughts. They rode up to the station and tied their mounts on the porch railing.

"Dylan, would you take Gladys, Knuckles and Handsome to the lean-to? I'll check in with Joe and get Baby into the trailer and we'll head for the ranch." Gentry was already on the steps into the station.

"Will do."

As Dylan led the horses away, Lauren followed Gentry into the station.

Hungry Horse Station was a well kept log cabin style building with two floors and a small holding cell. They were greeted by Joe, even more the cowboy than Gentry.

Towering over both Gentry and Lauren he held out a very large hand and grasped Lauren's hand. The resulting shake rattled her all the way down to her toes.

"Nice to meet you, Ma'am," he said smiling and continuing to shake vigorously.

"Gently, Joe," laughed Gentry, "You're about to loosen her shoe laces."

"Oh, sorry Ma'am," said Joe, dropping her hand and stepping back. He took off his hat and held it sheepishly over his chest, revealing a head of short cropped dark hair.

"No problem," grinned Lauren, patting his arm. "I'm a lot heartier than he gives me credit for, and you can call me Lauren."

They visited while Gentry found the paperwork he needed to complete documenting the last days activities and slid it into an empty file folder. He also found the letter from his favorite serial killer and stuffed it into the file. He had no interest in reading it, he already knew what it said, but it would be placed into evidence with the other letters.

"We're going to have to run, Joe. Thanks for taking such great care of the place for me. This has been a bit of a load for both of us, but you've done a good job."

Joe grinned and blushed, nodding to both of them as they headed out the door. Dylan was just returning from the lean-to after getting the two mares and the mule settled there. He helped Gentry get Baby loaded into the trailer and within a few minutes they were off.

Chapter Twenty-One

They pulled up to the beautiful log cabin and Dylan was the first to speak.

"This is *your* house? Why is it I've never been invited out for a barbecue?"

Gentry laughed and leaned over the steering wheel staring out the front of the truck at his home. It was a view he never tired of.

"Must be my fear those blue eyes would scare off all my guests," he said smiling.

Ignoring the comment, Dylan cast him a disgusted glance and jumped out of the truck. He helped Lauren down while Gentry guided Baby out of the trailer. They followed him as he led the mare into the barn and set her up in her stall with fresh hay.

"This is beautiful," smiled Lauren, "it really is just beautiful, Gentry."

"Thanks," he said, patting Baby's neck and strolling out of the barn. "I guess you could say this is my fortress of solitude."

"I can see why," replied Lauren, still taking it all in.

They entered the house and the courier box was on the table, as requested. Sofia, his housekeeper, did an excellent job cleaning up the place and making it presentable.

"Let's see what I've got in the fridge," said Gentry, knowing they'd not had much of a breakfast in their hurry to get back to the ranch.

"Let me look," said Dylan, "I'm the cook, remember?"

Sofia stocked the refrigerator as instructed and Dylan found a homemade pizza ready to cook and serve. He preheated the oven and set about making a green salad. Once that was done he set the plates, drinks and napkins on the table and the timer went off for the pizza.

Gentry and Lauren were hard at it, already deep into two files silently reading the profiles inside them. Gentry looked up and sniffed the air.

"Where'd you get a pizza?" he asked with surprise.

"It was in your fridge. Hope it was okay, too bad if it wasn't."

Gentry chuckled and picked up the file he was working on, placing it on the stack at the other end of the table. Lauren did the same.

Dylan set the food on the table and sat down.

"You made enough noise in there, you old woman," teased Gentry.

"You could have showed me where everything was, and that would have helped a little," grinned Dylan.

"Oh, this is *wonderful*," said Lauren, digging in. "Honestly, you're both like a couple of old men. You always say women are bad, but I believe most of the banter this trip has come from *your* lips, not mine."

Lauren shook her head, took a bite of pizza and grabbed the file she was working on, reading and chewing.

Gentry watched her as she worked, wishing she would do *something* unattractive, something that would make his heart shut down and know she wasn't the one. She was even beautiful when she ate.

The real source of his discomfort was how his admiration went far beyond what he saw on the outside. She was smart and resourceful, she cared and felt compassion for the victims of the crimes she investigated, and she hadn't lost that as the years went by. That was the most striking thing about her…well, that and her lips and cheekbones, and her hair wasn't bad either.

Dylan coughed and Gentry looked up. Dylan made a twelve-year-old moony face at him and it was all he could do to keep from making some snide remark about his eye color, or tell him this was exactly why he'd never been invited to a barbecue, or maybe just tell him to go suck eggs. However, Dylan's cough did get him back to work, after a thorough scowl. Gentry couldn't help but laugh at his antics. Dylan was a funny guy, and a good friend.

The hours went by quickly, and after all the files were thoroughly reviewed, Lauren looked at Dylan.

"Oh, no…she moaned, "I think I left my duffle bag back at the station. It's probably sitting right on the front porch where I left it when we walked in."

"Well, if Gentry will let me drive his truck, I'll run back and pick it up for you."

"That would be so nice! I'd really appreciate it."

Something was off with the whole exchange and Gentry could see it in Lauren's face. She wanted Dylan out of hearing distance, and as much as he'd love to think she wanted to spend some private time with him, he knew there was something else on her mind and it didn't look like a particularly good thing.

Gentry tossed his keys to Dylan and waited for the door to close and the truck to start.

"Okay, spill it," he said to Lauren, "what's up with the errand for Dylan?"

"You know how we requested a copy of each person's bank records?" she said, her face somber.

"Yeah, we've reviewed them and nothing was wrong, that I could see."

Gentry continued to study Lauren's face.

"Well, check this out."

She handed a bank statement over to him with three highlighted deposits. He didn't look at whose statement it was, just at the deposits. The three amounts were $3000 each, deposited exactly two weeks apart over the last six weeks. Once he saw the deposits, his eye was drawn to the owner of the account. The statement belonged to Dylan Sandusky.

Gentry shook his head and stood up, walking to the window that overlooked the valley below.

"You're wrong, Lauren. There's a perfectly good reason for each one of those, I'll guarantee that."

"Gentry, listen to me. Who was the only one left alone at the campsite, ever? And who took a walk off by himself when the bomb squad was up there? He could have planted those letters and the recording device at any one of those times."

Gentry listened, trying very hard to remain objective, but this was Dylan she was talking about. A man he'd known for too many years to count. They'd gone through the law enforcement portion of training together. He knew this man like he knew his own brother, and Dylan was not the man she was thinking he was.

"I know what you're thinking," she began, "but we know Bantus is devious. We have to check this out, you know we do. Not to mention his life could be in danger if at some time Bantus planted one of those radio devices at the base of his spine. We have to go about this very carefully."

"Planted a what? Where?"

Clearly Gentry hadn't been briefed on that little hidden piece of information.

"Never mind," she said, realizing she'd said too much already. "I just need you to let me ask him *any* questions regarding this, do you understand? This is very important, Gentry. You need to stay away when I question him. You don't understand all we're dealing with here."

"You're the one that doesn't understand," said Gentry, his eyes filled with anger and indignation. "That's just not the kind of man Dylan is. He'd *never* do something like that; he'd never allow himself to be charmed into being a part of something so evil. He's not capable of it. I *know* him and it's just not possible."

Gentry's voice was rising with every sentence. Lauren rose and started for Gentry.

"Don't," he said, holding his hand out at arm's length, "you do what you have to do, but don't try to convince me you're right. You're *wrong* on this one, Lauren. You have no idea how wrong you are."

Gentry strode angrily to his room, shutting the door firmly behind him. Lauren was exactly where she knew she should never have allowed herself to be…torn between believing the words of someone she cared deeply about and doing what had to be done.

She stood and paced along the dining room windows that looked out over a beautiful valley. She could understand why Gentry loved living here; it was peaceful and calming.

Lauren had no idea how long she'd been staring out the windows, but she was pulled back to the present by the sound of Gentry's truck pulling up to the house.

Dylan came through the front door and set the duffle bag on the floor.

"Where's Gen…" He saw the look on Lauren's face before he even finished the sentence. "What's going on?"

"Sit down, Dylan," she said softly. "I just need to ask you a few questions."

"Sure," he said, shrugging his shoulders, "but where's Gentry?"

"He's in his room," she said. Sitting down next to him and turning her chair to face him she showed him the bank statement.

"Yeah, whose state-"

His eyes moved to the top of the page and widened with amazement.

"Sweet!" he exclaimed before the impact hit him. "This is *my* account? Where'd these deposits come from? I haven't made any…deposits…for that…amount."

"Who made them, then, Dylan," Lauren spoke softly, knowing he was putting the picture together in his mind.

"Oh, no you don't," he said, shaking his head. "Oh, *no you don't*. I have no idea where those deposits came from. If they were mine, don't you think I'd have spent them? That's not my money and I have no idea *where* those came from."

"Dylan, until I know for sure what's going on, I'm going to need you to come with me to the police department. We'll need to place you in holding until we can clear you, you understand?"

"No, I don't understand. I don't understand at all! How can you hold me in lock up if I don't even know where those deposits came from? I'm telling you, that is not my money."

Dylan was angry now and Gentry could hear the tension rising in his voice. He'd listened from the other room for about as long as he could stand and now came back into the dining room where the conversation was quickly becoming heated.

Dylan stood up and began pacing back and forth.

"Dylan, I need you to sit down," said Lauren, worried he'd bolt through the front door if he had the chance.

"I'm not going to sit here and listen to you attack my character. How could you think I'd ever be a part of anything like this? Who are you to come in here and attack my integrity like this? You have no right…"

"Dylan, sit down, now," Lauren's voice was firm.

Gentry stepped in front of his friend.

"Dylan, we're going to get this figured out, there has to be an explanation and we're going to find it. Please, you have to give us a chance to clear your name." Gentry was holding onto Dylan's arm, trying to keep him still long enough to listen to reason.

"You believe this?" he said his voice filled with disbelief. He jerked his arm out of Gentry's grasp and stuck his hand in his pocket.

"No, Dylan, I don't believe this, I will never believe this. Just do as Lauren says for now and we'll find out how it happened as fast as we can. I promise you, we'll get to the bottom of it."

Lauren came up behind Dylan and cuffed his left wrist, pulling his right arm around and attaching the handcuffs to his right wrist. Dylan's face was twisted with anger and fury.

Lauren led him to a dining chair and sat him down.

"Please call the local police department and get them out here ASAP," she said to Gentry.

Dylan shot Gentry a traitorous glance then stared at the floor. The look sent Gentry's stomach into spasm, guilt rushing over him like a rock beneath rushing water. He walked into his bedroom, picked up his phone and put in the call.

The next few days seemed to run together, as Gentry tried everything he could think of to clear his friend's name. It seemed the deeper they dug, the more guilty Dylan looked. His sick days coincided with the time of death for both girls in the casket. About the same time, Dylan's father died. Had he really passed away? Gentry never once questioned him about that, why would he?

Gentry scoured the county records for Dylan's father's place of death and looked up burial records. He had indeed died and was buried when Dylan said he was, but Lauren was quick to ask what he'd died of. Would Dylan have killed his own father to make it look like he'd gone to a funeral? Would Bantus have killed Dylan's father to get him the time off he needed, and never disclose that to his new apprentice?

The coroner ruled the death a heart attack, and Lauren began checking into an exhumation. Gentry was becoming more and more confused by the whole matter. He considered asking to be removed from the investigation, but he knew he couldn't leave Dylan alone to fend for himself. Bantus was responsible for this, he knew it like he knew he had elbows. He'd find the connection, and he'd show Lauren she was wrong about this good man.

Chapter Twenty-Two

The room was cold, with grey brick walls and a table in the center. The two way mirrored window on one side allowed a view into the room without the suspect knowing who was watching the interrogation.

Dylan sat at the table, alone, staring at his cuffed hands. Gentry watched from behind the window, feeling miserable about his friend having to endure this. It grated at him, and yet when Lauren explained it, he understood where she was coming from, but it didn't change the fact that she didn't know Dylan like he did, and she didn't know that he wasn't capable of something like this. It just wasn't in his makeup.

The other teams continued following up on leads in the search for Bantus, but the investigation into Dylan fell on the team leader, and that was Lauren.

Gentry watched as the door into interrogation opened and she came through confidently, never taking her eyes off her suspect.

"Dylan," began Lauren, "I have to ask you some questions so, if nothing else, we can clear you as a suspect. Do you understand?"

"Where's Gentry? I want him in here for this."

"He's not here, Dylan," she said softly, "this has been very hard for him."

Dylan scoffed.

"I'll bet it has. I almost feel guilty for having such a good time, sitting here with my hands cuffed."

"Dylan, where were you on the seventeenth of June?" Lauren leaned forward, elbows on the table.

Dylan thought about her question, trying to remember a day much the same as any other.

"Well, that was a work, day, so I got to work at eight, worked all day. I probably had lunch at the café not far from the station because I do that almost every day. When I got off work I guess I went home, because I usually do that, too."

"Did anyone see you after you went home?" Lauren looked him in the eyes and he answered her, staring back into hers.

"No. I live alone, I'm not currently seeing anyone and I don't have a dog," he was being sarcastic, still feeling anger at being a suspect.

"Dylan, what did you do while the search party was looking for Emma?" Lauren's voice stayed soft, probing.

"Oh, well, let me see, I programmed a few recording devices with a maniacal laugh, wrote a couple menacing letters to you and my best friend, Gentry, then I had a sandwich and some chips. *What do you think I did?* I worked, I monitored radio calls and coordinated the search effort from the command tent! You and Gentry assigned me that job. You know what I did…and guess what? No one saw me there either because *they were all out searching!*"

"How did your father die, Dylan," Lauren asked, her voice level.

"You keep my father out of this; it's none of your concern."

"I need you to tell me how your father died."

Dylan clenched his jaw and sat forward, leaning on the table.

"My father died of a massive heart attack. We were very close, and I miss him every day."

"Did he have a heart condition?"

"Not that anyone knew of. That's why it was so hard to come to terms with. He was a healthy seventy-eight year old man."

Lauren's phone rang and she answered, never taking her eyes from Dylan's face.

"Porcelli."

"I'll be right there."

She stood and walked to the door.

"I'll be right back."

Dylan sighed and leaned back heavily in his chair, his cuffed hands dropping into his lap.

Gentry met Lauren in the hallway, she looked slightly shaken, and that was unusual for her.

"What's going on? What's wrong?" he watched her lean against a wall, her hand on her forehead. She dropped her hand before she spoke.

"Dylan's parents had a boarder, a male boarder. He told them he was working his way through school and saving up for medical school." Lauren looked at him expectantly.

"Okay, but what's that got to do with Dylan?"

"Gentry, they showed Dylan's mother a picture of Bantus. *He* was their boarder. She told the agents that Walter left for school that day and never returned. It was the same day her husband passed away."

At least a dozen different realizations hit Gentry's brain all at the same time. His eyes widened with excitement and horror.

"We have to find out if Dylan knew his parents had a boarder. He never mentioned they rented a room, not once." He was certain this information would clear his friend.

"Not so fast, Gentry," said Lauren holding both hands in front of her. "He could easily have known and just hid the fact. He could have been influenced by Bantus, lured into working for him."

"Bantus killed his father."

Gentry knew this was going to be the hardest part for Dylan.

"We don't know that for sure," said Lauren, "but just look at us. We're wasting all this time on Dylan, when we should be looking for our killer. It's exactly what he wanted us to do. I've ordered the video feed from the bank for the date and time of those deposits. It should be here any time. If Bantus is making those deposits, then Dylan's not our man. That's the best way to know. I'm going to go see if they're here. Wait in the observation room, I'll be right back."

Gentry went into the room and watched his friend. It was difficult seeing this usually carefree man looking so lost, but there was hope and Gentry held on to every ounce of hope he could get. The relief he felt at his friend's possible innocence was offset by the knowledge that Bantus may have killed his father.

Lauren came into the observation room carrying a disk. She walked to the computer, slid the disk into the slot and sat down. In a few clicks, the two of them were watching the clerk at the counter waiting on a man, unable to see the tape clearly. There was no sound, just video. They waited, hoping they'd see the man's face clearly enough, holding their breath, when the customer at the counter turned to leave, looked up at the camera and smiled widely. It was Bantus, obviously wanting to be captured on the video.

"YES!" exclaimed Gentry. His hand formed a fist in front of his chest.

"In a court of law, this proves nothing," said Lauren, trying not to get his hopes up. "He could easily have had Bantus make the deposits for him. However, I can also see how Bantus has manipulated this whole event.

"Dylan's fingerprints have never been found on any of the evidence. I'll go in there now and ask him about the boarder. We'll see what his reaction is."

Lauren left observation and entered the interrogation room.

"Tell me about your parent's boarder," she said.

"My parent's what?"

"Their boarder, the man who lived with them."

"They never had anyone living with them. They know I'd have thrown a fit about that. It wasn't a safe thing to do. I told them I'd give them money and help them out if they needed it. They didn't have a boarder."

"Dylan, they did have a boarder, he lived with them for about three months. He left the day your dad died."

Lauren let this thought sink in for a minute. She could see the wheels turning as his eyes filled with dread.

"They never said a word to me. They knew I'd-" gradually he made the connection and his next words came slowly, deliberately. *"Who was their boarder?"*

Lauren gradually slid the picture of Walter Bantus across the table. Dylan's eyes raged with fire, his jaw clenched as he glanced at the face staring up from the table at him. He couldn't touch the photograph and he quickly averted his eyes, focusing on the wall.

"Did he…did he kill…my dad?"

Lauren stood and walked around the table, taking the keys to the cuffs from her pocket. She unlocked the cuffs and removed them from his wrists.

"We don't know," Lauren said softy, laying her hand on his shoulder. "My best guess is…yes. He probably poisoned him after he got the information he needed about you so he could perpetrate this hoax. Your dad may have said or done something to lead Bantus to believe he was a threat. Maybe he started seeing the holes in his personality like his other victims did. We just don't know for sure. But what I do know for sure is that you're not part of this, and I'm sorry to have doubted you. I just had to know for sure."

She turned and left the room, leaving Dylan alone to process the events of the last couple days.

Chapter Twenty-Three

Gentry watched his friend from observation. If Dylan ever needed a friend, it was now, and the thought made Gentry's feet move in the direction of the interrogation room. He didn't know what he was going to say, or how he would be received, but he had to go.

He knocked softly on the door and opened it as Dylan looked up and quickly looked away.

"You're about the *last* person I need to talk to right now."

The bitterness in Dylans voice cut into Gentry like a knife.

"Dylan," he began, "I tried to tell her there was no way you were capable of anything like this. I really did."

"Yeah, I'm sure you did, right after you finished making out with her. Real professional, Gentry."

"You know that's not true."

"Do I?" Dylan's anger level was rising fast. "I thought I knew you, I thought you'd be the one to stand up for me! Where were you? Hiding in observation so you wouldn't have to face me? GET OUT! You're no friend of mine. The Gentry I know would have been there for me and you went into hiding so you wouldn't offend your *girlfriend.*"

The door opened and a furious Lauren strode into the room, slamming the door behind her. She strode up to Dylan and released the full force of her fury standing in front of him with her hands on her hips.

"Your *friend* did everything he could to keep me from bringing you in. He told me about your character, about the kind of man you are. He assured me on several occasions you were not the man who did this, that you could never do this. You are just as guilty of abandonment as you're accusing him of being."

She turned and walked back to the door, placing her hand on the doorknob.

"The two of you better figure this out, and fast. We have a job to do."

She pointed her finger at Gentry and continued.

"...and *you* will keep your hands to yourself, or I'll have *you* thrown in jail before you take your next breath. Dylan is absolutely correct on this issue. Getting involved with you will taint my perspective, he's right to question your intentions *and* my professionalism. We're done. I don't like having my job performance questioned, and it won't happen again, I can assure you. Now kiss and makeup or go back to your park. I don't have time to deal with this."

She stormed out the door, slamming it behind her for good measure.

Gentry was looking at the floor and rubbing his lips with his forefinger. Dylan ran his hand slowly over the back of his neck.

"I guess she told *you* how it's gonna be," Dylan said, masking a smile.

"No, not actually," grinned Gentry, hiding his mouth behind his hand, "I believe that was for you. You've really stepped in it now."

The two men looked at each other and broke into all out laughter.

"Dude...*she's* got a *tempe*r," laughed Dylan. "She could start a forest fire with those sparks!"

Gentry walked to his friend and clapped him on the shoulder.

"She has *no* idea who she's dealing with," he laughed as he guided Dylan to the door. "She totally wants me."

They both roared with laughter and walked into the hall.

"That was fast," she said, a little confused.

"Why, yes…yes it was," said Gentry, still laughing and putting his hat on his head. "And that, for your information, is how *real* men 'kiss and make up'."

Dylan was gasping for air as the two of them half walked, half stumbled down the hallway.

Gentry glanced back over his shoulder and watched as Lauren grinned, shook her head and followed after them. This caused a whole new round of laughter.

***

Gentry, Lauren and Dylan sat around Gentry's dining room table once again, re-checking the files they'd viewed previously. They were getting nowhere. The records were impeccable; with nothing shouting out that even one of them would have connected in any way with a crazed serial killer. It was clear they were going to need to think of another way to find the accomplice.

Though Dylan was no longer angry at Gentry, he was becoming withdrawn and quiet as the day progressed. Gentry kept an eye on him, keeping him talking and involved with the case thus far. Gentry knew he was thinking about his dad, grieving all over again for a life cut short, not by a failed heart, but a murderer. Gentry saw Lauren checking on him as well.

"Dylan," she began, "you may need to talk to someone about your father's death, a counselor, someone to help you process it."

Dylan looked up from his file, which he'd been staring at but not reading for the past thirty minutes.

"It's not complicated," he said, "It's just going to take some time to digest, that's all. I'll be fine."

"We haven't told your mother," said Lauren, "we thought maybe once we got him and he was under lock and key you could tell her his death may not have been a heart attack. Do you want to take some time off and go stay with her?"

"That might not be a bad idea, Dylan," said Gentry, "it would be good for you to be there in case he shows up at her door again."

"He won't," said Dylan, "but I appreciate it. They've got a twenty-four hour watch on the house, front and back. I don't think Bantus would dare show up there, unless he didn't think we'd figured the whole thing out. Even then, if he did, we'd get him and it's all good."

"That's an interesting perspective," said Lauren, staring out the window. "We may be coming at this thing completely backward."

Then turning back to the group she said, "Don't you think part of the reason for the whole charade between you two was that Bantus wanted a wedge between you? I haven't got a clue why, but I know the other part of his thinking was to throw us off his scent, which it did for a couple of days. But, let's just say for the sake of argument that he's not out of the park yet and he doesn't know you two are no longer mad at each other. He's assuming his little ploy worked, and you hate each other. If you, Dylan, went back to your mom's house, supposedly hating Gentry, he might try to contact you. This could work to our advantage."

"What would be the point in contacting me now?"

"Well, let's think like a serial killer for a minute," she said, continuing, "what if he could turn you to his side? You'd be a great informant, because you're working at the center of the investigation. He'd know every step we were going to take before we took it and we could possibly find who his informant is as well. This could work!"

Lauren's excitement level was rising.

"I don't know," thought Dylan, "this could be dangerous not just for me, but for my mom. I don't know that I'd want to risk that."

Gentry thought for a minute.

"Yes, you're right, but I don't think he'd even consider approaching the house. If we could keep your mother inside, I don't know, let her know the house is being watching and she needs to stay there because of Bantus…she'd be in no danger because the house is under surveillance."

"Yeah," said Dylan slowly, considering the ramifications, "can I have some time to think about it? I'm beat. It's been a day, and I'm exhausted. I'll hit the hay and give you my decision in the morning. Will that work?"

"Sure, you know which room is yours," said Gentry, "towels are in the hall closet."

"Thanks."

Dylan walked up the stairs and Gentry listened for his bedroom door to close. Once it was shut, he glanced at Lauren. She was staring out the window, concern and determination registering on her face.

"What are you thinking?" he asked, bringing her back to the present.

"I'm thinking how dangerous this would be, for both of them, and wondering whether or not it's a good idea." She continued to stare out the window, unblinking.

"I think that's up to Dylan at this point, and he deserves to choose, since Bantus is the reason his father is dead."

"We don't know that for sure."

Gentry looked at her in disbelief.

"Serious? You can't mean that. There is no such thing as a coincidence, Lauren, not where this monster is concerned."

"Gentry," she sighed, turning back to face him, "I can't form an opinion based on conjecture. It doesn't track in my line of work. I have to have cold, hard facts, and I can't honestly say I know beyond a shadow of a doubt Bantus killed his father. I *suspect*, yes, but do I know that? No, I don't. What I think won't hold up in a court of law, what I can prove will. His body will have to be exhumed and tested in order to know that for sure, and that's a call only the family can make."

Gentry rose and went into the kitchen. He pulled a container of coffee from the cabinet and proceeded to make a fresh pot. It was going to be a long night, and they would need it…and it gave him time to think.

Lauren hadn't said anything about her tirade at the police station with he and Dylan. Had she meant what she said? Did he dare even approach her on the subject? He wasn't real sure how the whole thing made him feel. Laughing about it with Dylan was a stress reliever, for both of them. It felt good and went a long way to repairing what was broken. But once he'd had some time to think on it, he wasn't sure how he felt about it.

He made his way back to the table and sat down while the coffee brewed. Lauren was staring at him and he dared not look at her. She stood and walked to him, pulling him to his feet.

"I'm sorry, Gentry," she said, standing in front of him, holding onto his hands. "I didn't mean to say what I said…the way I said it. I just meant that the situation was a perfect example of why we have to keep this professional. It's so easy for facts to be compromised by poor judgment."

"So…you won't arrest me if I do this?" he asked, putting his arms around her and pulling him to her.

She leaned into him and smiled softly.

"Only if you try to stop me from doing this," she said wrapping her arms around his neck.

She gazed up at him, with moist, warm eyes.

"This has to be kept private, Gentry," she said, her face tempting, welcoming him. "No one can know we have feelings for each other, not even Dylan."

"Your secret is safe with me," he said pulling her close to him. Their lips met and the passion burned once again. "Just don't start something you're not willing to finish."

Her intensity answered his demand, igniting his desire and pushing him for more. He wanted more, he wanted all of her, right then, unbridled and free of all commitment…but he knew that couldn't be, and so did she.

Gentry released her and stepped back.

"I would never want to interfere with your work, Lauren. What you do…what *we* do in this investigation is save lives, and we have to put those lives first."

He sat down in his chair and she followed him, standing between his legs and leaning into him. She caressed his face, the green in her eyes shining like emeralds and boring into him with a fiery focus that threatened to sear him alive.

"You and I," she said still holding his face in her hands, "are going to solve this case, and then I'm going to be on you like white on rice. Do I make myself clear?"

Gentry swallowed hard, his mouth felt like a scorched forest after a long burn. He leaned into her stomach, resting his head and breathing in her scent.

"Yeah, I think I got a pretty good mental image etched into my brain. Thanks for that."

She threw her head back and laughed that wonderfully musical sound that made him ache with wanting her.

"But for this to work," he said, moving her back and standing, "You're gonna have to get ugly and stupid real fast. Am I clear on *that*?"

This made her laugh even harder as she slid into her chair and sat back. The coffee was ready.

Chapter Twenty-Four

Next morning they met in the kitchen for breakfast. It had been a late night for Lauren and Gentry and they looked it. Dylan was back to his goofy self, which was a comfort to Gentry. It was good to have him back, and he wondered what his decision would be.

Dylan was in the kitchen when Gentry entered. Moments later Lauren came down the stairs from her room in a robe with hair that looked like it'd been done by Bigfoot himself. It made Gentry grin, but she was so tired she didn't care.

"Something smells good," said Gentry. "You've been busy, Dylan. What time did you get up, anyway?"

"Coffee." It was the only word out of Lauren's mouth.

After hearing her tirade the day before, Dylan was sure he didn't want to cross her first thing in the morning so he went quickly to the coffee pot and poured her a cup. She sat down at the table just as Dylan brought the cup over and set it in front of her.

"Thanks."

"You're...welcome," he said hurrying back to the safety of his kitchen.

"Oh stop being so skittish," she said, disgusted, "I'm over it, you get over it."

Gentry couldn't help the grin that slid over his face.

"Wow," he said, "you're *so* not a morning person. What happened to the nice lady that's been staying at my place for the past few days? I was certain she'd be here when I woke up."

"You wanna live to breathe another day?" she said with a teasing, but warning look.

"Shutting up," he said as he stood and headed into the kitchen.

Dylan started laughing and handed plates, silverware and cups to Gentry. He carried them to the table, and could tell the coffee was having the desired effect. Her smile was back to its normal sweet look and except for the Bigfoot hair, her demeanor had softened. He breathed a sigh of relief as he placed the plates around the table.

Gentry helped bring the food to the table and they all sat down to eat. It was a delicious meal, by all accounts, but no one was quite ready to address the elephant in the room, which was what Dylan had decided to do.

Finally, Dylan cleared his throat and began.

"I just wanted to thank you for being patient with me. It's been a hard thing for me to try and reconcile the death of my dad and be able to willingly participate in a plan that would require me to work with the man that killed him."

Lauren cleared her throat.

"Uh, you know we don't know that for certain, right?"

"I know it for certain," he said bitterly, "it's the only explanation that makes any sense. That he would suddenly keel over from a heart attack with no previous problem is just too much for me to swallow, knowing what I now know about Bantus and knowing the connection there."

Gentry watched his friend struggle to control the bitterness inside him. Eventually the anger left his face and his shoulders relaxed.

"I want to do this," Dylan said resolutely. "If I can do anything to bring this killer in, I'll do it. You're going to keep the guards posted at the house?"

"Absolutely," affirmed Lauren. "They're going to be there until I tell them to leave, and I won't do that until I hear it from you."

"Okay, let's get these dishes done and get down to business." Dylan smiled. "Don't think you're getting off without doing the dishes, Gentry, because I cooked. And Ms. FBI over there outranks the two of us, so she gets to…go…comb her hair."

Gentry stifled a laugh.

"I don't see that as particularly fair. She's from *Seattle*, after all."

"Hey; and what's wrong with Seattle?" Lauren stiffened at the insult.

Gentry carried the dishes into the sink.

"It's not a park, and a National Park outranks any city, no matter the size. I don't make the rules, I just enforce them."

"He says as he clears the table like a good little boy," she muttered.

"I heard that."

Lauren went upstairs to shower while the boys loaded the dishwasher, wiped the table and counters, then waited for her to come down. They were both thinking the same thing when Lauren returned to the table; the plan, whatever it would be, was going to have to be Bantus proof, and no one at the table was sure that could be done.

"Okay," began Lauren, settling herself at the table, "this is what we know. Our killer is incredibly intelligent, he's detail oriented, and everything he does, he does for a purpose. There are no accidents with this man, and there are no second chances. If you tick him off, the best way to get back into his good graces is to submit to his requests, act submissive. I know this is going to require a lot of excellent acting, Dylan, but you're going to have to do it or he will discover your deception. That is the last thing we want."

Gentry watched Dylan swallow hard. From the look on his face, he knew he was doubting his acting ability, but there was determination there as well.

"You can do this, Dylan," he said.

"Yeah," said Dylan, "I can do this."

They talked through the morning and into the afternoon, planning how they would set up the operation and who would know about it. It was determined for the sake of safety no one would know, except for the three of them and Lauren's Team Leader. Everyone else on the team would assume Dylan went home to spend some well earned and incredibly needed time with his widowed mother.

His contact with the team would be through burner phones, untraceable and discarded after each call is made. Dylan was instructed to check in with them two times a day, morning and evening. If he missed one check in, a call would be made to the agents watching the home and they'd be instructed to go in with weapons drawn.

"This feels pretty secure, the details of the op, I mean," said Dylan. "I'm even kind of looking forward to spending some time at home. With my folks living on the outskirts of Kalispell, I don't get down there as often as I'd like, and now that dad is gone, I'm ashamed I haven't taken the time to go see my mom as often as I should. This will be a good thing. I know you'll keep us safe."

Dylan left the group to go to his apartment and pack for the days he would be spending with his mom. A discussion ensued about where Gentry and Lauren would set up their base of operations. His ranch wasn't going to work as it was too far from Dylan's home on the south end of Kalispell.

Lauren put in the necessary paperwork to set up a command center in a hotel not far from Dylan's home. Within twenty-four hours the necessary equipment arrived along with the personnel to install it. Because there were problems when Greyson and Aspen set up their command center, extra precautions were taken with double and triple identification scans completed by a high security detail before anyone was allowed into the room to set up the equipment.

Sleeping accommodations included two adjoining rooms. The equipment would be set up in Gentry's room, with one queen bed removed to make the necessary space to house all of it. For security purposes, all of the set up was done before either Lauren or Gentry checked in, and their check in times would be separated by at least eight hours.

The details were never ending and before it was over, there were still only four people who knew the story behind all of this work. It was strictly need-to-know and each part of the plan was put together by a separate team, no one team having the whole story on all the parts.

Amazingly, the plan came together in the required forty-eight hours. Lauren was grateful Dylan hadn't heard from Bantus yet. Had he called too soon, they would have been playing catch-up, and that was never a good thing where this killer was concerned. They needed to be several steps ahead of him from the beginning, and now they were.

Gentry had no idea when they would hear from Bantus, if he was out of the park, or if he'd gotten medical care. The teams that were sent to the larger metropolitan areas outside the park reported no sightings and nothing from the local healthcare facilities. Small urgent care facilities that catered to the homeless population were also put on alert. So far, nothing came up from any of them.

"I'm concerned about not finding him," said Lauren, pacing back and forth in her room. "there are still so many holes, so many facilities that may not stay alert and end up treating him and letting him go."

"Well, if that happens," said Gentry, "then Dylan is the backup plan. If he gets treated and gets away, our plan kicks into gear."

"Yes, *if* he decides to contact Dylan," Lauren was on edge, the stress was beginning to show.

Gentry carefully took her by the shoulders and stopped her.

"We're on it, Lauren. You've done an amazing job at getting this all together as quickly as you have. We're gonna get him this time. There's no way he can know about this set up, no way at all."

"My experience has been there's always a way," she said, frowning and moving around Gentry to continue her pacing. "But, yes, I think we've done everything we can."

The blinds in both rooms were to remain shut; they would order their meals in, neither one leaving the rooms unless absolutely necessary. Housekeeping was instructed to leave clean towels outside the room each morning, picking up the dirty linens left there for them. It was as foolproof as they could get it. Gentry's main concern was how long before the two of them started going stir crazy. Hopefully, they wouldn't be there long enough to know.

Dylan was in place, the guards at his home were set up, Lauren and Gentry had their rooms, both were checked in and all the equipment was installed and ready to go. All that was left to do was wait, and so they waited, behind closed doors, with curtains drawn and a no touch rule that was going to make Gentry wish he'd been born a woman.

"Nice," he thought to himself. *"This couldn't be more frustrating if she was standing in front of me naked and I was tied to a chair."*

Chapter Twenty-Five

The moment Gentry let that thought enter his mind, it was a constant fight to change the picture. But he didn't have to work on it for very long, because the long awaited call came in and the locomotive was beginning to move.

Gentry and Lauren were at the computer, reviewing case notes and brainstorming about the different places Bantus could have holed up to recuperate. The line tap was always on and ready and when that line began to ring, they jumped to turn the recorder on.

"Hello."

As discussed when they set up the sting, Dylan answered the phone.

"Dylan, I've been wondering if you would be with your mother," he said smooth, like gasoline on water. "I'm so glad to speak with you."

"Who is this?" he asked, knowing full well who it was.

"This is Walter, Dylan, Walter Bantus."

"Why would you call me? You cost me my job. I'm not talking to you."

"DON'T HANG UP!" cried Bantus, speaking quickly. "There was a reason for that; it was all part of my plan. I have an unlimited supply of money, Dylan, and I'm willing to share with you. You lost your income, right? I can replace it, in return for a few…favors."

Lauren glanced at Gentry and quickly scrawled "money?" on a notepad. Gentry shrugged in surprise.

"I'm listening. Make it fast and make it good, you're not my favorite person right now." Dylan was doing great, his anger sounded real.

"I have need of a warehouse, not too big, but not small, either. I'm going to need to…to…hang some things there, you know, keep them there for a while. Make it about ten to fifteen thousand square feet. You understand?"

"What's in this for me? I have expenses because of you."

"Yes, yes, I know," said Bantus, almost apologetically. He was working Dylan for all he was worth. "I'm prepared to pay you ten to twenty-thousand dollars per assignment, depending on size."

"What's my guarantee you'll pay me? How do I know you won't send one of your weaselly little notes to Gentry Beauchene tellin' him what I'm doing?" Dylan figured he'd pushed about as far as he was going to be allowed.

"I'm a man of my word," said Bantus. "I've set up a Post Office box at the station in town, box number 231A. Go to the front desk of the Post Office and they'll have an envelope with the key in it. Bring your ID, they'll ask for it. I have a good faith payment in that box for you, for your work on this job. Just know I won't usually pay until the job is done, but I'm paying you now to show you I have the money. And just so you know, Mr. Sandusky, if you ever refer to me or anything I do as 'weaselly' again…I'll kill you."

"Uh, sorry. I guess I'm pretty angry still, but if the pay is good then I can channel all that anger where it belongs, on Gentry Beauchene. He deserves everything he gets."

"Now *that's* what I like to hear," cooed Bantus, back to his sickly sweet patronizing tones. "I can see we're going to work very well together. I'll call you back in forty-eight hours to hear your progress on that warehouse. Don't let me down, Dylan. You never want to disappoint me."

"No sir," Dylan said firmly, "you can count on me."

Gentry and Lauren waited for the dial tone and then hung up from their end. This was what all the prep had been for, the waiting was over. Within minutes a call came in to Lauren's cell phone from Dylan's burner phone.

"Hey Lauren," he said, "that was tough, especially having to apologize. I wanted to puke."

"You did very well," said Lauren, relieved. "That was impressive. I don't know if I could do what you just did."

"Well, thanks," he said, "where do we go from here? How am I supposed to know how to find a warehouse?"

"Call the Real Estate office downtown. Tell them you need a good commercial agent, the best they've got. They'll have the agent call you, but stress you need a phone call back within the day. You've only got forty-eight hours before Bantus will want his update."

"I can do that," sighed Dylan. "You guys stay safe. Thanks for the guards on the house even though my mom keeps telling me it's a waste of resources. I haven't told her anything about why the FBI wants to find Bantus, but I think she'll eventually figure it has to be something big."

"Don't worry about that for now," replied Lauren, "just keep your focus on acquiring that warehouse. As soon as you find the one and secure it, give us the address. We'll take it from there."

Dylan hung up the phone and Lauren turned to Gentry.

"I hope we're ready for this. I think this ball is going to start rolling pretty fast."

"We're ready. I don't know how much more ready we can be."

Gentry was in the same boat as Lauren, hoping they'd done all they needed to do.

***

Walter Bantus grinned at his good fortune. Gentry Beauchene's best friend hated him, and it'd been the easiest thing he'd ever done. A few recorders placed here and there, a note or two, and then, the finest part of all…the smartest idea he'd ever had…those deposits. He enjoyed grinning up at that camera; he wanted them to know *he'd* been the one to make them.

He smiled inwardly at the confusion that would have caused them. Bantus was sure they would decide Dylan was working with him when they saw that. They'd assume he and Dylan were business partners. He chuckled out loud.

Walter winced as he moved his leg. A large black brace covered his knee and most of his thigh and calf. He'd colored his hair and was growing a beard. Although his new beard growth wasn't long enough to color, it also wasn't long enough to tell what color it was going to be. He knew he'd lucked out getting medical attention and was sure the change in his appearance helped him a great deal.

He sat in his easy chair at the expensive hotel where he was staying, his fingertips pressed together in front of his face. The room smelled of expensive deodorizer and fresh cut flowers. His mother said he'd never amount to anything. Now he wished he'd not killed her, she would be amazed at his success. Even *he* was amazed by it.

Others would have never been clever enough to figure out the plan he put in place. He couldn't help grinning, and a small chuckle escaped his lips.

"What's making you so happy?" said the cheerful voice bringing him his coffee. She smiled at him, glad for his good day, and set the silver tray on the end table beside him.

She was a lovely child, at least now that she'd had a shower and change of clothing. He gazed at her beautiful blonde hair, large blue eyes and long lashes. Her teeth were a mess, and he thought of having them repaired, but she wouldn't be around long enough to make it worth his trouble. Drugs did such nasty things to teeth. She'd been clean for a year, she said, and it must be true, because she didn't shake or sweat like someone who needed a fix. She was healthy enough to die for him. And die she would.

Chapter Twenty-Six

Gentry watched the young woman, obviously homeless but surprisingly well dressed, enter the police department. He stood quietly in a corner beside the police station front door. It was one of the rare days he and Lauren got to dress up like someone else and meet with the other agents for updates on their investigations. The meetings were the only thing that saved his sanity and Lauren's as well. He was about to head to the conference room for the meeting when the young woman walked in. She piqued his curiosity.

The girl gazed furtively around the room and finding the information desk, made her way toward it.

"Can I help you?" asked the woman at the desk.

"Uh, yes," she said, still scanning the room, "I'd like to report a missing person."

"Can you tell me a little bit more about that?" asked the woman, "like, where she lives, when she went missing and if anyone saw who she was with?"

"Yes, we live…uh…outside, and she left with…" the girl looked up on the wall of wanted posters. "…with him."

Gentry's heart stopped when he saw her point. He couldn't be sure, but it appeared she was pointing at the poster of Walter Bantus.

He hurried to the information desk and peered at the young lady. He walked to the poster of Bantus and pointed directly at it.

"Is this the man that took your friend," he said, seeking confirmation.

"Yes, that's him. He said he lived at a fancy hotel, I can't remember the name, but that he would let her live with him and have anything she wanted. He tried to get me to go with him, too, but I saw through him right away. I told Lisa not to go, but she wouldn't listen to me. I'm worried about her. She hasn't been back since the night she left with him."

"I'll take it from here," Gentry said to the woman at the desk. "Oh, and would you please call my partner? Let her know I'm visiting with…" he looked at the girl expectantly.

"Charity," she said when she realized he was asking her name.

"…with Charity in the small conference room. And have her bring in some breakfast for the three of us."

The woman raised one eyebrow, but nodded and picked up the phone as he and Charity walked down the hallway.

He brought her into the room and showed her to a place around the table. He strode to the other side and sat down, facing her.

"We're looking for the man you pointed out. He's not a very nice man, and we need to find him quickly. When my friend gets here, she's an FBI agent; I'm going to have you tell us as close to exactly as you can get what your conversation was with him. I'm going to go take care of a few things so if you want to," he moved some paper and a pencil across the table to her, "you can write down anything you can remember. It would help us a lot."

"Okay," she said tentatively, eyeing the door.

"Don't worry," Gentry assured her, "you're safe here."

He rose and walked to the door, half wondering if she would bolt when he left. He entered the hallway and closing the door, motioned for a uniformed police officer to watch the door for him. He hurried down to the entry and waited for Lauren.

Gentry saw Lauren walking up the stairs into the building carrying a McDonald's bag. She looked more like a less showy version of Marilyn Monroe, but definitely not like Lauren Porcelli. Seeing her made him wonder who, exactly, he looked like but he was too excited to stop and think about it. He hurried out to meet her and she could tell by the look on his face he had big news.

"What's happened?" she asked. "You're not supposed to be seen with me. What's the matter with you? You'll blow our cover."

"I think we may have just gotten that break we were hoping to find," said Gentry ignoring her wrath.

He explained about the girl and where she was at the moment.

"You left her alone?" Lauren was horrified. "She could take off and we'd never find her again, Gentry!"

"No," he said calmly, "I posted a guard outside the door. Her name is Charity, and she seems to have a pretty good head on her shoulders for her age."

Lauren sighed and they went quickly to the conference room. As they entered, Charity was writing on the paper Gentry had given her.

"Hi Charity," said Lauren holding out her hand, "I'm Lauren."

Charity stood and shook Lauren's hand.

"Hi," she said, looking Lauren in the eye.

"Please, have a seat," said Lauren.

Lauren inspected the filthy, but expensive clothing the girl wore, right down to the high end tennis shoes.

"If I could just say," Lauren said, eyeing Charity like a nicely ripened tomato, "You don't seem like the homeless type. Where are you from?"

"I lived in New York City before coming to Kalispell. I...I ran away."

"Why did you run away?" asked Lauren.

"It's a long story, kind of convoluted, I guess."

"Is there a short version?" Lauren smiled gently at her.

"Well…my parents are filthy rich, they wanted me to have a 'coming out' party, I didn't want one, didn't like the lifestyle and just wanted to be free of it."

She stared directly into Lauren's eyes, as if defying her to change her mind. Lauren stared back and was contemplating where she wanted this conversation to go when a thought struck her mind.

"You said your parents are wealthy?"

"Yes, very."

"Did you by any chance tell Walter Bantus you came from money?" Lauren tipped her head to the side and peered at Charity.

"Yeah, he knew me, my family, my home town and state. He knew everything about me, but I didn't let him get his claws into me. I could see what he was after and I refused to go with him when he made me the offer. My friend, Lisa, she jumped at the idea. I tried to talk her out of it, but she wouldn't listen."

"Oh," said Lauren apologetically, remembering the food. "I brought this for you."

She handed Charity the bag of food and watched her eyes widen with delight.

"Oh, thank you so much! May I eat it now?"

"You certainly may," smiled Lauren. "We're just going to step out for a moment, and we'll be right back. Are you okay with that?"

Charity was biting into one of the breakfast sandwiches and nodded her head with a smile.

Lauren motioned for Gentry to follow her and he did. Once outside the conference room with the door shut Lauren studied his face.

"Do you know what this means?" she asked excitedly.

"It means we may have just found out where Bantus is getting his money," grinned Gentry. "We're going to need to get that information from her and make some calls, I believe."

This was the best news they'd had since the investigation began. They calmed themselves down and returned to the room.

Charity was drinking some orange juice and still enjoying the breakfast sandwiches.

"It is the best luck that Gentry heard you talking to that receptionist, Charity," said Lauren. "Tell me, have you heard from your parents at all?"

"Are you kidding?" she said, astounded. "They don't care about me. If I don't want to play their 'look at me I'm rich' game, they don't want to have anything to do with me."

"You're sure about that?" Gentry spoke up this time, surprised at her response.

"I'm sure," she said biting into another sandwich.

"Charity, would you be willing to give me your parent's names and phone numbers, home, cell, work, anything you can remember?" Lauren leaned forward on the table nearly holding her breath as she waited for a reply.

Charity stopped chewing and laid the remainder of the sandwich on the table and sat back in her chair.

"I'm not going back there, and if you tell them where I am I'll just go somewhere else. They'll never find me."

She'd made it more than clear there was no debating this subject.

"I'm not asking you to return home," said Lauren, "that will be your decision. You're a smart girl, well educated and able to make your own decisions."

Lauren let that sink in.

"Then why do you want my parent's information?"

Gentry took over at this point.

"Because we are certain this Mr. Bantus has been extorting money from your parents. I'm betting he's told them he is holding you captive and demanding money from them, either one lump sum, or as he requires it."

Charity's eyes narrowed and her lips formed a single line.

"They better not be giving him a single cent," she said angrily. "He's a liar and a thief."

"That he is," said Gentry, "and the only way I know of to find out if they're being financially held captive by him is for you to give us a way to reach them. We will tell them you are safe, in good health and should you decide to let them know where you are, you will."

The young girl's face softened as she sat up in her chair.

"I...I never wanted to hurt them you know," she said, nearly whispering. "I only wanted them to *see* me. To see me for who I am and what I am. They could only view me as their daughter, their rich daughter who had nice clothes and a mansion to live in. They forced on me the idea that I should be thankful to them and do whatever they said because they'd made me rich. It was sickening, really, and I hated them for the longest time. I realize now that I do love them, and I miss them."

The determination returned to her face.

"But I'm not going back until they know how I feel."

"Tell me how they're going to know how you feel if you never speak to them?"

Gentry sat back in his chair and waited for her answer.

"I'll give you their numbers, but I don't want to talk to them...yet."

Chapter Twenty-Seven

Dylan rode with the real estate agent through the streets of Kalispell searching for just the right warehouse for a monster to kill in. Of course, the agent didn't know that, and Dylan rode along wishing *he* didn't know it, either as he listened to the small talk.

The agent's name was Renaldo…Renaldo something, but he couldn't remember the last name. He needed to pay attention to what the agent was telling him, but he was finding it hard to concentrate.

They pulled up in front of the last of three warehouses they'd seen that day and Dylan climbed out of the car.

Renaldo immediately began spouting out a bunch of statistics about the area and the warehouse itself. The price was right, and if the interior was what Bantus required, he'd have a third one to pick from. It was as perfect (though the thought made Dylan's skin crawl) as the other two. He told the agent as they left he would get back with him either tomorrow or the next day. He gave him the number to his mom's house and as he was dropped at the curb in front of it, told Renaldo to give him a call in a couple of days if he didn't hear from him.

Dylan went into his room to grab a clean burner phone. He dialed the number for the day to reach Bantus and waited as it rang several times. He was most likely working off of burner phones as well, as the number changed every day. The FBI managed to get the same number assigned to all of Dylan's burner phones to avoid suspicion on his 'partner's' phone. Just thinking about Bantus being his partner made him want to wretch.

"Yes."

It was Bantus and the syrupy sweet voice sucked Dylan out of his nightmare.

"Hey, Walter, it's me, Dylan."

"Yes, I saw it was you. How did the day go?"

"Well, I found three that might work for you. I'll text you the addresses and you can go have a look and let me know which one you want me to sign on."

Dylan waited while the killer did his usual thinking ritual where he said nothing and expected the caller to just sit quietly and wait. The guy was a piece of work, for sure.

"I'll tell you what, why don't you pick the one you feel will be the best and sign on that one. I'll need it for about three months, and the lease can start next month. Text me the address and the amount needed to close the deal and we'll be done with it."

"Okay, I'll call the agent tonight and have him work up some numbers and meet with him tomorrow to sign the papers. Let me know where you're staying and I'll run the keys over to you as soon as I get them."

This was the wrong thing to say.

"I *told* you *I'm* the one in charge here and you will stop asking where I LIVE! Why do you keep doing this when I've told you to never ASK me that?"

"Oh, I'm sorry Walter, it slipped my mind. I'll leave the key somewhere on the property and let you know where I've left it. Forgive me Walter, I'm really sorry."

"That's better."

Dylan was still feeling the gag reflex in his throat.

"It's just that I want Gentry to pay for what he did to me. I want him to suffer like I'm suffering every day. I guess I just get over anxious."

"That is not a bad thing, my friend," cooed Bantus. "Not a bad thing at all."

"I'll do whatever you need me to do, Walter, if it means I will get even with Beauchene. He's nothing to me, less than nothing. I want to see him squirm."

"Soon," said Bantus, "soon."

Walter ended the call without another word.

***

Lauren and Gentry were in their hotel room, having convinced Charity to stay in the hotel for a few days while they sorted everything out. She was less than enthused, but when they gave her their word her parents wouldn't know she was staying there, she agreed. Gentry saw the look on her face when they opened the door to her own room. As tough as she tried to appear on the outside, for a split second her expression gave away how delighted she was to have a soft warm bed and a bathroom. Those were the two places she looked first.

They showed her the adjoining door that led into Gentry and Lauren's rooms and told her she could order as much room service as she liked and as often as she liked, but somehow, Lauren knew it would be the standard three meals a day. Charity didn't seem like the type to abuse another's kindness, and Lauren could tell she was also good for her word. Gentry let her know they would just be one door over and if she needed them to just give them a call anytime.

Worried removing their disguises would frighten her, Lauren made sure when they dropped her at her room to let her know they were undercover and couldn't be seen outside the hotel without a disguise. She seemed fine with the whole idea, even going with them into their rooms and watching them remove the makeup and hair. She giggled as the real Lauren and Gentry were revealed.

"So, which versions do you like best?" asked Gentry with a smile.

"The other ones," she said laughing and headed back to her room.

Thanks to Charity's information Lauren assigned the teams in her charge to check every high end hotel in and around Kalispell. There weren't that many, and it netted them nothing. He'd either paid someone to keep quiet, or he was unrecognizable by the photograph. The first was most likely, but they couldn't strong arm people for no reason, and they wouldn't even know where to start. The whole process was incredibly frustrating.

Back in their own room, the phone tap rang out. Lauren and Gentry were at the desk and immediately hit the record button. Dylan did well with the conversation; he was becoming quite the pro. Gentry had to admit, however, the last conversation bothered him a bit. The threat felt real and it made him uneasy. He did know that Bantus was an empty shell, full of hollow threats and grandiose thinking and that helped.

The most difficult part of the operation with Dylan and his mother was not being able to communicate with him. A covert system was put in place allowing messages to be sent back and forth, but it took twenty-four hours at least to hear back. Gentry worried about Dylan, worried about what was going on inside his head when he was forced to speak to the man responsible for his father's death.

It had to be difficult, but he also knew Dylan to be a man of integrity, and Gentry knew he was doing what he did because it was the right thing to do. He admired his friend a great deal, even though he'd always found about every opportunity to tease him. Both men knew it was a form of brotherhood, and remembering that brotherhood brought him back to the beginning of his train of thought. He was worried about his friend.

Gentry glanced to Lauren who worked feverishly entering the most recent conversation between Dylan and Bantus into the log. This woman was someone else he admired. His feelings went far beyond admiration, but, began at admiration. She was strong and determined, a good leader and a great kisser…wait…that thought wasn't supposed to be in there. Still, since it found its way in, he'd allow himself that brief moment to feel the memory of her in his arms.

Never had anyone ignited the passion in him the way she did, and yet he could have a conversation with her that made sense. She was intelligent and quick witted…and she loved horses. Was this kismet? Was this an example of two people walking independent paths and then one day those paths overlapped and love happened? Gentry grinned softly and shook his head. Is that how it was? Somehow it seemed kind of random to him, but wasn't life full of small incidents of randomness?

Lauren turned and peered at him.

"You're doing it again," she said, masking a smile.

"Doing what?" he asked innocently.

"Over analyzing *us*," she grinned.

"I was not," he said with mock defense, "I was over analyzing life in general, and since we're both part of life, then yes, we were in there somewhere."

"I'm going to call Charity's parents. Are you ready for that?" she said, the grin fading from her face.

"Ready."

Don and Shannon Newman were beyond wealthy. They owned several large insurance companies with branches in many countries throughout the world. They may as well have been called Mr. & Mrs. Insurance, because most all insurance companies could trace their roots back to the Newman's.

Lauren put the phone on speaker and dialed the number. It rang several times before someone answered.

"Newman residence."

"Yes, may I please speak with Mr. or Mrs. Newman?"

"Who's calling please?"

"My name is Lauren Porcelli. I need to speak with them about their daughter."

There was silence on the line and the voice finally spoke.

"One moment please."

Several minutes passed before they heard another voice. It was strained and tenuous.

"Hello? This is Mrs. Newman."

"Mrs. Newman, I'm calling regarding your daughter. Do you have a minute to talk with me?"

"I…I'm so…sorry…You…I, I mean we…well, we don't have a daughter," she said, struggling for each word. "You must have the wrong number." The line went abruptly to dial tone.

Chapter Twenty-Eight

Lauren held the burner phone in her hand for a few seconds before glancing at Gentry.

"She's disowned her daughter for running away?" Gentry couldn't believe what he'd just heard.

"I...don't think so," said Lauren, still contemplating the conversation. "I'm willing to bet she thinks her lines have been tapped."

"Bantus tapped her lines?" Gentry's mind was reeling with the different scenarios flying through them.

"No...I'm thinking he's told them something to make them *believe* he's tapped their phone lines."

Lauren was still holding the phone in her hand and placed it on the desk in front of her.

"Oh, come on," said Gentry in disbelief, "someone with that much money and power wouldn't have that checked out immediately? No way, it's got to be something else."

"Would you have it checked out if your life or the life of a loved one were threatened? Would you take that risk?" Lauren wasn't looking at him; in fact, she wasn't really speaking to him. He could almost see the thoughts bouncing around in her head.

"What are you thinking?"

"I'm going to arrange for some undercover agents to pay a visit to the Newman Mansion. They'll figure out a way to speak with them, let them know we have their daughter and she's fine and see if that opens up the lines of communication."

Lauren was already dialing her office in Seattle as she spoke.

***

The two FBI agents pulled up outside the very large home belonging to Don and Shannon Newman. They'd arrived in a paneled cable company van and wore the uniform of the company, complete with monogrammed ball caps.

Large marbled columns lined the front of the three story home, extending upward for the first two stories. The property covered nearly twenty acres of exquisitely manicured lawn and gardens. It was a very impressive home in an exclusive neighborhood in the suburbs of New York City.

With clipboards in hand, the two men headed up the long walk and approached the house. On one clipboard in large lettering were printed the words, "Charity is in FBI custody". The paper on the second one said, "She is alive and in excellent condition, say nothing."

They rang the doorbell and it was promptly answered by one of the household staff.

"May we please speak to the lady of the house?" asked Agent Billings, holding his clipboard in front of him so it could be easily seen.

Agent Lentsworth was holding his in front of him as well.

The woman at the door gasped, but Agent Billings held his finger to his lips. She composed herself right away.

"Please come in," she said calmly. "I'll let her know you're here."

Not knowing for sure if the monitoring of the household was audio or video, the two men rotated the pages on their clipboards revealing yet another message and turned them inward, silently waiting for Mrs. Newman.

Within a very few minutes Mrs. Newman approached them. She was a tall woman, with blond hair and piercing green eyes, eyes now filled with hope and terror all at the same time. The two agents began their dialogue about getting a call for repair of their internet lines. As they droned on about what they needed to do to repair the lines, they held their clipboards out once again, the one now reading, "Your daughter is alive and well", while the other one read "Is your monitoring done through audio or video, please point to the correct one".

With Mrs. Newman in front of the men the words were hidden from any video equipment that may be present.

In the beginning she appeared frozen with fear, eyes wide, her body unmoving. However, the two agents helped calm her as they rattled on about the repairs and eventually she pointed to the word video.

Agent Billings set the sign down on the floor revealing another one.

"We're going to check your home for bugs now, say nothing."

Mrs. Newman quickly picked up the sign from the floor and flipping it over scrawled a note across it. She turned it so the agents could see the handwriting.

"He told us our phones were tapped and monitored by him, that he would know if we spoke to anyone at the police station or FBI, but he didn't say how."

Agent Lentsworth pointed to the phone with raised eyebrows. Mrs. Newman nodded.

He quickly checked it for bugs, and shook his head. The two men proceeded to check the entire home for bugging devices and found nothing.

"You're safe to speak freely now. I'm sorry to say you've been the victim of a scam."

Agent Billings was sitting on the couch in the drawing room across from Mrs. Newman. Mr. Newman joined them after the staff filled him in on what was happening.

"Where is our daughter? When can we talk to her?" he said, sitting down next to his wife. His graying hair was cut short on top and stood up, accenting a strong jaw line and tanned skin. He's dark eyes moved from one agent to the other desperately seeking answers yet with a demeanor that said he usually got what he wanted.

"Your daughter is safe, and that is all the information I have for you at this time. Neither your home phones, nor your cell phones have been tapped and the video you have appears to be only what you have installed for home security."

"It's been a nightmare," said Mrs. Newman, her eyes filling with tears.

She leaned into her husband and wept softly.

Mr. Newman put his arm around her and held her as he spoke.

"Charity left us nearly four months ago. She was angry with us for forcing her to do the things normal young ladies of her stature do. We were ignorant and selfish; we wanted her to be like the other girls her age who were excited about their 'coming out' parties and formal balls. However, I'm afraid we drove her away with our selfishness. She is fiercely independent and refused to do things the way we wanted them done. In our ignorance, we lost our daughter."

Mrs. Newman sat upright and dabbed her eyes with a handkerchief.

"This awful man told us he had her and would kill her if we didn't do exactly as he said. We had to make deposits into an account number he sent us and we had to continue until he told us to stop or he would kill Charity." She began weeping softly again.

"If you'll excuse me," said Agent Billings, "I'm going to make a call."

"Certainly," said Mr. Newman.

The room fell quiet as the reality of their daughter's safety settled in on the two of them. They hugged each other, finally realizing they were not only free of the dreaded phone tap, but their daughter was alive and well.

Agent Billings returned.

"Mr. Newman, if we could use your computer we can set up a video link with the agents that are caring for your daughter. Would you be willing to do that?"

"Yes," he said, rising. "It's just this way."

Once they had the link ready, Agent Billings dialed Lauren. Within seconds her image exploded onto the screen.

"Mr. & Mrs. Newman, this is Lauren Porcelli. Go head Agent Porcelli."

Lauren didn't really know where to start, but even before she could speak, Charity's father jumped in.

"I want to talk to my daughter. I want to see her, to know she's well like you say."

"Mr. Newman, we are going to have to take this slowly. If you force her to talk to you, she's already told us she will run to another city, a bigger city and get lost in the homeless population there. You're going to have to leave the ball in her court for a while, or risk losing her forever. You may never get another chance like this."

"But she's a minor and we are her parents. As such we have rights."

"Yes, that is true and because of that I am bound to do what you say, but if you do this, she'll run at her first opportunity. Think this through before you make your demands."

Mrs. Newman touched her husband's arm softly, a pleading look on her face.

"We're doing it again. We have to stop sometime, and now seems like a pretty good time."

Mr. Newman sat back, his shoulders drooping.

"I can't believe I'm picking up where we left off. You're right, Agent Porcelli, you're right. I'm sorry."

"Mr. Newman, I need the account number you've been making your deposits into. We'll need to put an IRS hold on that account. I'm afraid what you've put in there may be gone, but at least you're done feeding the monster."

"I appreciate that," said Mr. Newman. "I'll get the account number now."

He rose and walked to his desk. Lauren watched as he pulled out a leather bound portfolio and opened it to the first page. He read the account number to her and she read it back to him for clarification. He told her the name of the bank and closed the leather cover, replacing it in the drawer.

"Thank you," said Lauren. We'll take care of this right away."

"Hi mom, hi dad," came a firm voice from behind Lauren. She turned and there was Charity standing behind her, staring into the monitor. Lauren stood and motioned for Charity to have her seat. She sat down, staring into the monitor.

"Did you mean what you said? You're really willing to let me be who I am and not who you want me to be?" Charity's tone was neither apologetic nor meek.

"I did," said her father, "I do mean what I said. We never learned to appreciate you for the individual you are. I'm ashamed that I drove you away."

"I love you, Daddy, and you, too Mom," she said, tears filling her eyes. "I want to come home."

"And so you shall," said her mother, tears rolling down her face. "On your terms and in your way, we promise."

Gentry and Lauren went into the other room and let the family speak in private. Lauren quickly made a phone call to her office in Seattle and ordered the hold on the bank account.

"That's going to make our little gremlin angry," she grinned.

It was a huge victory, and as they heard giggling from the next room, they realized the best victory was a young lady heading home, both she and her parents smarter and more humble than when she left.

Lauren was facing Gentry, and looked up into his eyes. The joy of hearing Charity talking with her family, the relief of one child still living, the love he felt for Lauren exploded in him and he wrapped his arms around her. He couldn't seem to get her close enough and she responded to his embrace, melting into him like hot wax. The room swam and he wondered if he would be able to stay upright.

The fire suddenly stopped as they heard Charity signing off with her parents.

"I love you, Mom, love you Dad. I'll see you tomorrow."

"Good-bye, Baby," said her mom, tears choking her voice.

"We'll see you tomorrow, honey," said her dad.

Gentry and Lauren quickly composed themselves and returned to the office. Charity remained seated, staring at the monitor that was now dark.

"How did that feel?" asked Lauren.

Charity smiled a big beautiful smile.

"Great," she said with a giggle, "it felt great."

Charity never went back to her cardboard box under the bridge. She stayed in the hotel until the next day. Gentry and Lauren said their goodbyes when a field agent arrived to take her to the airport. Her father booked the flight as soon as they ended their call the day before. As they watched her walk to the elevator, she turned and waved. She certainly didn't look like the same girl that walked into the police station earlier that week.

Lauren and Gentry shut their door and returned to the task at hand. Charity was a wonderful reprieve in the filth of dealing with Walter Bantus. Now it was back to the dirt and the grit.

Bantus had apparently not been made aware of the IRS hold on his checking account. Gentry was certain they would know the minute he found out.

It took less than twenty-four hours for the news to reach him. Gentry and Lauren were at their computers when the wiretap phone rang. Lauren pushed the record button and set the speaker.

"Sandusky."

"Your friend Gentry has sealed his fate this time!" Bantus was furious.

"First of all, he's not my friend, but what's happened?" Dylan was attempting to mask his thrill at the anger in Bantus.

"They somehow got their hands on my money, and I'm going to kill them both. I'm going to slit their throats and watch them die, watch them bleed to death. *I'm going to kill them.*"

"How would they be able to get to your money?" asked Dylan, still hiding the smile in his voice.

"*I DON'T KNOW HOW THEY DID IT! THIS CHANGES EVERYTHING!*" Bantus sounded like he was strangling on his own words. "I'll kill them…I'll kill them all and I'll smile as I watch them take their last breaths."

He was calming down, the talk of killing calming him and bringing him back to a place in his mind where he could think clearly, his focus gradually returning.

"I have enough money on me to finish my work here in Kalispell. We're going to bump up the timeline, Dylan. I need you to quickly finalize the deal on the warehouse. I've left the money for you in your PO Box. Go there tomorrow morning and get it, take it to the realtor and sign the paperwork. I have work to do, and it starts tonight."

Chapter Twenty-Nine

Those last words sent a chill ripping through Gentry. It was *never* a good thing to hear a killer say he had work to do.

"Okay, we know where the warehouse is he's chosen. We'll set up surveillance on it and send the local LEOs out to watch over the homeless camps, at least as much as they have available."

Gentry was frustrated.

"Is it still necessary we stay in this room while everyone else is out there working? I need to get out of here. We could use our disguises again."

"Gentry, we have to keep this as low as we can. If there is even *one* minor slip up, he'll bolt like a rabbit. We have to let this play out and make sure he's not just blowing smoke to see what effect it has."

They were still seated at their desk. It was late afternoon and they'd now been sequestered in their hotel rooms for a full seven days, with one day out for a meeting at the Kalispell Police Station. Having come from Glacier Park, Gentry was definitely more stir crazy than Lauren. He needed to be *out*, somewhere…anywhere. However, he knew by staying hidden, he was protecting Dylan.

Gentry sighed and sat back in his chair, his hands folded across his lap.

"Yeah, I know you're right, but it's like sending lambs to the slaughter. You heard him! He has "work" to do. He's going to start killing and we can't stop him."

"We can, Gentry, if we are patient," Lauren rested a hand on his. "We can hope that he has to spend a few nights finding and charming his victim before he kills them. By his own standard, we have at least a couple nights before he kills. Everyone is on high alert; we'll get him this time."

She stood and leaned over him, kissing him gently on the forehead. As she walked into her room, Gentry wanted to follow her in the worst way. Every part of him struggled to maintain a sense of professionalism when at each turn of events he wanted to throw that same professionalism right out the window. However, he knew he'd lose her if he did, and that was one thing he wouldn't let happen. It was the one thing in this whole evil affair he actually had control over…and come to think of it, it was the one thing he'd rather lose control of.

The thought made him smile, and as Lauren strolled back into the room she saw him.

"You smiling because you're just happy being you, or is there another reason?" she poked him playfully in the side as she sat down.

"Oh, nothing really," he said trying to hide his thoughts. "I'm only feeling good about how well this seems to be working out."

"Well, don't jinx it," she grinned. "We law enforcement types are pretty superstitious, you know."

"Yeah, whatever," he said flatly, "you are anything but superstitious. It's hard work that makes or breaks a case."

Lauren grinned and turned to the monitor, checking the surveillance teams in the neighborhood surrounding Dylan's home as well as the team watching the home. Everything was quiet and things looked to be progressing well.

"You know," she said smiling seductively at Gentry, "I don't think I've ever known anyone like you."

"Well," said Gentry, his most charming grin spreading across his face, "there might be three Beauchene boys, but as my mother always said, 'thank the heavens there was only one Gentry'."

"Your mother," she said still smiling, "sounds like a very smart woman."

Lauren turned back to the monitor.

"I mean it, Gentry. You're the most genuine person I've come across in my lifetime. I like that you have no pretense, no mask. You're the real deal and I've come to rely on that in this investigation. Dylan said you were just going along with me because I was 'your girlfriend'. Little did he know how hard you were fighting for him and how you never gave up on him."

She smiled again, and rose. She stepped to his chair and lay herself across his lap, arms around his neck. He embraced her, placing his mouth, hungry and warm, over hers. She ignited a heat inside him like he'd never experienced, and she responded to him with a tender yet heated desire.

Gentry let himself fall into the moment, into a place in time where it was just the two of them. To a place where there were no serial killers, there were no children in peril. This was a quiet nook, away from the chaos, and it belonged only to the two of them. His body burned with an excitement fueled by her presence in his arms, and the peace and tranquility that presence brought him.

"I think I love you, Gentry," she whispered breathlessly into his ear. *"I think I love you."*

He let her fall back into his arms and saw the fear on her face.

"Your face tells me that is *not* a good thing," he said carefully, "but your body is telling me you agree with your mouth."

Her face paled and she sat up. Before she could get out of his lap he carefully grabbed her arm and held her there. Their eyes met, still hot from the encounter.

"I think I love you, too, Lauren. I think I've known it for a long time now," he chose his words very carefully. "We don't have to be afraid of that."

Lauren sighed and stood up. Gentry rose and they embraced.

"I'm afraid of that feeling," she said softly into his ear. "It scares me because I've never felt it before. What if it ends, what if you go your way and I go mine and it just ends?"

"I can't imagine that happening, Lauren, but if it does, if you change your mind about how you feel about me, we'll part friends and continue our lives. Just don't think for one minute *my* feelings are going to change. They're not."

Dylan's home phone began to ring into her phone and Lauren quickly released Gentry and turned on the recorder.

"Sandusky."

"I distinctly told you *not* to pick up what was in the Post Office Box until tomorrow. Do you not know how to follow orders?"

"I...I was downtown and by the Post Office, so I thought I'd see if it was--"

"Shut your mouth! Just shut up! When I say doing something in the morning, I mean do it in the morning. You have no idea what my timeline is like and one false move, one unplanned pickup can ruin everything! Do you hear me?"

"I'm…I'm so sorry…I didn't know-"

"Well now you know, you *fool*. Do as I say or die. You got that? *Do as I say or die.*"

"Got it," said Dylan, trying not to spit the words.

"Did you also meet with the real estate agent today instead of tomorrow?" Bantus' voice was mocking and hateful.

"No...no I didn't. I set up the appointment for ten o'clock tomorrow morning."

"Well at least you aren't a complete moron."

"Maybe we could meet and discuss the warehouse," said Dylan, attempting to keep him on the line just two more minutes to complete the trace.

Bantus' voice became evil and menacing.

"If I didn't know better, I'd think you were trying to keep me on the line because only a complete idiot would ask me to meet when I've told him over and over *we.will.never.meet.*"

Bantus ended the call and Lauren heard dial tone. She closed the line and turned off the recorder.

"How much more of this can he stand?" asked Gentry. "The man killed his father and he has to treat him like a superior. That has to be eating his stomach lining like bleach on fine linen."

"No doubt," said Lauren, "but he did very well. He's staying strong, and it doesn't appear he'll have to keep up the charade much longer."

***

Walter Bantus paced the room in a wild fury, throwing chairs and lamps as far as he could. His leg was in a straight brace and he felt the restriction more keenly than he had before, wanting to tear the brace from his leg, but knowing he couldn't yet walk without it.

Just then Lisa entered the room and his eyes went vacant. She hated it when he got that look, it always meant something bad was about to happen.

He tried to smile, but she began to back away from him.

"Where do you think you're going?" he ask, sickly sweet, yet evil.

"I…I need to run to the store. We're about out of milk. Are you hungry? I can pick you up something while I'm out, or I could-"

He limped to her, holding out his hands.

"No, no don't go anywhere. Come here to me, let's cuddle."

Lisa turned to run, but somehow he was already on her and grabbed her arm.

"Come here, my Lisa. Come to me; rest on the bed with me. We'll spend some time together and then you can go to the store."

Lisa froze in place and he took her hands, pulling her to the bed. She was trembling and the trembling turned to stark terror.

"Please," she begged, "please, I want to go back to my friends. I want to go back."

Abruptly Bantus pushed her back onto the bed and sat on her stomach, his braced leg hanging over the side of the bed, his other leg bent beside her. His hands stroked her face and traveled down to her throat as he spoke softly to her, calming her.

"But you're so happy here, my sweet. We get along so well together, don't we? Surely you don't want to go back to that dirty camp…" His words continued on as his hands grasped her neck firmly and began to squeeze, gently at first, then harder and harder.

Lisa fought back, grabbing his hands and trying to pry them from her neck. She kicked her feet, trying to kick his head from behind but it was no use. She gasped for air, fighting, clawing at him until there was no air left in her and she lay limply on the bed, her eyes staring vacantly up to the ceiling.

Bantus felt the thrill of the moment, reveled in it, breathed deeply of the air in the room and threw his head back, filling the room with laughter. He truly loved his work.

***

It was after six when Gentry finally looked at his watch.

"We should eat something. Want some pizza? We could have it delivered to the front desk and the staff can bring it up."

"Ooohh…" said Lauren. "That's an excellent idea. I could definitely eat pizza."

Gentry put in the call and then let the front desk know there would be a delivery for them. He asked that they pay for the pizza and charge the fee to their room. This was the usual agreement between them and the hotel and it was working nicely.

Lauren and Gentry worked at the computers, continuing their radio checks with each surveillance team. The night was quiet, all teams checking in and the two dug into their pizza.

Gentry wondered how much longer they would be hunkered down in this room, swearing to himself he would never stay in another hotel as long as he lived.

He shook his head, unable to shake the feeling that something was wrong. He hated it when he felt like this…come to think of it…he'd never felt like this, and it really, really bothered him.

Chapter Thirty

Gentry woke the next day unable to shake the feeling that something was wrong. He even talked to Lauren about it, who couldn't be happier with the way things were going. He wished he felt the same way she did.

They ordered room service for breakfast and ate in her room, away from the computer and phone equipment. It was the only way they ever felt like they got a break.

The two of them visited about the case, Gentry worried about Baby, but he knew Joe was taking excellent care of her.

"When did your love affair with horses first start?" Lauren asked, pouring a generous slathering of maple syrup over her stack of pancakes.

Gentry chewed on his bite of pancakes and thought for a moment.

"I guess I was eight years old," he began. "My grandpa had these big old Clydesdales, a pair of them that he used for pulling a sleigh in the winter. They were so gentle, and *gigantic*. I remember standing in front of one of them and putting my feet together, side by side, and both my feet still weren't as big as one of their hooves."

He grinned and continued his story.

"My grandpa used to set me up on that horse and I was sure I was sitting on top of the world. It felt like I could see for miles. He'd lead him around the pasture with me frantically grasping his withers, trying to hold on. Grandpa would always remind me to hold on with my knees, and eventually I did. After that, I was hooked.

"I'm still lulled into another place in time when I hear the rhythmic thud of hooves on soft ground. It's hypnotic. Either the sound of the hooves or the sound Baby makes when I give her a carrot, you know…that muffled crunch. Baby is the first horse I've ever owned that whinnies softly when she sees me. There's just nothing like it. How about you?"

"Me?" she said, smiling at the memory. "I was probably about the same age as you and it was my dad who first introduced me to horses. He wanted to get a couple horses for the new ranch he'd just bought. We'd moved in and he'd shown me the barn, but it was empty. So he took me to a friend of his who owned purebred Arabians," she stopped and her eyes grew distant. "Magnificent animals."

"And…" said Gentry, coaxing her back to the present.

"Oh, sorry," she blushed, "I was just remembering how it felt to have that huge animal under me, so much power and strength. I was bareback, like you, and felt every muscle as she moved through the barn. Dad had her harness, so I felt safe. She was a very gentle soul, it felt like she knew I was a child and she needed to move carefully. I'll never forget that feeling. From the moment we connected in that way, where it felt like I was aware of her feelings for me, I, too, was hooked and in complete surrender to the wonder of a horse."

They visited about their years growing up on a ranch and their favorite memories.

"I don't understand," said Gentry, shaking his fork as he spoke, "how you could grow up immersed in the outdoors and end up with a job that keeps you indoors."

"Well," she said, thinking about her response. "For me you're actually talking about two different things. The FBI is about helping society, taking dangerous elements off the streets and protecting people so they can hopefully live the kinds of lives they want to live. Growing up on a ranch helped me to become strong. It taught me commitment, and how to finish what I start.

"Don't get me wrong," she said, continuing, "I will always have a love affair with the outdoors, but I also have this responsibility to help our society be a safer place."

Lauren's cell phone began ringing and Gentry sighed. He was really enjoying putting the world outside for a little bit.

"Porcelli."

Gentry stood up as the color drained from Lauren's face. She quickly hung up the phone.

"What? What-"

The phone rang again and she checked the number. It was Dylan.

"Get out of the house, NOW!" she screamed into the phone and hung up.

"What are you doing? Why are you screaming at him?" Gentry couldn't understand what was happening.

"It was Dylan," she said trembling.

"I saw that, but what-" he stopped mid-sentence when he realized what she was saying.

"He must have gotten mixed up on the phones…he called my cell phone from his home phone, Gentry, and we know Bantus has to have known that. He's aware of every call that goes in or out on that line. His cover may have been blown."

"What do we do? We have to warn him!" The look on his face was sheer panic.

"I've done everything I can," she said, still pale. "I told him to get out of the house."

Suddenly a horrendous explosion ripped through the air, shaking the windows of the hotel. Sirens began wailing down the street, heading away from the hotel. Gentry and Lauren stopped breathing, looked at each other and headed for the door at a full run. They took the stairs and ran through the lobby and out to their car. It felt like it took forever to start it, put it in gear and get out onto the street. They both knew where Dylan's home was, and they raced through the streets as fast as they could.

They turned down the street, the sight was chaos.

"Oh, no…" said Lauren as they screeched to a stop.

There was very little left of the home that belonged to Dylan's family. What was left was burning, along with the homes on either side, though they were only scorched from the explosion. There was nothing left. It took only seconds for Gentry to realize his friend was gone. There was no way to even hope he'd made it out of the house with his mother, no one could've moved that fast. He may not even have realized what he'd done until it was too late.

Minutes passed as Gentry stood on the sidewalk, numbly watching the fire burn. He didn't know how long he'd been standing there, didn't even know for sure if he was breathing. Lauren stood beside him with one arm around his waist, staring at what was left of the still burning home.

Gentry bowed his head, and when he looked up, his eyes fell on a figure in the crowd. He quickly looked back down, not wanting to let Bantus know he'd just been made.

"Don't look, Lauren, don't move your head. If you can move your eyes, look just a little to the right of us into the crowd."

Lauren scanned the crowd as best she could and gasped. He was there, like he didn't have a care in the world, grinning and glancing around the crowd, seemingly enjoying the reaction of the crowd.

It was all Gentry could do to keep himself from bolting through the crowd and nabbing Bantus where he stood.

"Don't move, Gentry," she said sharply, still watching the blaze. "We have to think this through."

"Well, don't take too long," he answered, "I'm willing to bet he's not going to stick around."

Lauren turned and walked slowly to one of the agents involved in the surveillance of the home. She touched his arm and while solemnly glancing at the fire, tried to act like she was talking about the fire itself.

"Bantus is in the crowd. I want you to take your partner and get low. Make your way around the group and come up behind him. Take him into custody as quietly as you can, but make it fast."

"Yes, Ma'am," he said and stood watching the fire burn for a few more seconds as Lauren made her way back to Gentry.

The mood was tense as Gentry continued to watch the blaze and check frequently for Bantus' attendance in the crowd. Within a few minutes Bantus was gone, and so were the agents. His hope rose as he touched Lauren's arm and let her know he didn't see Bantus.

The two of them began walking toward the spot where he was standing and arrived there the same time as the two agents, but it was too late. He was gone.

Gentry was angry and wanted to scream. His friend was dead, along with his friend's mother and nothing would bring them back. He felt empty inside, hollow. If he hadn't encouraged Dylan to cooperate in the undercover operation, he'd still be alive. He couldn't lift the guilt that weighed so heavily on his shoulders.

The agents came back around and reported that by the time they got there Bantus was nowhere in sight. The fire continued to burn. Firefighters kept water on the homes on either side of the blaze to keep them from igniting in the heat. Lauren and Gentry stayed by their car and kept watching the fire with eyes that occasionally scanned the crowd, which was beginning to thin. Their chance to snag a killer had passed, which meant the killings would continue.

Eventually the blaze was calmed down, but it would be impossible to walk through the remains of the home until the hot spots were out and the burn was cold. Lauren and Gentry headed back to their hotel, the sequestering no longer an issue. Bantus knew they were there, knew they were aware of his 'warehouse' and he would somehow make adjustments to his plan.

***

Lauren sat up on the bed in her room painstakingly reviewing the profile and its updates from their crime scene over and over again. What would his next move most likely be? Would he still use a warehouse? Would he find another city altogether?

She highly doubted he would move on because he still had a score to settle with Gentry. However, she wondered if this new development would settle that score in his mind. She wanted to call Aspen Beauchene and see what she thought. Glancing at the time, she realized it would be close to one in the morning in Alaska.

Her mind wandered to the room adjoining hers, to the man who'd lost a good friend tonight because she'd placed him in harm's way. He would blame her for Dylan's death, and she would deserve the blame, at least for the time being. Would this ruin any chance they might have had of a relationship? Would he ever be able to see past the pain she'd caused him?

Once again her feelings for Gentry were interfering with her ability to do her job. She'd never had issues with focus before, ever. There was just something about standing next to him that made her heart beat faster and her body ache in ways she didn't know was possible.

Lauren sighed and stood up, walking to the window and standing before it with arms folded. No need now to keep the curtains drawn, Bantus knew they were there. She knew they'd put a decent sized crater in his plans, and forced him to switch things up. For someone like Bantus, that was huge, and would take some time for him to recover. If his profile rang true, which it had to this point, he would be in a panic to pull it all together. He could make mistakes if he were in a hurry.

What was confusing her at this time was his complete lack of panic at the fire tonight. He seemed calm, like he was enjoying his work, gloating over it. He didn't seem panicked at all to look at him, but then, maybe that's how he'd wanted to appear; carefree and satisfied with his work, but terrified on the inside he wouldn't be able to complete it.

She quickly walked back to the bed and sat down, once again pulling the profile into her lap. Would he want to appear carefree? Could he? She would figure this puzzle out if it took all night, and from the time on the clock, it was probably going to.

Chapter Thirty-One

Gentry lay in his bed, hands behind his head, staring into the darkness. He'd asked himself the same questions over and over again, wondering if he'd ever be able to *stop* asking those questions.

How could he ever have been so ignorant, so careless as to think someone like Dylan could pull off an undercover operation of such magnitude? Gentry knew the caliber of man they were dealing with. As a sniper, he'd been assigned to teams of assassins tasked with removing opposition leaders in the Middle East. He'd often worked undercover to infiltrate these groups and identify the leadership. It was dangerous work and required every ounce of brain matter to keep the op moving and keep himself and his team members safe.

Dylan was invested in this operation from the moment he made the connection between Bantus and the death of his father. His investment was emotional.

'Why didn't I see it? Worse yet, why didn't I stop it?'

That should have disqualified Dylan from the operation from the very start. He let his friend walk into an incredibly dangerous situation with emotions leading him, not facts.

Gentry tried to reconcile the fact that Dylan was insistent, but it made no difference. His insistence was emotional. That would forever haunt him. He sent him in without stressing the importance of fact, thinking with his head not his heart. Now Gentry would pay for that decision the rest of his life as his friend had paid with his death. It left a feeling of bitterness in him he couldn't ignore. A good man was gone, far too soon, and it was Gentry's fault.

In angry solitude he added to his responsibility the death of Dylan's mother as well. She knew nothing of the danger she was in. She'd had no warning, no clue. Another death to scratch into the cold, stone wall he felt surrounding him and he made the mark with his very soul.

The weight of the guilt combined with the grief and loss he felt kept his eyes open for hours, wondering how he could have talked Dylan out of the decision to do what he did. Hundreds of scenarios played in his head hour after long, painful hour, acting out all the different ways he could have stopped him. If he'd only done this or if he'd only said that...it made no difference. Dylan, his father and his mother were dead. Father, Mother and Son all killed by the same man.

The night slowly peeled away each dark layer until daylight began making its way into his room. He hadn't slept at all, his grief keeping him deep in thought all night. He slowly dragged himself out of bed and stood, stretching and walked to the window.

Kalispell lay out before him as if nothing had changed. Gentry knew a black burned out pock mark on the landscape remained only a few blocks away, where once a home stood. It would appear everywhere he looked, he'd be reminded of how he'd killed his friend.

Gentry showered, shaved and dressed mechanically. It's what he did every day, and he'd continue to, just as the city moved on with its days. The world continued to live, but Dylan was dead.

He sat down at his computer as the door into Lauren's room opened and a very disheveled FBI agent walked through. It was the first time he'd grinned since the fire the day before, and he stopped immediately.

"What?" she asked, "No snappy comebacks? No comments on my hair?"

"Sorry," he said turning back to the monitor, "just not in me today."

"Gentry," she said sliding into the chair beside him, "the deaths weren't your fault. There is no way you'd have let him take part in this if you'd thought for a minute he and his mother would end up dead."

"But that's just it, Lauren," he said turning to her, "we did know it could happen. Dylan didn't, and it was my responsibility to make sure he knew, to make sure he didn't make the stupid mistake he did."

"Listen up," she said, "I lost a partner last year, someone I cared very much about. For months I carried the guilt with me. I wore it like a new suit. It was *my* fault, *I* should have done this or if I'd *only* done that it wouldn't have happened. But the truth of it is I didn't pull the trigger. I learned after far too long a stay in self pity I wasn't the killer, I would never have killed my partner. Gentry, put the blame where it belongs; don't give Bantus the joy of seeing you suffer for his crime. *He* did this; he set the blast up that killed Dylan and his mom. Let him have the guilt and the shame for what he did."

"He could care less and you know it," spat Gentry, the bitterness welling up inside him.

"That's not your concern," she said, spitting right back at him. "How he handles the responsibility of what he's done doesn't matter. It only matters that *you* don't take it on yourself. Let the blame sit where it belongs, and it doesn't belong on you. Here's what's going to happen if you hang onto it…you'll be useless to me. We won't be able to finish what we started and Bantus will continue the killing rampage he began months ago. *He* started this."

"And what if we can't stop him?" said Gentry, "What if he just keeps on killing?"

"Then everything we've done here will be added to the investigation and will help someone else stop him."

She was quiet for a moment and let the words sink in. Finally, she stood and shoved her chair into the desk.

"Fine," she said turning and walking to her door. "Enjoy your grief. Go back to your park and live out your life with your very own crown of guilt. You're no use to anyone the way you are, least of all yourself. Pack your things; I have to find a new partner."

Lauren slammed her door.

Gentry jumped from his chair and pulled the door open almost loosening the hinges in the process. He stood there, anger seething in him, his jaw firm, his teething grating against each other.

"He was my FRIEND!" he yelled, "My *friend*! I should never have let him do what he did, he was too emotional. I should have stopped him."

"Because...why?" she yelled back. "Because he was only ten years old and couldn't see a serial killer when he's standing in front of him? Because he was too immature to know danger when he saw it? You think he was *stupid?* Or was he your friend? Because he can't be both, Gentry. He can't be stupid and immature *and* be the caliber of man he'd have to be in order to be your friend. You don't have a corner on the integrity market you know! Dylan was strong, he was smart and he was incredibly brave to do what he did. You're not honoring his memory. You're staining it! WAKE UP! He did what any decent human being would have done. He stepped up to the plate to stop a killer! He's a hero and he deserves our respect, not our pity."

Lauren stormed into her bathroom and slammed the door.

Gentry stood in the doorway feeling like he'd been hit by lightning. He wanted to be angry, to walk to the chest of drawers and begin throwing his clothing in his duffle as fast as he could. He wanted to march out the door and never look back, but when he thought of doing that something stopped him. Logic stopped him.

Lauren was right. Dylan was a hero, he'd been strong in the face of danger and he'd died in an effort to keep others from dying. Could he ask his friend to be anything less than that?

Gentry felt the pain beginning to soften, gradually replaced with a sense of pride in what Dylan had actually done. He realized he'd been looking at the whole thing wrong. Dylan was aware from the very beginning how dangerous Bantus was. He'd seen the casket in that meadow. He knew…and he went anyway.

Gentry bowed his head as he leaned on the doorframe. What he really felt was loss. He'd miss Dylan every day of his life. Losing a friend was hard and he quickly realized it was okay to feel that loss, but respect must be acknowledged and he respected his friend.

He strode into Lauren's room and to her bathroom door and knocked softly.

She opened the door and gazed up at him.

"Do I need my gun?" she asked, a slight smile gracing her mouth.

"No…no you don't," he said looking at his feet. "What you need is an apology. So, first of all, I'm sorry for losing it-"

Lauren started to interrupt him and he put his finger to her lips.

"And second, thank-you. You're absolutely right. Dylan died a hero, and so did his mom. I needed to hear that."

Lauren blushed slightly at the compliment and tightened the sash on her robe.

"You're so very welcome," she said as she kissed his cheek. "Now, may I please finish getting dressed?"

"Certainly," he said grinning slowly, "I'll just wait right here."

"Uh, no," she said pushing him back playfully, "You'll wait in there."

She pointed to his room and shut the bathroom door.

Gentry walked into his room and to the same window he'd stared through in mourning only minutes before. This time, it was pride and honor that filled him. When he looked at that same burned out home, he'd feel strength and certainty that a good man had given everything he could.

Lauren came out of the bathroom looking as beautiful as ever.

"Let's go see if the structure has cooled enough to do some investigating. I want to know what Bantus used to blow up that home, and see if anything can be gleaned that may give us a little more information."

"What information?" asked Gentry, "I would think there wouldn't be a recognizable thing left."

"Sometimes," she said raising her finger to make a point, "it's what you *feel* when you see evidence, not what you see."

As they drove to the burn site, Lauren clarified her feelings on Dylan's death.

"You know, Gentry," she began, "I'm not saying you shouldn't miss Dylan."

"I know," he replied, "I do know that. But I wasn't grieving, I was blaming and you showed me that was two different things. I get it."

Lauren smiled.

"You're a quick study, you know that?"

"Yeah, I guess," he said, smiling softly, "but I sure will miss teasing him about his blue eyes. I mean, seriously, did you ever see eyes that blue? Really?"

Lauren laughed and they spent the rest of the drive remembering Dylan. The mood was lighter as they pulled up in front of what was once Dylan's home. They both sighed and got out of the car, the moment quickly turning somber at the destruction before them.

They said nothing more and walked to the home, now just a pile of charred beams and broken glass. They walked around the perimeter examining pieces of roofing and eaves.

They hadn't noticed the car parked out front when they pulled up and were surprised to see the fire inspector come around the unattached garage, slightly scorched but still standing.

"Hello," he said, "can I help you?"

"Hi," said Lauren, holding out her hand, "I'm FBI Special Agent Lauren Porcelli; this is my partner Gentry Beauchene."

Gentry shook his hand at the introduction.

"Jake Martel," he said as he shook their hands.

"What can you tell me about the explosion?" asked Lauren.

"Well, it was definitely a bomb that started it, but not what actually burned the structure."

Chapter Thirty-Two

Lauren stared at the man for a moment before speaking.

"How do you mean?" she asked, confused.

"Well, it was meant to be a big bang, which it was, but the home was heated by natural gas. The explosion ignited the gas and up she went. Had the home been heated by electricity, the bomb itself wouldn't have been enough to more than blow a hole in that south facing wall where it was placed."

"Would you mind showing us?" asked Lauren.

"Not at all, follow me," he said.

He directed them to where the natural gas line entered the home and showed them the shrapnel like pieces left from the line.

"It definitely exploded right here," said Jake, "but it was put where it was because the person who placed the bomb wanted nothing left. Do you know who did this?"

"We have a suspect," said Lauren, "but so far he has evaded custody. We're working on finding him."

"Good luck, he seems to know what he's doing when it comes to explosions."

With that, Jake returned to his work behind the garage.

Lauren watched him go, interested in what he was looking at back there because it wasn't burned in the fire.

"Uh, Mr. Martel?" she asked, following after him. Gentry stayed with Lauren, curious as well.

"Yes?" he said peeking around the end of the garage.

"What are you looking at back here?"

Lauren asked her question as she and Gentry made their way to where he stood.

"Oh, nothing really, just curious. It's more a matter for you, I guess, or the police."

"Why do you say that? What are you seeing?" They came around the corner of the garage and stopped.

"This," said Jake, pointing to a section behind the garage.

Lauren and Gentry walked to where Jake pointed. The area was flattened, like someone had been there for a period of time. Two large bunches of Iris plants lay smashed, trampled by someone or something.

"Could water from the fire trucks have hit this spot?" asked Lauren. "That's certainly would be enough force to flatten the Iris'."

"I don't think so," replied Jake, "I was told the fire trucks were parked close to this end of the home, which would make their hoses pointing more northward. It could have maybe hit back here when they turned them on the neighboring homes to keep them from burning, I guess, but I doubt it could have done this. I think this was human."

Lauren looked at Gentry. They were obviously rolling the same questions around in their heads. Could Bantus have been placing the bomb the moment when Dylan made the call? Was he going to blow up the house anyway? Did the call from Dylan have nothing to do with the explosion? It just seemed like too much of a coincidence, but stranger things had happened.

***

The pitiful amount of cash he had on hand wouldn't be enough to see him through all the upcoming expenses. Bantus ground his teeth with clenched jaws.

"If that idiot had done what I asked of him and picked up the money when I told him to, it would still be waiting at the Post Office. What an idiot. People just need to do what they're told."

It had been an incredible strain to get Lisa's body out of the hotel undetected. Back doors and maintenance elevators were a boon in his business, and he'd even managed it all with a bad knee. He was very impressed with himself. Sometimes, these little wrenches that were thrown into his life had a way of making him even more proud of himself than he already was. His smile grew wider as he thought of the previous evening.

The fire at the Sandusky home was quite impressive. He couldn't help but have a look once the home was completely engulfed in flames. That was the best part of a fire. He'd worked very hard to get himself spotted by that FBI witch and her little flying monkey. How beneath him they both were. If they weren't so inconsequential he'd kill them both, but now, with his timeline in shambles once again he'd forgo the joy and concentrate on what needed to be done.

They'd be hard pressed to find his little hideaway now, and this new place worked far better for his purposes than the stupid warehouse. Life was good and incredibly rewarding.

***

Getting back to the car, Gentry tried to brainstorm with Lauren about what could have caused that depression in the flower beds on the back of the garage. Lauren was quiet on the subject and Gentry couldn't get her to participate in the conversation.

"Okay," he said, yielding to her change in attitude. "What's up? Why aren't you running with this?"

She hesitated for a moment before speaking and it seemed he almost saw a sense of guilt in her.

"Because," she said, uneasily, "it gets us nowhere. We can only ask questions and we get no answers. We need to focus on what we know."

"O…kay…" he said, eyeing her suspiciously. "But first, tell me what you're not telling me, because something is eating at you."

"No," she said, quite unconvincingly, "there's nothing. I just feel like we need to think about the questions we *can* answer."

Gentry leaned back into his seat. He wasn't buying it for a minute, and if she was keeping something about this investigation from him, he was going to find out what, if he had to shake it out of her.

He sat quietly in the car for the remainder of the ride.

"I think we should get some lunch, don't you? We didn't eat breakfast and I'm starving." Lauren was changing the subject.

"Sure," he replied, searching for a way to make her open up to him.

"Gentry," she said as they pulled into the restaurant parking lot, "please trust me. There are things I can't tell you, things that have to stay within the FBI, please."

"O…kay," he said again, "but isn't that why we're 'partners' like you said? I mean, if I'm your partner, shouldn't I be privy to the same intel you are?"

"Usually," she said slowly pulling on the door handle, "but not this time. Just trust me."

They walked into the restaurant together and sat down, ordering their meals and eating in silence. He didn't know what to say to her, didn't know why she would keep needed information from him, but he would trust her.

He played with the french fries on his plate, and nibbled at his hamburger. The thought kept coming back to him that maybe he needed to be at the FBI instead of in the park. Could he make himself leave a lifestyle he loved for one that was filled with the ugly side of humanity? He wasn't sure he could do that, wasn't sure he wanted to do that.

"What are you thinking so hard about?" Lauren said as she swallowed a french fry.

"Oh, I don't know," said Gentry, "not much. Just, you know, thinking."

"Yeah, I know," she said smiling, "I can hear the wheels turning clear across the table."

Gentry smiled weakly and tried to eat. For some reason, he had no appetite, due in part to the decision he knew he'd have to make in his career, but also in part to the events of the last couple days.

"So, here's what I'm thinking," said Lauren, trying to open up some communication. "Bantus isn't going to stick to the warehouse Dylan found for him. We didn't have the address of the warehouse yet, but he's not going to know that. However, I've got teams on all the vacant warehouses in the city, which isn't that many in a city this size, fortunately. They're keeping a low profile, but watching the buildings 24/7. I also have the local LEOs watching the homeless camps to see if Bantus shows up there."

"I don't see how that's going to do any good," said Gentry. "He has to know we are aware of his activities now. He'll keep his visits to any homeless camp pretty hidden."

"Yes, I'm aware of that," said Lauren, "but we have to be vigilant. It's our job to now go from the obvious to the not so obvious. Where would he go that we wouldn't expect him to go?"

***

Bantus limped out of his newly found rental to his car. Luckily, he'd purchased a nice car with early funds from the Newman's. He was really going to miss that money and wondered if he'd killed their daughter, he'd still have money coming in. Dead girls tell no tales.

He chuckled at his own joke.

"Maybe I should write a book," he laughed.

It wasn't long before his scowl returned, however, and opening his trunk he threw some duct tape onto the two dead bodies there. Once night fell, he would be bringing these two into the house, or should he say, casket. This time he wouldn't have to build a casket, the house would serve that purpose quite nicely.

***

After finishing their lunch Lauren and Gentry were headed back to the car when Lauren's phone rang.

"Porcelli."

The voice on the other end of the line was panicked and speaking very, very fast.

"Wait…wait…" said Lauren, stopping in her tracks, "slow down and say that again."

Lauren listened intently as the fire in her eyes began to take hold.

"We'll be right over," she said, "don't leave, we'll be right there."

Lauren grinned over the car at Gentry.

"What?" he said, his impatience growing.

"Bantus' landlord just called us. He saw his picture on the news last night as a suspect in an arson case."

They quickly jumped into the car and raced to the home of the homeowner. They came up the walk and the landlord greeted them on the porch.

"Please," he said, "come inside."

They stepped into the house.

"I'm Acton Wilson," he said, greeting each of them.

Lauren introduced the two of them and was invited to be seated on the couch. Once they sat down, she pulled out a picture of Bantus and showed it to Acton.

"Yes, I believe that's him. His hair is a dark color now, and he has a leg brace."

"You were right to call us," she said, "he's a very dangerous man. We're going to put a surveillance detail on your home for your protection. We'll need to get the address of the property he rented from you."

"Here's a copy of the rental contract. I wanted a year lease, but he said he'd only need it for a month. Since it's been vacant for so long, I decided to let him have it for a month. One month income is better than nothing, and he paid cash, including the deposit."

"Did he say anything else to you? Give you any reason he needed only a month?"

"No, he said very little and seemed to be in a hurry so I didn't press him. But he said he didn't need to do a walk through because he'd looked in the windows and it looked like it would work perfectly for him."

"Okay, we'll keep an eye on the property," said Lauren, "and we'll keep in touch with you, as well."

"I don't have to give the money back, do I? I mean, he has actually rented the property." Acton looked hopefully at the two of them.

"No, you don't," Lauren assured him, "no need to worry about that."

Acton looked relieved and ushered the two of them to the door.

"Thank you for calling us," said Lauren, "you did the right thing."

Acton nodded and they headed to their car.

"We've got him," said Gentry, "we've finally got him."

"Not yet," smiled Lauren, "but we will very soon."

Between this break and bumping into Charity in the police station, it was beginning to look as if the investigation was starting to turn in their favor.

Chapter Thirty-Three

Lauren and Gentry were set up in a vacant house across the street and a few houses down from the home Bantus rented. They had a good view of the front of the home from the upstairs bedroom and another team of two agents watched the back of the home.

Bantus had gotten sloppy in his hurry to repair the gap in his 'timeline'. He'd allowed himself to be seen and that made Lauren very uncomfortable, but she wasn't the only one.

"This is too easy, Lauren," said Gentry, staring out the passenger window. "This shouldn't have happened."

"Yeah, I know," agreed Lauren, "why would he want us to know he'd rented a place, and then make it so easy to find out where the place was? It doesn't make sense."

"Unless…" Gentry was pulling at his lower lip as he thought the sentence through.

"Unless?" urged Lauren.

"Unless he'd already been living there."

"But, why would he-" Lauren gasped.

"Charity said he had a fancy hotel room," said Gentry, "she said that's where he lived. But he could've had this other place already scoped out and been doing his dirty work from there long before renting the motel room."

"He played us," said Lauren, "again."

"Maybe," said Gentry slowly, "but maybe not. He might just be in enough of a hurry to complete his 'stay' in Kalispell that he's gotten sloppy."

"Not likely if you've studied his profile like I have." Lauren was angry and disappointed. "He's not sloppy, and everything he does is calculated to the fullest extent. He leaves nothing to chance; at least, he hasn't thus far. Walter Bantus is a master at making every bad experience work in his favor."

Gentry picked up the binoculars and searched the neighborhood around the house. Lauren called for a check in on the handheld radio.

"Any activity in the backyard?" she said, releasing the button on the radio.

"All clear in the back," came the reply.

She pressed the button again.

"All units check in."

"Team one clear," came the first reply. "Team two clear, team three clear."

"Leader out." Lauren laid the radio on the folding table they'd brought in. Waiting was the hardest part of the job, especially on this op. She had to fight to keep herself from picking up the radio every five minutes for a check in.

"I can't believe I'm going to say this," grinned Gentry, "but would you sit down? You're making *me* nervous."

"I can't help it," said Lauren, raising her hands helplessly, "there are so many ways this could go, so many reasons it will work and won't work at the same time. I want to strangle the man with my bare hands! I really do."

"I can see that," he said, still grinning.

"How come you're so calm," said Lauren, eyeing him with suspicion.

"Because," Gentry replied, "this one's for Dylan and his mother. I'm certain he's up there directing traffic."

"Up where?" asked Lauren, that guilty look from earlier in the day returning.

"You know," laughed Gentry, "You're a lousy liar, and by 'up there' I mean he's watching over us. He's right here with us, and he's going to help us catch this…this…whatever he is."

"Jerk? Imbecile? Monster?" said Lauren, only half listening and staring out the window.

"All of the above," said Gentry, picking up the binoculars and scanning the neighborhood once again.

Lauren looked through the high powered scope set up at the very edge of the window. It allowed her to see the nose hairs of anyone walking to or from the house. This proved useless because no one *walked* to or from the house. She sighed and stood up, beginning to pace back and forth across the empty room.

The house they were in was an old home, built in the thirties from the look of it and updated rather nicely. In doing the updating the owners had done an excellent job of maintaining the beauty of the original home, right down to the squeak in the floor boards. This was most annoying to Gentry as Lauren paced back and forth continually.

"I can see why partners argue on stakeouts," laughed Gentry.

"Who says partners argue on stakeouts?" ask Lauren, without really caring about an answer.

"Well, you always see them discussing things on TV and getting into these squabbles about ridiculous subjects."

"When do *you* have time to watch TV?" Lauren chuckled, "and what doofus cop shows are you watching?"

"Oh, I have time every now and again, and it's none of your business what I watch."

"Yeah, well, TV stakeouts are *way* more interesting than real ones, as you can see. But, just why do you think we're not getting along?"

"Oh, we're getting along, but I'm about to tie you to your folding chair over there if you don't stop pacing back and forth. The squeak in this floor is making me crazy."

She took another step just as he said that and started laughing at the creak that echoed through the mostly vacant room."

"Oh," she laughed, "sorry. I guess I didn't hear it."

"I guess not," he said, teasing her.

It was beginning to grow dusk and soon they would be using the night vision scope and binoculars. Lauren was sure this would be when the activity would most likely begin, and was anxious for nightfall.

About an hour later, as darkness fell over the city, a car pulled up in front of the house with its lights off.

"Here we go," said Gentry looking through the night binoculars. "Yup, it's him. He's going to his trunk."

Lauren rushed to the scope and confirmed it was Bantus. He wore a hoodie, but there was no mistaking the brace on his left knee. She picked up the radio and pressed the button.

"All units, heads up. The suspect has arrived. I repeat the suspect has arrived."

Each unit checked in with "roger that".

Lauren and Gentry watched as Bantus pulled what looked to be a suit bag out of the truck and balanced it on one shoulder. He steadied himself, shut the trunk and limped slowly into the house.

"Was that what I think it was?" asked Gentry, a sick feeling in his stomach.

Lauren picked up the radio once again.

"All units, stay back. I repeat, stay back. No one approaches the subject without my authorization."

Again "roger that" came over the radio three times.

In a few minutes, Bantus appeared at the front door empty handed and made his way down the walk to the trunk of his car.

"No," said Gentry in disbelief, "not another one."

Opening the trunk, he struggled yet again with another heavy suit bag, making his way slowly up the walk and into the house.

Lauren picked up the radio.

"All units, on my mark." She held the radio in her hand and waited for the door to close behind him. "GO! GO! GO!"

Lauren grabbed the radio and the two of them raced down the stairs and out the front of their house. As sirens blared from the other units, they ran toward Bantus' home. Before the units could get to the home there was a horrendous explosion. Shards of glass flew from the window frames; fire erupted and completely engulfed the home in seconds.

Gentry and Lauren skidded to a stop and crouched down, trying to avoid the flying shards of glass. Once the debris settled, they stood slowly, horrified by the scene in front of them. Were there girls yet alive inside there? Had he already killed them? Did he escape prior to the blast? Was the explosion premature and he was killed as well?

Gentry didn't even know where to start with the questions rushing through his brain. It was too much to process, too much input at one time combined with the explosion and fire. He watched Lauren, no disappointment showing on her face, only anger and frustration.

She stood with her hands on her hips, looking at the ground and shaking her head. He could see the muscles in her face twitching in the firelight.

Within moments fire trucks barreled up the street, the firefighters quickly jumping to their work. Both Lauren and Gentry knew they were too late for anyone who may have been alive in the house, if indeed any were. They wouldn't know until the morning if there were people inside. They knew for sure they would find at least two bodies and the thought sickened Gentry. The one question remained over all of them. Would they find the body of a serial killer amongst the charred beams and boards?

Gentry scanned the crowd that formed across the street from the fire. They were quickly ushered back to a safe distance, and he checked each face in the crowd. Bantus was not there.

Lauren put the radio to her mouth.

"All units, did you see anyone exit the back of the house prior to the explosion?" She sounded not hopeful for a good answer.

"Negative," came the reply, "we were pulling away when the house blew and didn't see anyone exiting."

Lauren dropped the radio to her side. Her face fell completely and she ran her hands through her short hair. Did that mean they got him? Dare she believe it was over? A small thrill of excitement rushed through her, but she squelched it, afraid to hope it was true.

They walked in silence back to the house where they were set up. They packed up the equipment and took it out, stowing it in the trunk of the car and headed to the hotel. The ride was quiet, nothing to say, nothing worth speculating on. Disappointment hung thick in the air sucking all the life out of the two of them.

They carried the equipment up to their rooms and set it down in the corner. Lauren collapsed in her chair and Gentry followed suit.

"Lauren," he began, "we'll check through the debris tomorrow as soon as the fire department lets us in. The fire inspector will be there, he'll be able to help us out. Maybe Bantus is in there, maybe the explosion was premature and he didn't make it out."

"Sounds like a lot of maybe's to me," she said, still not hopeful. "But we'll see what we find. I'm going to bed. I didn't sleep last night, but hopefully I'll be exhausted enough tonight that sleep will be the order of the night. I certainly hope so.

"Yeah, me too. I'm going to do the same thing. Sleep well."

Lauren scoffed as she closed the door.

Tomorrow would be very telling. As Gentry readied himself for bed, he reviewed the events of the past two days. These would be events he could tell his grandchildren about. Then, thinking that through a little further he thought, *"Well, maybe not. I never want my children or grandchildren to know the world is this ugly."*

Chapter Thirty-Four

The next morning as they were getting ready to go examine the charred remains of the home, Lauren's phone rang.

She bowed her head as she usually did when she talked on the phone, studying the toes of her shoes.

"We can do that," she said firmly, "what time do you want us there?"

She listened to the caller and then ended the call.

"They want us down at the coroner's office," she said. "They need help with the remains."

"When?" asked Gentry, not looking forward to the experience.

"Right now," she said, "we'll grab some breakfast on the way."

"You can't be serious," he said staring at her, "just what I need, food on my stomach before I go view charred bodies."

"You're *such* a weenie," she said grinning. "We'll eat after."

"Oh, that will really help," he said, "I'll totally want to eat something *then*."

They walked out of the room, closing the door behind them and headed to the elevator.

"Did they say if one of the bodies had a brace on the leg? Could they tell?" Gentry couldn't control his curiosity.

"Didn't say," said Lauren, now lost in thought.

"Why didn't you ask?" he asked, shocked. "Aren't you curious?"

Lauren shook her head as the elevator door slid open. They stepped onto the lift and pressed the button for the first floor.

"I guess I didn't want to hear the answer. I didn't want to know."

They stood side by side and Gentry placed his arm around her shoulders.

"I hear that," he whispered.

The doors opened and they walked through the lobby and out to their car.

"They had to practically dismantle the whole inside of the cabin where Greyson and Aspen were held to find Bantus' hiding place," said Lauren. "He'd made a fake wall in the kitchen closet and used slider bolts on the inside of the wall. When he replaced it after crawling through and investigators tried to move the wall, it felt firm, like a nailed piece of sheetrock. When they did finally remove the wall and found the bolts, they investigated further and found a hole dug in the dirt under the house. There was a tunnel ending probably fifty feet from the house, in the brush where he had a short ladder and even a cover over the exit which he'd hid beneath dirt and brush. Sound familiar?"

"What…is this guy part mole?" Gentry was astounded. "How long do you suppose it took him to do that?"

"It had to take months, but he didn't have months. The only conclusion was he'd paid others to help him. They checked around, but got nowhere. They figured he catered to illegals who needed work under the table. It would only have taken a few days with enough help."

Lauren pulled into the parking lot of the building that housed the coroner's office. She removed the keys and sat back in her seat with a sigh.

"What will we get in here, relief or regret?" she smiled weakly. "Let's go find out."

They got out of the car and headed into the building, walking to the front desk.

"Hi," she said flashing her badge again, "Lauren Porcelli, FBI. I'm looking for the coroner's office."

The receptionist smiled and pointed left.

"Take the elevator to the basement. Head left off the elevator, room eighty-seven. You can't miss it. It's the one with the double doors."

"Thanks."

"You know," said Gentry, smiling weakly, "it could be him."

"I'm afraid to think that, even allowing myself one tiny maybe..." she let her voice trial off.

They entered the elevator and rode down in silence. Once the doors opened again, they followed the directions they were given and easily found the office.

A short man, slight, with spectacle-type glasses and thinning hair greeted them.

"You must be Agent Porcelli," he said, his dark eyes scanning her face, "I'm Dr. Randall Castell."

"Yes I am, nice to meet you Dr. Castell," she said, "this is my associate Gentry Beauchene."

"Let me show you what I've found, it's a bit peculiar, to be sure," said Dr. Castell, hurrying back to the operating table.

He led them past four sets of remains, charred beyond recognition and brought them to a fifth set and stopped. These remains showed what was left of a metal leg brace, still somewhat attached to the left leg.

Lauren's heart jumped.

"We found one male body with the female bodies. He appears to have been wearing a leg brace on his left leg. Is this in keeping with the description of your perp?"

"Yes, it is," said Lauren, smiling with satisfaction.

"Well than this is good news," smiled the doctor. "I did find one anomaly, though. I'm wondering if you can help me identify what it is."

"Certainly," said Lauren.

Dr. Castell went to a small plastic dish. He handed the dish to Lauren.

Inside were the remains of what appeared to be a small computer chip. Lauren looked at it with foreboding. Gentry leaned in to see what was in the dish.

"Where did you find this?" she asked, brows furrowed. Lauren already knew the answer.

"It was rather interesting, actually," he said taking the dish back and scrutinizing it with a magnifying glass. "It appeared to have been implanted at the base of his spine."

Lauren's shoulders fell. She rubbed her forehead as she stared down at the remains.

"This doesn't look like good news," said Dr. Castell.

"No, it's not," said Lauren with a sigh, "and I'll need you to keep this information to yourself."

"I'm sure you're aware that everything we do here is confidential. You need have no concern there."

"Thank you, Dr. Castell. You'll be contacted for transport of these remains once you've finished your work here."

Gentry and Lauren walked to the elevator, nothing said, nothing needing to be said. Bantus hired an actor to pose as himself and leave the bodies in the house. He was still out there, more people would die, they'd failed to stop him.

***

It was late afternoon and the sun was shining through the trees, leaving giant shadows stretching dark and silent across the grass. They'd been back to their rooms, sent out a general and disappointing announcement that Bantus had escaped and put the teams on high alert.

Three of the local teams were sent to the airport. Lauren knew he would already be gone, but she asked them to check around, find what airline he was on and where he was headed.

The two decided to have their own memorial for Dylan and his mother. They wanted to go to the cemetery, find a nice quiet spot under a big beautiful tree and talk about Dylan. In so doing, they would also be talking about his mother, as she was at least half the reason he'd grown to be the man he was

"I'm sorry, Lauren. I know you've worked hard on this case, I've seen it. I'm just sorry we didn't get him." Gentry walked through the cemetery, his arm around her.

She smiled up at him, a lot more cheerful than he would've thought she'd be. He chocked it up to her ability to put on a good face.

They found the right spot and sat down on a wooden bench strategically placed under a large old oak tree.

"You knew him much better than I did," she said, laying her head on his shoulder. "You go first."

Gentry sighed and rested his head on hers.

"I don't know what to say, other than the man had the bluest eyes..." he began.

A voice behind them interrupted his thoughts and brought him quickly to his feet.

"Can you think of *nothing* else to say about me? 'He had blue eyes?' *Really?*"

Dylan stood behind the bench, smiling broadly, his mother beside him.

"What? You're...you're not *dead*?" Gentry was on his way around the bench and hugged his friend, then clapped him on the back. Gentry hadn't been to Dylan's house and met his parents, but in his excitement he hugged Mrs. Sandusky as well. She grinned and patted him softly.

"Well, no, I'm not dead, but I did think of getting myself a nice set of brown contact lenses and really throwing you for a loop."

Dylan hugged him again, his mother patting both of them.

"How did this happen? We saw the fire, heard the explosion!"

Gentry looked over the bench to Lauren who was smiling widely, a tear trickling down her face.

"You *knew?*" he said, his eyes filled with disbelief. "You knew about this and said nothing? Your little speech, 'he's a hero', 'he deserves our respect not our pity'-- all of that was fake?"

"You said that about me?" Dylan was straightening his shirt and looking smug.

"Yeah, pretty good, eh?" Lauren chuckled.

"I couldn't say anything," she said turning to Gentry, "you could only know if you were FBI, which of course, you're not."

"What was that depression in the flower beds behind Dylan's garage then? You were very sketchy on that." Gentry pressed her; he wanted to know it all.

"*That*," she grinned, "was left by agents waiting to transport the two of them to the resort once it was dark. I'd have to admit, that was sloppy and they're going to hear about it."

Lauren went on to explain how the phone call from Dylan's house phone to her cell was a set up to force Bantus' hand. They were hoping to make him speed up his time frame, which it did, but he'd simply used his 'assistant' to call their bluff. The call hadn't actually been made from their home; it was made from a phone at a motel, forwarded through their home phone to make it look like he'd called from the house. It worked, but was not as effective as Lauren hoped it would be.

"We still lost him," she said, "but at least we could get these two out of hiding. There's no need for Bantus to think them dead now."

"What have you two been doing all this time? Where have you been?" Gentry couldn't believe he was having a conversation with the man he'd believed dead. It was hard for him to wrap his head around, to really believe this was real.

"We were in a cabin in one of the park resorts," he said smiling. "And we were treated like royalty, under the name of Sir Nathan of Rigsby. And this lovely lady was introduced as the Duchess of Rigsby."

Dylan's mother grinned.

Gentry turned to Lauren with disbelief.

"You're kidding me, right?"

"Not actually. We had a hard time getting around them not having an accent, but told the staff they were really practicing their English and had almost lost the British accent." Lauren was grinning broadly.

"They were masquerading as a Duchess and her son?" Gentry's voice was becoming more and more incredulous. Dylan couldn't hold it any longer. He burst out laughing, his mother as well and they watched the realization gradually creep over Gentry's face.

"No..." scoffed Lauren, joining in the laughter. "They were just themselves, but they *were* at the resort."

Gentry shoved Dylan's shoulder and walked back around the bench to where Lauren stood.

"I don't know whether to kiss you or...or..." he wrapped both arms around her and gazed down at her, shaking his head. "Just for that, I say the FBI owes us dinner, you think?"

He stared into her green eyes, still holding her close to him.

"So, it's payback, is it?" she stretched up and softly kissed his lips. "Well, then you're leaving the generous tip."

"Me?" he said, astounded. "Why? What'd I do?"

"I don't know, but I'll think of something." She kissed him again and they turned, four people heading out of the cemetery where only two had entered.

Dinner was fun, filled with laughter and reminiscing, and Gentry still in awe his friend was alive. He and Lauren sat across the table from Dylan and Mrs. Sandusky. They laughed and smiled, teased and joked, having far more fun than anyone else in the restaurant.

"So," said Lauren, kissing Gentry softly on the cheek, "do you forgive me?"

Gentry paused, and the table grew quiet.

"Marry me," he said, staring into her eyes, "Marry me and we'll make beautiful babies together."

"I guess that's a yes on the forgiveness thing, huh?" she laughed. Then she thought for a minute.

"But for a marriage to happen," she said staring into his eyes and studying his face, "you'd have to cherish me as much as you do Baby. I don't know if you can do that, even if I asked you to."

He smiled down at her as Dylan chuckled softly across the table.

"I can do that," he said without a pause. "For all my life, I can do that."

"Then, yes," she said smiling, "I'll marry you."

Their waiter approached the table just as those last words left Lauren's mouth. He turned to the other customers and made an announcement, quite loudly.

"Ladies and Gentlemen, the young woman at this table said yes!"

Applause rang out throughout the restaurant, everyone more than aware of what that 'yes' meant. Those at tables stood and cheered, toasting the couple with shouts of 'here here' and 'congratulations' before sitting back down and gradually resuming their meal.

The newly engaged couple kissed. Was it to hide their embarrassment at the attention poured out upon them? No, this kiss represented the quiet realization they would never have to put the love and the passion they felt for each other second to anything, ever again.

Epilogue

The knee was healing well. Bantus gritted his teeth at the loss of time the injury had cost him. He'd more than made up for it in kills, which brought a satisfied grin sliding across his face like oil. Still, it was an interruption to his process and he didn't like it.

With money nearly depleted, he thought about a job, something he could do to get enough stashed away so he could continue his work. He thought an orderly at a hospital might work; he'd have to make sure his references checked out. That might be a bit tricky, but he'd never let that bother him before.

He stared out the train window as the scenery passed lazily by, the steady click, click of the wheels over the tracks lulling him into numbness.

Suddenly his shoulders tensed, his back straightened and his eyes took on a dark, sinister tone. It was time to kill. He knew it. His mind was telling him it was time and when it was time, there was nothing he could do about it. There was nothing he *wanted* to do about it, but kill.

He quickly hailed the conductor.

"What is our next stop?" he asked kindly, trying to hide the evil boiling inside him.

The conductor shrank back, but tried to conceal his disdain by looking at the schedule he held in his hand. He knew the schedule, he knew exactly where the next stop was, but he couldn't look at the passenger sitting before him.

"That would be Stockton, uh, sir," he said looking into the darkness of his eyes. "It's another thirty minutes."

"If I wanted to get to Yosemite, is there a train that will take me there from Stockton?"

"You're going to want to take the San Joaquin 712 to Merced and then from there you can take the 8412 bus to the Ahwahnee Hotel. There are buses to other hotels as well; you can take your pick from the station."

He couldn't get away from the man soon enough.

"You've been very helpful, thank-you."

Unbeknownst to the passenger, the conductor would not soon forget him. In fact, he would endure many nights where this specific passenger would haunt his dreams, making a lasting impression on his mind.

Other books by JL Redington

Young Adult

The Esme Chronicles:

A Cry Out Of Time
Pirates of Shadowed Time
A View Through Time

Romantic Suspense

The Broken Heart Series:

The Lies That Save Us
Solitary Tears
Veiled Secrets (Title change from Hearts in Hiding)

Passions in the Park Series:

Love Me Anyway
Cherish Me Always
Embrace Me Forever (Coming End of March 2014)

Also coming in 2014:
For all of you who have wanted to know if Max, Alexa's father, ever finds love. Watch for a prequel to The Broken Heart Series and a sequel this spring/summer. I'll keep you posted!

Come join me on Facebook:

Author JL Redington

On Twitter:

@Author JL Redington

And on the Web:

www.jlredington.com

Made in the USA
Charleston, SC
07 February 2014